D0252837

SCHOLASTIC PRESS | NEW YORK

To everyone who knows right from wrong.
And to Thom and Linda for being the best of everything.

Copyright © 2015 by Jeffrey Salane

All rights reserved. Published by Scholastic Press, an imprint of Scholastic Inc.,
Publishers since 1920. SCHOLASTIC, SCHOLASTIC PRESS, and associated logos are
trademarks and/or registered trademarks of Scholastic Inc.

No part of this publication may be reproduced, stored in a retrieval system, or
transmitted in any form or by any means, electronic, mechanical, photocopying,
recording, or otherwise, without written permission of the publisher. For information
regarding permission, write to Scholastic Inc., Attention: Permissions Department,
557 Broadway, New York, NY 10012.

Library of Congress Cataloging-in-Publication Data Available

ISBN 978-0-545-45031-7

10 9 8 7 6 5 4 3 2 1   15 16 17 18 19
Printed in the U.S.A.   23
First edition, April 2015

The text type was set in Gotham Narrow Book.
Book design by Phil Falco
Illustrations copyright © 2015 by Nancy Stahl

Never pray for justice, because you might get some.

MARGARET ATWOOD

CHAPTER 1
THE WRONG QUESTIONS

"I always knew I had a purpose. . . ."

M Freeman stirred at the sound of her own voice. It was distant, grainy, airborne, and it wasn't coming from her.

"I'm sure you do, Ms. Freeman, but allow me to ask you a few questions first."

The second voice jolted her to the core. "Watts?" gasped M.

Her eyes flicked open and she whipped her head around, searching her new environment, but Lady Watts was not in the strange room. M was alone, but from the looks of the place, she wouldn't be alone for long.

The room was unlike any space she had ever been in. It was entirely made of glass. Glass walls, glass ceiling, glass floor, glass furniture; it was all crystal clear and cold to the touch.

In fact M was sitting in a glass chair at a glass table. It was not a comfortable or cozy place. She tried to move her hands, but they wouldn't listen. Instead they stayed firmly glued to the table in front of her.

M stared down at her unresponsive hands, then she looked past them, through the glass table and the glass floor into the room beneath her. It was a control room of some sort, crammed with oversized servers and people focused intently on screens, typing and speaking into their headsets. But even with all of the activity below, the only sound in her room was the soundtrack playing over an intercom system. It was a recording of her Lawless School interview.

M wasn't sure if it was the lack of a horizon that made her stomach lurch and her head spin, or if it was hearing the sound of her own voice from several months ago. Several months ago when she was innocent, just a seminormal kid with a hardworking, single mother; a loving but deceased father; and a slightly wacky homeschool education.

But the Lawless School hadn't changed *everything*. She still had a hardworking mother — only now she knew that her mother's business was stealing works of art. And her father was still gone — but new and disturbing truths about his life and his death meant that he hadn't been the person she'd thought he was. The schooling had been the only change she had voluntarily signed up for, sort of. She'd been so excited to attend her father's alma mater. But she hadn't expected the criminal masterminds of Lawless to pull back the curtain on every other aspect of her life.

The Lawless School felt far away now, like a distant dream, but the audio confirmed that it wasn't. No, it hadn't been a dream. It had been a nightmare.

"An art historian can be a demanding job. Is your mother around much?"

That was Zara's voice slithering into the room. Zara, her roommate and guardian at Lawless. Zara, who she'd begun to think of as a friend. Zara, the girl who should not be trusted. Where was she now? She had been on the Lawless campus when disaster struck. When the Fulbright agents had unleashed a junior-sized black hole — with M's unwitting help.

All signs pointed to an air-sucking ending for Zara. But M supposed if anyone could survive such a gravitational grab, it was probably her.

The prerecorded interview kept on playing over the intercom, which M finally pinpointed directly above her, just a set of tiny holes in the glass ceiling, showering her with ghostly voices from her past. As she listened, she began to hear the true meaning behind the Lawlessly slanted questions from Ms. Watts.

"If you found a wallet on a street near your house, what would you do?"

"Can you tell me about a time that you have worked with a team to solve a problem?"

"And if you were in this restaurant and you had to leave, how would you do so?"

M had known the interview was a test, but hearing it a second time, she noticed there was clarity about what the Lawless School had expected from her. And, boy, from her answers, she had really lived up to the hype.

Outthink the world. Build a team. And always have an escape route.

Ms. Watts was definitely still alive. M didn't know how she knew, but she knew. It's next to impossible to get rid of vermin like that. Ms. Watts could probably survive a nuclear explosion and a zombie apocalypse . . . mostly because odds were that she would have been the one who sold the nuclear codes and unleashed the zombies. M had experienced Ms. Watts's diabolic sweet talk firsthand, and now she felt like a pawn that had been pushed to every corner of the chessboard — from South America to London to Germany and back, all in search of the *umbra mortis*, a doomsday weapon M never would have sought if she'd had all the facts. But finally M was free.

She tugged at her restraints. Well, free of Ms. Watts, anyway. She may have escaped the woman's velvet handcuffs, but these new handcuffs were made of glass.

M studied the room again. No doors. No visible ventilation or air ducts to crawl through. No obvious way out as far as she could tell. There looked to be an empty hallway that surrounded all four sides of the room, but beyond the hallway, everything was dark.

"Ms. Freeman, in this envelope is the ticket to your future. Or maybe not. I don't know; that is, I have not been informed as to your acceptance or rejection to the Lawless School. I am only a point person chosen to ask you several questions and hand this to you. I have my own thoughts on the matter of your future, but I have been instructed to keep my thoughts to myself."

The intercom erupted into a scramble of deafening white noise that made M cringe in her glass seat. This was the point in the interview in which Ms. Watts had clicked her pen and the buzzing in the room had started. The woman had known that their interview was being recorded and she didn't want what she said next to be heard.

Now over the mind-twisting hiss of static, a booming voice echoed through the small room. "M Freeman, what were you told here?"

"Not until you answer my questions first," M said calmly, though her heart was racing. "And show yourself, why don't you? Let's sit down and discuss this, Lawless to Fulbright."

The recording ended and the room fell deathly silent.

"What were you told?" the disembodied voice repeated.

"Where's my mother?" M asked. "And my friends Merlyn and Jules, what have you done with them? Answer me, and then maybe we'll talk."

"What were you told?"

"What's the matter," M said, smirking, "afraid of a little girl in handcuffs?" There was no doubt; she had learned a thing or two from Zara.

Suddenly bright white lights illuminated the hallway that wrapped around M's interrogation room. Now she knew how a shadow box felt. A line of masked Fulbright soldiers marched into the hallway and stood at attention. She counted forty Fulbrights, each standing over six feet tall and facing M, forming a blockade of black suits that were coiled with glowing wires and green ember eyes. Behind them, M could see movement. Someone was hidden, walking behind the goon squad.

A seamless door slid open in the far glass wall and the row of Fulbrights there stepped aside. Into the room walked a boy with a military-grade haircut. He must have been close to M's age but was a good foot taller than her. He was a rope of muscles twisting under his black uniform and his clear blue eyes didn't betray any emotion that M could read as he purposefully slipped off his gloves and walked toward the empty seat across from her. The door behind him slid shut with a *shush* that made it feel as if the air itself had been stolen from the room.

The boy sat down, staring deep into M's eyes and waiting for her to say something. M's eyes, though, were flittering over every inch of her silent captor. His suit held no information about him. It looked like every other suit worn by every other Fulbright who had attacked her in the past. There was no name, no rank, no badge to declare what this secret society was or where this boy belonged in its structure. Leaning back in his seat, the Fulbright put his hands casually on the table between them. He was wearing a strange, thin ring on one hand. It fit around his middle two fingers, but the top of the ring stretched the length of his fist, like a delicate set of brass knuckles.

The stare-down didn't last much longer than a minute. Then the boy rapped his knuckles on the table. At the command, the entire mob of soldiers outside the room turned their backs on M.

"You're right," the boy said with a British accent. "We should do this a different way with you. You've earned that. My name's Ben Downing and I'll be your direct, assuming all goes well in this interview."

"Oh, that's what you call this?" asked M. "Feels more like an interrogation."

"You say tomato," Ben answered with a slight smile. "Believe me, if we were interrogating you, we'd know what we wanted to know already. Now, you had questions. Fire away."

"My mother," M started.

"Alive and well," finished Ben. "She's in our protective custody."

"That's a nice way to say it," said M, keeping eye contact with Ben. "Another person might call it holding her hostage."

"Hostage?" Ben said with a small laugh. "I'm afraid you've got us pegged all wrong. *We* saved your mother's life. Lady Watts had your place swept clean five minutes after you left for that school of hers. There was barely time to extract your mother before the Lawless losers made their house call."

"Merlyn and Jules, where are they?" M asked.

Ben shrugged. "Eaves and Byrd are under surveillance in another Glass House."

M looked around the room. "So that's what you call this place. . . . Real original. Why are you holding my friends?"

"We're not sure where their allegiances lie."

"Oh, but you know mine, right?" snapped M.

"Maybe *you* don't know whose side you're on." Ben smiled. "But we have it on good authority that you're one of us."

She recalled Devon Zoso's comment back in the hangar at Lawless: *You've always been the weapon against the Lawless School!* But if M had been helping the Fulbrights against Lawless, it hadn't been by choice. "How do you expect to get away with creating a black hole on Earth? What kind of monsters are you, anyway?"

"Black hole? I'm not sure what you mean," said Ben. "You must be referring to the world's largest sinkhole, which has recently opened up in a remote forest in Peru. It's a media flash in the pan that filled a news feed between some actress's new haircut and what fashion trends to expect this spring."

"You killed people, you know."

"We made the world a safer place," Ben said without emotion. "With your help. And now we'd like to help you in return."

"Help me what?" asked M coldly. "Make the world a safer place with you?"

"In time, maybe," said Ben, "but today we would like to help you figure a few things out. You've got a lot of questions, but you're asking the *wrong* questions. Let's start with your so-called friends. Do you know anything about Merlyn Eaves's family?"

"I know Merlyn," said M pointedly. "And I know I can trust him."

"The Eaves family," Ben continued, "have been behind numerous cyberattacks across the globe. They have shut down entire law enforcement divisions, intercepted emergency services communications, incited riots, and in more than a few instances, laid the groundwork for uprisings and riots with higher casualties than what you witnessed at the Lawless School."

"It doesn't mean Merlyn wants the same thing," said M.

"Well, we don't know that, do we?" claimed Ben. "And the Byrd family is a breeding ground for grifters. Miss Juliandra

Byrd herself helped steal a set of rubies that were on loan to Sotheby's from the British royal family."

"That doesn't sound so bad." M shrugged. "A kid's got to eat. A thief's got to steal."

"Yes," agreed Ben, "except two guards and an innocent bystander went missing during the heist. The insurance covered the jewels, but the people were never found and were presumed dead."

"I . . ." started M, but she couldn't think of what to say.

"Lawless raises irredeemable thugs," Ben said. "But you're a special case, aren't you, Freeman? You didn't know what you were in for with that pitiful excuse for a miseducation. And we know you didn't mean to help Lady Watts track down her precious lethal weapon, either. You were just retracing your father's footsteps. So no harm, no foul. Jonathan Wild's fabled *umbra mortis* ended up in Fulbright hands at the end of the day. And we used it to wipe that school clean off the map."

Ben sat in his chair with perfect poise, oozing the smug, relaxed attitude of someone who thinks he has the upper hand in an argument. M realized something then. Unlike Ms. Watts, this kid didn't know there was another moon rock — one half of the *umbra mortis* — still out there. And if he didn't know, chances were the rest of his people didn't, either. Which meant M had a secret. It was a small secret, but it empowered her to be bolder with the Fulbright, even in this glass room surrounded by other Fulbrights, deep inside what was probably the Fulbright hive.

"How do you know what I did or didn't mean to do?" she asked. "How do you know the first thing about me?"

"Simple," said Ben. "Your father told us."

A double agent. The phrase left a bad taste in her mouth. M's father had attended Lawless, but, if recent sources were to be believed, he had ended up working for the other team. And while M wasn't exactly on Lawless's side anymore, to align herself with the Fulbrights felt . . . wrong.

"The destruction of the Lawless School was a happy but unexpected outcome of your involvement in our centuries-old crusade," said Ben. "But the battle isn't over. Fox Lawless, Lady Watts, Lendium Bandit, and dozens of other maniacs are still out there, preparing their next move. And we know that your involvement isn't over, either, even if you haven't figured that out yet."

M fidgeted in her seat. The room was not getting colder or hotter. The air was not stale or moist. There was no obvious temperature tactic meant to make her uncomfortable, which made the fact that she felt so awkward, well, all the more awkward.

"Prove it," she said through her clenched jaw. She felt like she was dismantling an explosive. "Prove to me why I'm involved and why I should care."

"Oh," said Ben with a smile. "I thought you'd never ask."

He turned to face the glass wall to his left and M followed his gaze as the lights around the room dimmed. An oversized projection flashed to life upon the wall, showing a still-frame image of a photo booth. The empty black bench was worn down from years of use and vandalism. Initials + initials were written onto and carved into the wood. The tattered red velvet curtain shrugged carelessly in the wind: The picture was moving. The picture was a movie. A movie whose star stepped into view then, his huge face lighting up the room with beaming brown eyes, a shock of brown hair, and the same tired smile M would never forget.

"M, if you're watching this, congratulations on a job well done . . . and I'm sorry. I'm sorry that I can't be there in person to have this talk with you. Because if you're watching this, I'm most certainly dead."

M's father always knew how to make an entrance . . . even from the afterlife.

Seeing him again, six years after his death, touched M in unexpected ways. Her legs started bouncing like they had when she was a child. It was a nervous habit that she'd rid herself of years ago, but she couldn't stop herself now. Seeing the younger photos of her father at Lawless had been one thing, but this was her real father, exactly as she remembered him — laugh lines, receding hairline, and all. This was the father she knew best.

"There's so much," her father said, "so much more to tell you, but you've probably figured out a lot on your own by now. You're a smart girl. M, you've inherited a very heavy load. I'll take the blame for that. But listen, my time is running out. You'll be safe with the Fulbrights for now. Trust me. And if you get in trouble, I'll come back for you."

M could see from his sly smile that this was obviously a joke.

Just like her dad to send a sarcastic message from beyond the grave.

Then turning quietly serious, her father continued, "There's evil in the world, M. The Fulbrights are going to need your help to combat that evil because it's bigger than even they can imagine. Please, for me, help them before the evil consumes the world and burns it to the core."

An audible scuff of footsteps came from the video and M's father peeked through the red curtain before turning back to the camera. He was nervous about whatever was out there. Softly, someone whispered his name. There was someone else with him. Someone standing guard anxiously, pacing around, someone who also whispered, "Speed it up. They're getting closer."

"M, I'm proud of you," said her father, regaining his composure. "I love you. Always remember that you are greater than the sum of the parts your mother and I gave you. I'll be watching you from above, ever in awe of what you've done and of what you're going to do. Be the best, M. It's a tall order, but the world needs you."

Her father's face froze, eyes forward. She could see herself in him. Then as the lights around the Glass House came back on, her father faded until his picture disappeared completely.

What an unexpected gift that had been, to see her father, alive and well, talking to her just like old times. But these weren't old times. They were new times, strange times, times in which she was trapped in a glass room surrounded by guards.

"So?" asked Ben from across the table. "Proof enough?"

She held still and weighed her options. If what her father said was true, the Fulbrights needed M. "If I help you," she said, "what's in it for me?"

"The Fulbrights represent the greater good," said Ben. "We don't encourage personal interests."

"Well, I'm not a Fulbright yet," said M. "And I have a few demands. First, you let me out of this handcuff restraint. Second, you bring in my friends. If you want me to help you, they have to be part of the team. I need to be with people I can trust."

Ben smiled. "I've never heard of Lawless slime sticking together."

"In case you haven't noticed, I'm not the standard Lawless slime," said M. She didn't show it, but she was a little taken aback at Ben's coarse words. It was the first time he'd shown any ill will toward her. Well, besides the whole handcuffed-prisoner thing.

"Let's hope we can say the same for those friends of yours," he said. "So we have a deal, if you get out of the cuffs and we reunite the old crew?"

M nodded slowly, thinking that this arrangement was a little too easy.

"Great, then first things first," said Ben as he stood up and pulled out a syringe. Uncapping it dramatically, he leaned over the table and showed it to M. "This is the first step toward becoming a Fulbright."

The hypodermic needle's gauge was very large, gaping, even, with a blade-sharp edge that gleamed in the light. The syringe was filled with an amber fluid that roiled with a shimmering glow. Ben slid M's left sleeve up to reveal her soft white wrist. Her veins pulsed and jumped against her skin as she readied herself for what would surely happen next.

Slowly, almost as if with pleasure, Ben pushed the needle into M's forearm. The pain jolted her upright, but M held her eyes on Ben, determined not to show him any weakness. But she could feel the fluid pour into her. It ached like a sunburn, seething under her skin, and she could trace its path as the solution moved up her arm, past her collarbone to her chest, until the odd sensation blossomed through her entire system. She broke out into a heavy sweat, the temperature of the room going from perfect to infernal.

"What was that?" asked M woozily when Ben had removed the needle.

"A little magic potion that will tell us more about you," said Ben.

M studied him and noticed that he wasn't sweating. The heat was coming from inside her. She slumped over in her seat when her muscles went dead all at once. The only thing holding her upright was the glass handcuffs. As she struggled to regain control of her body, she whipped her limp neck around to see Ben walking through the open glass door.

"Oh yeah," said Ben, turning around absentmindedly. "You wanted those cuffs off." Then, with a press of a button, the cuffs clicked open and M fell to the hard glass ground with a resounding thump. She could see the people below her again, sitting at their computers' flashing screens. No one looked up at the girl lying facedown on their ceiling.

M heard the door slide shut. She was alone again. As she lay there, a background buzz came back on over the speakers.

"Did she take the bait?"

It was Ms. Watts's voice again. The recording had restarted. There was something more that the Fulbrights wanted M to know, apparently.

Hook, line, and sinker, answered Zara. *I'm on my way to collect her now.*

Keep her alive, said Ms. Watts as offhandedly as if she were asking Zara to pick up milk from the grocery store on the way home. *She might not look it, but she's very important to someone very important to me.*

Affirmative, said Zara.

There was the sound of a door closing, the shuffling of papers, and the clicking of Ms. Watts's high heels. It was like Ms. Watts was a ghost in the Glass House with M. The sound bounced and resonated off the floor, ticking and ticking against M's immobile body.

M puzzled over Watts's last words as the thrumming pain inside her finally conquered her efforts to stay awake, and a heavy sleep smothered her like a thousand-pound blanket.

CHAPTER 2
A DANGER TO OTHERS

The new room was bright, but at least it wasn't see-through. From her cot, M saw a ceiling and four walls . . . but that didn't mean she wasn't being watched. When she attempted to roll over and inspect the rest of the room, she was met with a flare of pain blistering all over her body.

"Not yet," commanded an unfamiliar voice. "You shouldn't try to move yet. The serum isn't out of your system."

M flipped over again to face the voice and instantly wished she hadn't, due to the sharp, splitting feeling that almost cracked her in half. She grimaced and clenched her teeth. Next to her sat a girl who held a tablet in her hand. The girl's eyes moved from the tablet to M's arm to M's eyes and back to the tablet in a carousel of motion. She looked vaguely familiar, but M couldn't place her face.

"You're looking for something," said M.

"Just reviewing your vitals," said the girl.

"How are you doing that?" asked M.

"The shot was a serum that cleans your system, so to speak," said the girl as her eyes continued their circuitous route. "Like being scrubbed clean on the inside. Cleanses the spirit, we like to say."

That was exactly how the shot had felt.

"When's it go away?" asked M. "The pain."

"Depends," the girl answered. "You should get your rest. Life's not going to get any easier from here on out."

"You're not a doctor," noted M as she studied the girl's features. She was young, only slightly older than M, with blond hair. She was dressed in a standard Fulbright uniform, except for a knee brace that she wore on her left leg.

"You don't remember me, then?" asked the girl.

"The night by the jet," M said, the memory suddenly clicking. "You're the Fulbright who attacked me."

"Attacked you," the girl said with a laugh. "If I had attacked you, you wouldn't be here now. You wouldn't even have reached that plane. No, I was apprehending you."

"Well, good job there," M said sarcastically. "I gave you that brace?"

"What's a hyperextended knee between roommates?" asked the girl. "It was nothing two surgeries and months of rehab couldn't fix. I'm almost field ready again. Just in time, from the looks of things."

"Great, you're my roommate," repeated M as she lay helpless in her cot. "Listen, it looks like we've gotten off on the wrong foot. I don't even know your name."

"Oh, I'm Vivian Ware," she said, grabbing M's left hand and giving it a sturdy shake. It felt like she was ripping M's arm right out of her socket. "It's a pleasure to finally meet you officially."

The sudden movement colored the room a blinding hue of violent white. M felt like she had been struck by lightning. Her eyes unfocused, and Vivian became pixilated into millions of pieces. It was like a body-length stitch had been tugged and now M was spilling out of her own skin. Drool trickled down her chin as she sat as still as possible, trying to recover.

"Okay, we're even," M said after a few minutes. "Can you show me what's on the computer now? I've always wanted to see my insides."

Vivian flipped the tablet to share the screen with M. There was an exact outline of M's body flickering with wild tones, like flames lapping within a fire. Blues, whites, reds, and yellows ebbed and flowed through her digitized self.

"I'm told you need a steady red before you are cleared for action," Vivian said.

A dark purple node showed on the screen at M's wrist, where Ben had administered the shot. "What's the purple blotch?"

"Tracker and dog tag," answered Vivian.

"I always figured the Fulbrights had a way of making people feel wanted," said M jokingly. "Are they afraid I'm going to run away?"

"No," said Vivian. "They are afraid you are going to be captured, killed, or worse. Every Fulbright gets one." She held up her left wrist and a glowing knot pulsated through her skin like a beacon. "Standard issue."

"And this serum, it takes a couple hours to pass?" asked M.

"If you're lucky," said Vivian.

M breathed steadily and slowly eased herself onto her back. There was no way around it — she needed to take it easy for once. But she wished she could see Jules and Merlyn. Thanks to her agreement with Ben, they were probably unwillingly going through the same painful entry into the Fulbrights. M felt like a dragnet of trouble, sweeping up everyone who came into contact with her, friends and enemies alike. But Jules and Merlyn had been trapped in the Box with M back at Lawless. They had heard Ms. Watts ask about the remaining moon rock, and they had witnessed the dire level of destruction said rock could cause. If they were still speaking to her after all this, M hoped they would be in for another crazy ride. Whether or not it's what her dad had been hinting at, it was up to her to find that missing rock and make sure it would never fall into the wrong hands again. Not Ms. Watts's or the Fulbrights' or anyone else.

As M was lost in thought, the white room dimmed into darkness.

"Um, is this stuff supposed to mess with your vision?" she asked. "'Cause I might be going blind."

"It's lights out," said Vivian stoically. "Mandatory bedtime, so stay in your bunk."

"Oh, I'm not going anywhere," said M. She closed her eyes under the oddly soothing false night. Perhaps it was the serum beginning to work its way out of her system, but she felt good. She felt confident about her new situation. It was daunting. It was insane. And it was exactly where she needed to be.

As M drifted off, she felt like she was sleeping during a thunderstorm. The echo of heavy drops of rain surrounded her and brief flashes of bright lightning erupted in her dreams, casting shadows where only darkness had been beforehand. Glimpses of her dream placed her back in her family home, but before she could make sense of her imagined landscape, the walls of her Fulbright dorm illuminated.

They cast a soft light that bloomed under M's closed eyes and drew her gently out of a deep sleep. She remained stone still at first, not wanting to move for fear of waking the mind-numbing ache from yesterday, but the new morning brought with it a highly reinvigorated M. She sat up, suddenly hyper-aware of her entire body, from the tips of her toes to the slightest shift of her eyelashes. She yawned and stretched harder and longer than she ever had before in her life.

Vivian's cot was already neatly made, and she was seated in the corner, reading a book.

"Wow," said M, looking at her hands and arms as if they were totally new appendages. "I feel amazing!"

"That's because your body chemistry has been realigned with essential nutrients, stimulants, and compounds that are not typically found in humans," said Vivian without looking up from her book.

"Did you guys make me into a superhero?" asked M playfully.

"It's a chemical boost, not superjuice," answered Vivian, who obviously lacked a sense of humor. "Now you're almost fit for the field. Put this on and follow me."

Vivian tossed M a white robe. For the first time M realized that her clothes were gone, replaced with a white hospital gown. Catching the robe, she wrapped herself in it and swung her legs out of bed. The ground felt amazing against her bare feet. Warmth was emanating from beneath the impeccably clean white floor. M stood and looked around the room again and noticed something was missing. Windows. Normally she would feel trapped and constrained in a room without windows to the outside world, but this room felt spacious and open.

"Why no windows?" asked M.

"I said, *follow me*," said Vivian from the room's doorway, "not *if you have any questions, just ask.* So let's go before we're late for breakfast. Don't want to get a demerit on your first day."

"I can see why they didn't give you a room with a view, Miss Sunshine," said M as she followed Vivian out into a hallway filled with unmasked Fulbrights. They were all young — students, M realized. But the typical chaotic hustle of students that she was accustomed to at the Lawless School had been replaced here with two orderly, single-file lines of kids moving up the hallway on one side and down the hallway on the other. They were all dressed in their pitch-black uniforms, which made M stand out like a sore thumb in her white robe. And the other students noticed, too. She could tell by their swift glances, quick cuts of the eye toward M, like they were watching an accused thief walking into a courtroom. Their eyes held a mix of curiosity, anger, and judgment, but their legs marched along as if the day was no different than any other day. Maybe it wasn't for them, but it definitely was for her. M stepped into traffic and did her best to stay in line with Vivian, but walking in unison wasn't really her forte.

Around corners and down unending halls, Vivian led M through the white-walled labyrinth to an unmarked room with a table and chairs and nothing else.

"Wait here," said Vivian as she turned, and disappeared beyond the door.

M listened as Vivian's uneven, knee-braced footsteps faded into the distance. Seizing the moment, she jumped onto the table and ran her hands along the ceiling, searching for a speaker, an air vent, a camera, anything, but she found only another smooth white surface. There weren't even any lights. The rooms themselves glowed to create the sense of morning, evening, and night. The message of the architecture was very clear: The outside world does not concern you while you are in these halls.

"Get off the table, Freeman," said Ben when he entered the room. "I brought you some breakfast." He placed a tray of bizarre-looking food that resembled a Technicolor TV dinner on the table and helped her down. "Come on, recruit. Down the hatch."

M took a small bite of a pink gelatinous substance first. It tasted amazing, like bacon and grits smothered in butter. "What is this?"

"Bacon and grits, of course." Ben smiled. "And the green

stuff is fried green tomatoes in a spicy tomatillo sauce. The brown ice cubes are chunks of banana, which is great for your high sodium level. What have they been feeding you at Lawless? Your numbers were more askew than I've ever seen from a recruit."

"I honestly can't remember," said M as she wolfed her breakfast as if it were her first meal in years. "Food wasn't a priority there, you know?"

Ben laughed. "I suppose you had better things to do with your time. Well, at the Fulbright Academy meals are an extension of the training. Your portions are exact, your meal is planned out to give you the best diet possible, catered to your unique physiological needs. This tray is your standard kitchen experience, but we couldn't have you eat in the mess hall dressed in a robe."

M stared down at her empty tray and used the sleeve of her robe to wipe her mouth. "Wouldn't want to cause a scene on my first day here, huh? Well, I think you're too late. The other students got a good look at me already."

"Oh, don't be silly, M," came a voice from behind her. "I'm sure you'd cause a scene no matter what day it was." M twisted to see the doorway darkened by the tiny, vile person she had been happy to avoid for this long — Devon Zoso. Failed Lawless student, Fulbright double agent, and all-around creep, who had unleashed a black hole on the only life-sustaining planet in scientifically known existence. What wasn't to like about a girl like that?

"Ugh, I'm glad I finished eating. A scumbag like you can make a person lose her appetite," said M as she gripped her fork and knife tightly.

"Be nice, Freeman," said Ben. "You're on the same side, after all."

"That's the thing," admitted M. "I'm not sure we *are* on the same side."

"Words hurt, M," said Devon. "Just for that, maybe I won't give you your welcome-wagon present."

M tried to jump up, to grab Devon and shake some sense into her, but Ben forced her back down into her chair.

"Just bring her in, Zoso," said Ben, holding M in place. "And I want all bad blood squashed immediately. Fulbrights are nothing without each other. Just because you've been undercover doesn't mean you've forgotten everything we've taught you, has it?"

"Of course not, Direct," said Devon, flashing a smile that M couldn't read. It seemed snarky at first, but there was the slightest hint of fear behind her eyes at the same time. There was more than M and Devon's history clouding this windowless room. No, Devon and Ben had a past, too. "You two know each other, right?" asked Devon as she dragged another person into the room.

It was Jules, M's best friend and partner in crime. But the old Jules, with the graceful, athletic stature, was gone. The Jules who slumped into the room looked different, wounded, even. Her once-brown skin had turned ashen, her arms dangled listlessly at her sides, and this new Jules, dressed in a white robe, moved slowly, carefully, as if the life had withered from her.

"Jules!" cried M as she leapt up to help her friend, who was scorching hot with fever. "Devon, you should have let her sleep. She's clearly not over the serum yet."

"Hey, dear, you wanted the crew back together," said Devon. "Ben ordered a meet-up and I delivered. I can't help it if you're a danger to others as well as to yourself. I'm actually surprised you're so concerned about this sick little Byrdie here. You had the whole Fulbright Academy at your beck and call, and the only thing you asked for is to have your hench-twerps back by your side? You didn't even ask for your own mother's freedom. What kind of daughter lets her last living parent rot away in a cell like that?"

"I said, *squashed*, Zoso!" demanded Ben. "Now get out of here before you earn a demerit."

"Gladly," said Devon as her eyes stayed glued on M. She was testing M's nerves, but M stared right back at her until she turned and left the room. Then M bent over her friend.

"Jules, can you hear me?" she asked.

"M," mumbled the usually exuberant Jules. "Is that you?"

"It's me," answered M. "Just relax." She cleared the finished tray from the table and helped her friend lie down. "They gave you a shot. It's going to hurt like crazy for a while, but you'll be okay, and then we'll figure all this out together."

Jules smiled. "Same old M, huh?"

"Yeah, some things never change, do they?" M whispered. The pain from the shot had been agonizing, but watching Jules have to go through the same thing was ten times worse. "Why isn't she better yet?"

"The serum works differently on different people," said Ben. "And Miss Byrd seems to have a more . . . robust physiology than most."

"Sure. Her muscles have muscles," said M. "So?"

"So our special concoction has more to work with. Byrd's actually in such good shape that her body might even be fighting the serum, which wouldn't be the smartest thing to do."

"I can still hear you," said Jules from her prone position on the table. "And I'm not fighting anything. Look, here's my white flag. Just call off the chemistry, Captain."

"If I could, I would, Byrd," said Ben. "But you are part of a bigger picture now, so these steps are a necessary evil."

There was a knock at the door, and another kid stood in the entryway. He was skinny and awkward, unlike the other Fulbrights, and wearing a lab coat instead of the standard suit. His dark eyes matched his deep brown skin, which stood out dramatically against the stark whiteness of the Fulbright Academy's environment. "Direct, I have the new recruit ready. Should I bring him in?"

"Of course, Noles," said Ben. "Mr. Eaves, I presume?"

And in walked Merlyn, but M almost didn't recognize him. He was not the same geek she had met in the back of a limo on their way to the Lawless School. He wasn't even the same geek who had gabbed nonstop to the curator in the Black Museum a few days ago. Like Jules, he looked entirely different, but unlike Jules, these changes were for the better. His glasses were gone and his mop of hair had been trimmed high and tight, accenting his strong jawline and chiseled cheeks, which M had never noticed before. With his posture straightened, he appeared taller and more confident. Add in his new Fulbright uniform and Merlyn looked right at home here.

"M!" said Merlyn, running over to give her a hug. "I thought, well, I didn't know what to think."

M was scooped into his arms and felt a new strength in Merlyn that had never been there before. "What happened to you?" she asked. "You look so different."

"Oh yeah," he said bashfully. "Um, this is all Keyshawn's doing."

The kid in the lab coat extended his hand. "M Freeman, I've heard a lot about you. I'm Keyshawn Noles. I'm Merlyn's roommate, but I've also been assigned to help train your team."

"He's great, M," Merlyn interjected, like an excited, hyperactive child. "He gave me this shot and I just didn't need glasses anymore. Then he set me up with this crazy suit. And wait till you see his laboratory, it's . . . Hey, why is Jules lying on the table?"

"Don't mind me, you idiot," muttered Jules. "It's good to see the new you, too."

Keyshawn passed M and ran a small scanner over Jules. "She's not taking to the serum. Who's her roommate? I should have been notified about this immediately."

"She's with Zoso," said Ben. "I'll talk to her about it."

"Please do, Direct," said Keyshawn as he pulled out a syringe and plunged it into a bottle of violet fluid. Then, looking at Jules, he said, "This will help. Is it okay if I give you this shot?"

Jules gave a subtle nod and Keyshawn prepped her arm before gently inserting the needle. Instantly a wave of relief washed over her face and her body relaxed.

"She'll be loopy for a few minutes," Keyshawn told M and Merlyn. "Stay with her, and when she's feeling better, I'll see you in the lab. We'll get you set up with your uniforms so you can get out of those robes."

"Thanks," said M, "for helping Jules and Merlyn."

"That's what I'm here for," Keyshawn said with a smile.

"So the reunion's complete," interrupted Ben. "Noles, get back to your station and await further instructions." As Keyshawn left the room, Ben kept his eyes trained on M and Merlyn. "Sit, please, Miss Freeman, Mr. Eaves. I'd like to bring you up to speed."

Ben remained standing. The moment M and Merlyn took their seats, he spoke. "The past forty-eight hours have been quiet, due to the Lawless School's destruction, but the lines are lighting up with chatter now and we have a feeling that something big is being planned in retaliation."

"You sank their school," said M. "What did you expect? That this would end the game?"

"We expected a little more downtime, honestly," answered Ben. "The Lawless faction is not known for its ability to play together nicely, but it looks like they are getting the hang of it. There are a lot of conflicting reports coming in, but one thing is becoming clear: The Fulbrights will need you sooner than expected. Your father felt that you would be the key to disrupting the next Lawless plan and I believe him. For that reason, we'd like to get your team on an accelerated track in preparation for immediate fieldwork. You've shown promise in your Lawless missions, but let's face facts: You had dumb luck and older, more devious allies on your side."

What Ben was saying was definitely true. The Masters, Zara, Ms. Watts, Fox Lawless, Professor Bandit, Jones, even M's mother, they had all helped M navigate the treacherous maze of the last few months.

"So what do you want from us now?" asked Merlyn.

"I don't want anything from *you*, Eaves," said Ben in a cold, even tone. "Let's be perfectly clear about that. If it were up to me, you and Byrd would be at the bottom of whatever pit was left at the Lawless School. You are here at Freeman's request. We will train you only so that you will be helpful to her in any situation that may arise."

"Wow, tell us how you really feel, why don't you?" Merlyn said under his breath.

Ignoring Merlyn's comment, Ben looked at his watch and continued, "Byrd will need to be better by nine hundred hours. After that you'll report to Noles immediately. Do you understand?"

"Yes, Direct," said M.

"Good, then you have the room to yourselves," said Ben as he strode to the door. "I have a class to attend. And if you're late to see Noles, that's a demerit for each of you."

After he left, Merlyn and M rolled their eyes almost in unison. "Wow, he's a straight shooter, huh?" said Merlyn.

"Careful," said M. "It sounds like he's got his eyes on you. What do you think a demerit means around here, anyway? Does it go on your permanent record?"

"I don't want to find out," said Merlyn. "I have a feeling that whatever it goes on, it's going to be permanent . . . and it will probably sting like the dickens."

"Not worse than that shot, though," said M, rubbing the insertion point on her left wrist, which was still tender.

"Yours hurt?" asked Merlyn.

"You're kidding, right?" asked M. "I felt like a fish being gutted while getting a chemical peel."

"Really?" said Merlyn. "Keyshawn explained everything that was happening to me and gave me other stuff to stabilize the pain. It was over in no time."

"Looks like you won the roommate lottery, then," said M as she drifted back to the door to make sure the coast was clear. "Okay, let's get real. This place is psycho. We've seen what the Fulbrights are capable of and I don't think we can trust them, but I don't think we can trust anyone from the Lawless School, either."

"So what are we supposed to do?" asked Merlyn. "I mean, we're basically prisoners here, but out in the real world, Ms. Watts would hunt us down."

"You're right," said M, "so let's use that to our advantage. We're safe here and the Fulbrights think that we can be of use to them in the field."

"Why do they think that?" moaned Jules, who was now covered in sweat. Her fever had finally broken, but she looked far from better. Anger at Devon rushed over M again, but now was the time to remain calm and stay focused.

"My father. He left me a video," said M. "He seemed to think that I should stick with the Fulbrights, work with them toward some greater good. And he obviously convinced them that they should let me. Remember, he's the one who left me with the keys to solving Wild's *umbra mortis* mystery. What if there are other keys out there, waiting to be found?"

"Oh sure, and you want to find them while under the watchful eyes of the Fulbrights," said Merlyn. "That makes a lot of sense."

"It does, if you think about it," said M. "Ultimately we want the same thing as the Fulbrights. We both want to stop Ms. Watts from getting her hands on any more weapons."

"But that's not all the Fulbrights want," argued Merlyn. "They want to destroy Lawless at the same time."

"Let them try," said M. "They can have their war if it means that we can tag along and keep innocent people safe."

"It may be the fever talking, but that does seem like a good idea," croaked Jules from the table.

"Okay, you've got the invalid's vote," said Merlyn. "As long as we're talking about Ms. Watts, though, I've got one more question that's been bothering me. She really wants that second moon rock, right? But without Wild's meteorite, it's only a rock. She needs *both* if she's planning to fire off another do-it-yourself black hole."

Instantly M was taken back to her final showdown with Dr. Lawless. He had given up the meteorite way too easily; he'd hardly even made M work for it. And that led her to an inescapable conclusion. "Merlyn, you're a genius. Lawless only gave me a *piece* of the meteorite. I'd bet anything Ms. Watts still has the rest of it. . . . We definitely need to get to that rock before she does."

"Where do we even begin?" asked Jules.

"We find my mother. That's the best place to start," said M.

"But she could be anywhere," complained Merlyn, "and we don't even know where *we* are. No windows, white walls, we could be in a space station, for all we know!"

"Wherever we are, she's here with us," said M.

"That's why you didn't ask the Fulbrights for her freedom," said Jules. "You're not as clueless — or heartless — as Devon assumed."

A bolt of confidence and determination shot through M, though it could have been the serum taking a stronger hold of her system. "No, Devon is the clueless, heartless one," she said. "Can you imagine if I had asked for my mother to be released? Then we'd have no idea where she'd run and hide."

"Or what would be waiting for her when she got there," added Merlyn.

"It's better to have her here, even if we don't know where *here* is," said M. "This is our secret, guys. We can mount a search for my mother when the time is right. Apparently we're good at finding things that people don't want to be found. For now, though, we've got to work alongside the entire Fulbright

Academy. And I'm sure we're not the most popular cadets around here. Every Fulbright is training for one purpose and one purpose only: to capture and destroy Lawless students like us. They don't trust us, they don't like us, and they only see evil when they look at us. So get ready to become the unthinkable."

"What's that?" asked Merlyn.

"A good guy," said M.

CHAPTER 3
NEED-TO-KNOW BASIS

The endless turns of nondescript hallways made for the world's most boring maze, but thank goodness Merlyn had apparently paid attention to where Keyshawn's lab was located. Jules was up and about, with her almond complexion almost back in full. As the path splintered off into one long corridor after another, M became dizzy at the sprawling mental map of the school she was creating in her mind. And they were only seeing one floor! Who knew how high or how deep this place actually went. She was determined, though, to devote every inch to memory — she had to, if she had any hope of finding her mother. Every corner mawed into a new path, a new possible hiding place for something that wasn't supposed to be found.

And the doors! There were hundreds of doors that they passed along the way. What could be waiting behind each one? Were they dorm rooms? Classrooms? Weapons rooms? Jail cells? With each door lacking a handle, the unmarked entryways stood there like the ancient mysteries of Stonehenge, daring M to puzzle them out.

But time was not on their side, and M had enough mysteries to worry about. She hurried down the hallways, following

Merlyn's lead and looking over her shoulder regularly to make sure that Jules wasn't going to pass out. Whatever Keyshawn Noles had given her really helped. Taking stock of the new people in her life, M realized she had already formed opinions on who she could trust and who she shouldn't.

She trusted Ben, though the thought actually surprised her. He was not a fun guy, but he was at least honest. He didn't like Merlyn or Jules, and he didn't hide that fact from the world. M appreciated that. She also knew that Ben was following orders. He may be a direct, but he had a direct, too. That's the way things worked around here. She didn't need more than a few hours with the Fulbrights to put those pieces together.

The verdict was still out on Vivian. She was hard-pressed to keep a conversation going past a few cursory formalities, but that didn't make her a bad person, just an awkward person. And true, she hadn't helped M with the pain, but she had at least explained what was happening to the best of her ability. Still, M had laid her out pretty bad, and for a Fulbright, that had to be a hard pill to swallow. M put her in a mental maybe list of allies.

But Keyshawn, well, there was no question in her mind: She did not trust him at all. He was a plant so fake that she couldn't even see the roots. Cozy up to Merlyn first, then heroically save Jules from a Devon attack? He might as well have been part of the Smooth Criminal clique at the Lawless School — with his perfectly timed kindness and unassuming appearance. It was all a ploy to win M's confidence, and an obvious ploy at that. Not only was he great with her friends, but he also just happened to be the nicest and most earnest of their Fulbright liaisons? No, if it seemed like it was too good to be true, it *was* too good to be true 99 percent of the time. And Keyshawn was not a 1 percenter.

"This is it," said Merlyn as he turned to a door, which looked like every door they had previously passed.

"How on earth can you tell?" asked Jules.

"Oh, that's right. You don't have a suit yet," said Merlyn with a geektastic smile. "It's so mind-blowing that I'm not going to spoil it for you."

Then he placed his palm against the door and pressed gently until a sigh of air heaved from the frame and the door swung open. M took note of the lack of knobs and the pressurized, concealed hinges. The Fulbrights had not made this a criminal-friendly environment. In fact, breaking into any of these doors may be nearly impossible. Nearly.

The lab was the antithesis of everything cold and clean they had previously seen at the Fulbright Academy. Books with broken spines and well-worn covers were stacked in haphazard piles that stretched from floor to ceiling, and unfinished tech projects cluttered every remaining surface. Fulbright suits sprouted thin, stray wires like exposed arteries on an autopsy table, while open-faced motherboards of all sizes and complexities hung on a wall. It was like walking into a horror movie for robots that reveled in the gory side of artificial life, all guts and soldering irons ready for a modern-day Dr. Frankenstein to build, destroy, and start again. Five separate dry-erase boards were splattered with diagrams and messily written scientific formulas. Before the largest board, Keyshawn stood deep in thought.

"You made it," he said, turning around with a smile. "I was slightly worried. This place can be, well, confusing, if you're not used to it. I take it the suit works, Merlyn?"

"Absolutely," said Merlyn, with a giddiness M hadn't heard from him since their last class with Code, Lawless's prodigious programming professor. "Guys, Keyshawn built this thing especially for me."

"Well, don't get a big head," Keyshawn said while capping his pen. It was a subtle move that demanded attention. M had seen many different teachers use this exclamation mark to quiet their class. "I built one for each of you, coded to your strengths, your weaknesses, and made for only you to use."

"How?" asked M, running her hand along one of the empty uniforms, hung up like a pelt to dry.

"The suits react to the serum we administered," said Keyshawn with an obvious eagerness to explain the process.

Good, thought M. The more Keyshawn bragged about Fulbright tech secrets, the more light he would shed on their situation here.

"So there *is* a higher purpose for that insane roller coaster my body just went on," said Jules. "What was that amber stuff, anyway?"

"The amber fluid . . ." started Keyshawn, but then he paused to carefully choose his words. M knew that meant he was going to dumb it down for them. "It carries new chemicals through your body and deposits them along the way."

"And the chemicals bolster our health," finished M as she erased a stray mark on one of the dry-erase boards.

"Yes, some do," Keyshawn said excitedly. "But some map out the physiological makeup of the cadet. Those chemicals have been designed to serve as wi-fi devices for the body. So let's say you have an atrophied muscle — the chemical will send messages directly to your suit to ensure that when you use that muscle, the suit does the heavy lifting."

"Crazy, right?" said Merlyn. "That's how I remembered the way back here. It's like muscle memory! And the interface between the suit and the user is so natural that I can't tell where the suit ends and where I begin."

Merlyn may have been in seventh heaven with Keyshawn, but all M heard was that the suit was in control of the user. Which meant if the Fulbrights so wanted, they could turn their cadets into a programmable drone army.

"Why doesn't Vivian Ware have a uniform like this, then?" asked M. "She wears a knee brace, but your suit would fix her up, right?"

Keyshawn paused again at her question and M knew he was once again thinking carefully of the best way to phrase his answer. "Not everyone here chooses these suits."

"Because the suits are dangerous?" asked M.

"No, no, not at all," stammered Keyshawn. "The suits, well, some people think of them as a crutch. It's a stoic and out-dated way of thinking, if you ask me. The same people might

as well use a typewriter and carrier pigeons instead of computers, but it's hard to argue with that can-do mentality. For
Vivian, though, the suit wouldn't have corrected the issue
permanently."

"Meaning she'd only be able to walk when wearing the
suit," said M. "I'm not sold. Sounds so far like you've created a
remote-controlled second skin. So tell me, why should I get
into your suit?"

"Because one day you're going to need it," said Keyshawn.
"And you won't know you need it until the very second you
do. But what better way to prove its worth than to attend your
first drill? And trust me, you will want to have these on when
you do."

He gestured to the two dark suits behind him as if he were
presenting them as a generous prize. "I'll leave you to try
these on while I prepare the Maze."

As Keyshawn left the room through one of several doors, M
and Jules turned their attention to the empty suits. They were
sized perfectly. Their height, their measurements, it was if they
were looking at shadowy outlines of themselves. M's fingertips
sizzled when she touched her suit for the first time. As she
jerked her hand away, white sparks jumped between her skin
and the fabric. She shot a wide-eyed look at Merlyn, who just
smiled with excitement.

"It's electrifying, I know," he said. "But you'll get used to it.
That sensation is the chemicals recognizing the matching tech
components for the first time. Compare it to the first time a
QWERTY keyboard made sense to your hands, and instantly

every key was in the right place to spell out your thoughts without your having to hunt and peck."

"You know we're not computers, right?" asked Jules, who seemed to be having second thoughts about the new dress code. "And can mine come in pink? This black is way too drab."

"Just try it on already and stop being so girlie," joked Merlyn, but the looks that the girls gave seared through him and he appeared instantly sorry for what he'd said. "I'm going to pay for that one, aren't I?"

"Oh yeah," they said together with conviction.

"Now turn around while we slip into something more . . . technological," said Jules.

Brushing Merlyn's idiocy aside, M took the suit down and puzzled over its open back. She didn't see any Velcro or zippers. As she stepped in, though, the back of the suit closed around her automatically, like magnets locking into place. The effect was surprising, but nothing compared to what came next: a sudden light shock that danced over her entire body and gave her goose bumps, like millions of antennae were growing out of her skin. The suit was communicating with her body in a language that M's mental self couldn't understand but that her physical self did. "Whoa" was all she could say.

"I know!" said Merlyn without turning around, but M could hear his wide smile. "This must be how a Jedi feels!"

"Merlyn, I'm sure this is all incredibly exciting to you," she said quietly. "But you know we can't trust Keyshawn, right? This suit, it's great, but if it can do everything Keyshawn promises, it's basically a skintight jail cell waiting to happen. Can you hack into these suits and put us back in charge?"

Merlyn turned around, his smile replaced with an expression of shock. "Oh wow, you're right. I . . . I got too hung up on the next-level tech specs to think of the downsides of the design."

"Well, the suits apparently don't make you any smarter," said Jules with a wink. "Come on, Merlyn. I'm sure you've got an answer up there in that big Crimer head of yours."

"I can't believe I didn't think it through," said Merlyn faintly to himself.

"Are we ready?" asked Keyshawn as he came back into the room.

"You know that old saying, *The clothes make the man*?" M answered. "I finally understand what it means."

"I'm glad you like it," said Keyshawn. "But this suit is slightly more complicated than a nice shirt that makes you feel like a million bucks. In fact, this uniform *costs* a million bucks."

Keyshawn picked up a tablet and walked over between Jules and M, murmuring as he studied the small screen. "Yes, it looks like everything is responding beautifully. Better than I imagined, actually."

"What do you mean, better than you imagined?" asked M, whose nervousness was building in the pit of her stomach. "You've done this, like, tons of times, right?"

"A little less than that, if my math is correct," said Keyshawn distractedly.

"Let's assume you're great at math," she continued, "because if you designed these suits and wrote those equations on the boards over there, then your math is probably pretty brilliant."

M twisted and grabbed Keyshawn in a single, swift movement that caught them both off guard. Lifting the taller boy off the ground, she asked, "How many suits like this have you made?"

As Keyshawn's toes dangled and reached for the ground, he creaked out an answer in the tiniest voice M had ever heard. "Including yours? Four."

"Hold up," exclaimed Merlyn. "You're saying that we're the guinea pigs?"

"I'm saying that I have been given orders to introduce a new tech on a trial basis with a small team," admitted Keyshawn calmly while still in M's grasp. "I didn't know in advance who would be chosen for the team. And I was under the impression you knew about the test."

"Did it look like I knew what was going on when I was paralyzed on the table?" asked Jules.

"He doesn't care whether we're willing subjects or not. Do you, Keyshawn?" said M. "You only care about the suits and how they work." Then she tossed him heavily to the floor, where he landed hard.

Even though he lost his breath on impact, Keyshawn spoke through his windedness. "You have to understand. I've put so much time and thought into making sure these suits are in excellent working order. This is the future of the Fulbrights. With this, maybe, hopefully, we can end this conflict once and for all."

"Oh yeah, you care so much about ending the war that you created a supersoldier," answered M. "That makes you about as smart as the guy who invented the atomic bomb."

"Well, that guy *was* pretty smart," added Merlyn thoughtlessly. Then he caught M's look. "Oh, but, yeah, not in the way you're referring to."

"Who signed off on this trial?" M asked Keyshawn. "Beyond Ben, that is. I want to know who he reports to. I want to know who you all report to."

"John Doe," declared a new voice from the doorway. M, Merlyn, and Jules all turned, ready to fight. Between the harsh backlighting of the hallway and the dusty darkness of Keyshawn's lab, they couldn't make out the newcomer's face.

"And don't be so aggro on Keyshawn," the voice continued. "He may not be the most personable guy, but he means well. Besides, by now you must have figured out that all facts in the Fulbright Academy come on a need-to-know basis."

"Thanks for the straight answer," called out M with a cautious edge in her voice. "Now, why don't you come in and join us, friend?"

"Come on, guys, relax," said the figure as he strolled toward them. "It's just little old me."

And into the light of the room stepped the fourth suit, the mysterious voice from the darkness, none other than Calvin Fence — the Lawless student they had left for dead.

CHAPTER 4
MAZE, MAYHEM, MEDUSA

A gray smudge, floating lifelessly in the freezing river current, shoulders slack and sliding against the thick layer of ice that held him underwater — that's how M remembered Calvin Fence. She wished her most prominent memories of Cal were from their first days at the Lawless School, when he was a goofy, green-eyed, awkward kid. But those memories had been replaced with the sight of Cal in heavy, soaked clothes, arms like dangling ropes cut loose from their moors, and a body adrift like an unmanned lifeboat discovered in an ocean storm.

Even now as he stood before her alive and well, M knew she would never forget that terrible vision of Cal. She wouldn't let herself forget it because that underwater dead end had been her fault. She had led Cal to the painting. And while his own mother drove him into the frigid waters, M was the one who'd tried to save him and came up empty-handed.

In fact, just before the ice had cracked open to spit them back out into the breathable night air, M had let go of herself, too. It was a disturbingly tender experience that she and Cal shared, the letting go. It was a feeling she was determined to never feel again.

"Cal!" exclaimed Merlyn. "You're all right!"

"Better than that," said Cal. "And I have you to thank for it, M. I'm told that if you hadn't come after me, I would have been frozen fish food."

"We both got lucky," M said as she carefully held her arms out and gave Cal a hug. This time she did not miss her mark. "The Fulbrights probably would have let us drown if not for my necklace — it was the only thing important enough for them to save."

"It was more than the necklace," said Cal. "Give yourself a little credit. The Fulbrights came back for you later, didn't they?"

As she pulled away from Cal, M's hand absently rose to her chest, searching for the phantom necklace that was no longer there. It was a hard habit to break. Again, she was transported back to that fateful night in Hamburg, Germany, when Devon, in full Fulbright gear, had snatched her necklace, and Cal's unresponsive body had been dragged away like a lifeless bag of bones.

"What happened to you after Hamburg?" asked Jules.

"Switched sides like you, I guess," said Cal with a wry smile. "Which is to say the Fulbrights brought me here, nursed me back to health, then asked me if I wanted to help them defeat my mother. As you can imagine, I couldn't resist."

"Yeah," said Merlyn. "I definitely get that. Ms. Watts tried to do us in, too, you know."

"Makes sense," said Cal. "She never liked you guys all that much."

"The feeling is mutual," said Jules. "No offense, but your mom is the worst."

"Wait," interrupted M. "If you're here, did Foley make it, too?" Cal hadn't been the only member of M's crew captured that night. As far as she knew, there had been no sign of Foley, an older Lawless student and Cal's guardian, since their heist had gone wrong.

Cal frowned and looked toward the ground. "He's here, but he's under heavy surveillance — like, the locked-up kind. He's Lawless through and through. Even after he learned what my mom had been up to, there was no breaking through his criminal convictions. As far as he's concerned, we're in the belly of the beast. It didn't matter that the Fulbrights saved him from the fire."

"The fire that *they* started," said M. "That's mighty caring of them, isn't it?"

"Careful," Keyshawn piped up from outside the reunion circle. "If Ben or Vivian hear you talking like that, they'll lock you up alongside this friend of yours. Doe doesn't like bugs in his program, if you catch my drift."

"And just who is this John Doe, other than the guy behind the Fulbrights?" asked M.

"He's the *unseen* guy behind the Fulbrights," answered Cal.

"And the less we talk about him, the better," added Keyshawn.

"Because if we keep this up, we'll endanger your suit tests," guessed M.

Keyshawn paced nervously through the stacks of books. "Yes," he said begrudgingly, "and no. It's been my experience that avoiding John Doe makes for a much easier time at the academy. If you do catch his eye, it doesn't matter if you're the class pet or the class pest. Either way, you'll be led down a path best left untraveled."

"You do realize that just by having us here," said M, "just by having us take part in your experiment, that we're all on John Doe's radar?"

Keyshawn grumbled and tapped angrily at his tablet.

"How do you know about John Doe?" Jules asked Cal.

"His dad," answered M.

"John Doe is your dad!" cried Merlyn.

"No, no," said Cal, motioning for everyone to calm down. "I'm not related to John Doe. My dad's a Fulbright. But he never talked to me about his boss — if the guy even exists. I mean, it sounds like an alias to me. *John Doe* is actually the ID that police give to people who are unknown for one reason or another."

"Enough!" snapped Keyshawn. "John Doe is not your priority right now. I've only got two weeks to get you prepped for the field and if this experiment fails, then *I* fail, and I'll be —" Just as quickly as he had raised his voice in frustration, he stopped himself short. "And *we'll* be in a situation we'd all rather avoid."

M narrowed her eyes. "What happens in two weeks?"

"I don't know," answered Keyshawn. "But something is in the works. It's the reason my program was green-lighted. And it's the reason you're all here today instead of locked up. So, you've got two weeks to learn everything the Fulbrights can teach you, take it or leave it. If you want out now, say the word and I'll call Ben to take you away."

The perspiration beaded on Keyshawn's forehead. And in this perfectly temperature-controlled environment, M knew that his sweat spoke volumes.

"Two weeks is plenty of time," said M in a calming manner. She was doing her best to channel her father, making her voice jovial, hopeful, and casually reassuring all at once. It worked; Keyshawn let out a sigh of relief.

"So what's the first step?" asked Cal. "You guys got a Box hidden around here?"

Keyshawn wiped his brow with a handkerchief and motioned in the direction of the door he'd gone through earlier. "The Maze is a good place to start."

Through the door, the crew entered a long, wide room that seemed as big as a football field, but the tail end of the room was hidden in dark shadows. The ceiling was so uncomfortably low, they could reach up and touch it. The cramped headspace reminded M of her narrow escape from being crushed in the Box, the high-tech training facility at Lawless that Ms. Watts had reprogrammed into a deathtrap. There were dim lights recessed throughout the room in key areas, which barely helped shed any real light on what they could expect to happen next.

"Okay," said Jules with a sudden excitement. She was back in her element. Anything that raised her heart rate was a welcome challenge. "So what's the mission?"

"You just need to escape," said Keyshawn.

"Escape an empty room?" said Merlyn with a nasal snort. "Easy peasy."

Unfortunately M didn't share her friend's confidence. In her experience there was always more than met the eye to these tests. She felt her suit tighten around her at the thought, but decided that must have been her imagination.

"Less talkin', more walkin'," said Cal. He shoved Merlyn onto the main floor.

"Hey!" yelled Merlyn as he stumbled forward, flinching as if he expected something bad to happen next. But nothing did. Instead he stood, scratching his head, a few steps away from the rest of the group. Smiling nervously, he asked, "Is this one of those tests where it's more important to make the first move than to complete the journey?"

"No," said Keyshawn dryly, and a solid metal wall sprung up from the floor and crunched against the ceiling, trapping Merlyn on the other side. The others jumped at the wall's sudden, violent appearance.

"So it really is a maze," said M, as she touched the new wall. It felt warm, heavy, and unbreakable. "Isn't that kind of obvious? To name a maze the Maze?"

"I'm sorry if we don't have the same flair or swagger that the Lawless School boasts," said Keyshawn absently as he watched a dot moving across the screen of his tablet. M realized he was tracking Merlyn's movements. "Here we call it like we see it."

"Sounds too simple for my taste," said Jules.

"Oh, we may be straightforward, but you'll find your training anything but simple," replied Keyshawn with a renewed interest in the discussion. Clearly he was satisfied with Merlyn's progress...or nonprogress. "The Maze is trained to play against you. The walls rearrange themselves constantly based on changing algorithms; there are no defining characteristics to the paths, and what was a dead end one second can lead to an exit the next."

"So the object is to confuse the subject and see how quickly they can make key decisions," said M.

"Not how quickly," said Keyshawn excitedly. "Or not only how quickly, I should say. We're studying *how* you make decisions. After you run this maze several times, we'll know how you think — to the point that we could potentially predict your every move. Do you favor the right path or the left? Are you willing to travel backward to move forward? At exactly what point will you give up? It's fascinating stuff."

M realized that Keyshawn was giving them more information than what was strictly need-to-know, which was useful to her but perhaps very dangerous for him. He obviously lived for scientific study and wasn't modest about his achievements, either. But she sensed that he was a loner at this school.

The wall sank open again, but Merlyn was gone and so was the expansive room. In its place was a pitch-dark path that seemed to twist in the gloom. The sound of metal shifting heavily echoed from within.

"I'll be the next hamster," said Jules with a smile. She leapt full force into the slot and ran into the shadows. The walls closed around her and she disappeared, but M could swear that she heard Jules giggling, giddy at the challenge.

"Your friend is enthusiastic," noted Keyshawn. "Always a dangerous reaction to the Maze."

"How do you mean?" asked Cal.

"The Maze plays to your level, doesn't it?" said M. "The more you attack it, the more it attacks you."

"I can see why people are interested in you," Keyshawn said as the walls opened up again.

"Anything else you want me to know before I go?" M asked. Keyshawn and Cal both remained silent. "Okay, then, see you on the other side!"

M entered the Maze and left the Fulbright world behind her. The sterile, well-lit hallways of doors were nowhere to be found in here. It was like being underwater again. The metal chamber was a cold, damp nest of murky shadows, which beckoned her in every direction. Three distinct paths sat before her, each a yawning entrance of emptiness. A small light flickered dimly in the far distance of the middle opening, a sign of life. Or was it a sign of a trap? Before deciding what direction to take, M held herself still and cleared her mind. It was a nearly impossible feat, since every muscle in her body burned with the instinct to run. Her very bones were filled with an unconquerable urgency to escape the Maze at any cost. But M knew this was the Maze at work, so she held her ground.

It wasn't a long moment, but it was enough so that the Maze reconfigured itself. The changing shadows became a crosshatch of darkness that pulled her back to the memory of the relentless *umbra mortis* as its slow, sucking depths swallowed the Lawless School. M was frozen, trapped in her nightmare scenario.

Keep on moving, she thought to herself. *If you don't, the Maze will come for you.* With her first step forward M instantly banged her head against a lower section of the ceiling. "Ouch!" she cried out to herself. "Where did that beam come from?"

Ducking down, M felt her way along the beam, letting it guide her in the darkness. The first beam connected to a second beam. They were both hefty and strong, like the support beams from her basement back at home, which definitely wasn't the cheeriest place, but she couldn't shake the strange sensation that bumping her head here was no mistake. An obstacle like that was most likely designed to embarrass cadets, surprise and scatter them in another direction. But what if the Maze was working with her? M closed her eyes and stepped forward again. This time she ran into a low table with her knee. Sure, it smarted, but the bruise would be worthwhile. M knew this table. She knew this entire layout. And she began retracing her basement path from memory. As she moved past the remembered locations of the old, dusty boxes that littered her basement back home, the Maze allowed her to continue unhindered. The walls traveled alongside her, as if she were in a car surrounded by big-rig fourteen wheelers with cargo hauls blocking out the roadside, and the momentum was palpable.

On her left, M heard a low, muffled noise coming from an unseen room behind a dark gray wall. Straining to listen, she realized it was Merlyn talking to himself, logically parsing out his next move. She considered hollering to him, but then changed her mind. If the Maze had become her own basement, that meant everyone's journey through the Maze was different, and if she tried to help him, she might end up negatively affecting his results. Individual results were what Keyshawn was after, anyway, right? And if they had any hope of finding her mother and escaping this place to stop Ms. Watts, then they had better keep their heads down and at least pretend to follow orders.

M pushed farther, still counting and retracing her steps as if she were at home in the basement when she finally reached the last step. If she had really been back home, M would have been face-to-face with the far wall, with her feet sinking slightly over the cracked foundation that rooted up from the floor. That wall still held a collection of her father's tools. Hacksaws, screwdrivers, paintbrushes, boxes of nails, a flashlight, and well-rusted gardening shears hinged on hooks, banished to the basement, waiting to be useful again.

Back in the Maze, M took another deep breath before stepping forward . . . straight into a solid wall. Her nose and chest took the brunt of the blow, but when she tried to step backward, there was another wall in place behind her. Frantically she lifted her arms to guide herself sideways, but was again met by unrelenting walls. She was trapped in the spot, held in a coffin-confined space. M crouched down and jumped up as high as she could, working her arms up to grab hold of any ledge she could find. Nothing was there, not even the low ceiling. She braced her arms and legs against the walls and began to scale the slippery, upward path as best she could, but a new ceiling capped her exit. Determined, M leapt back down to the ground hard, with all her strength, crashing through the Maze floor. The sudden breakthrough surprised her and she flexed her hands, scratching at tunnel walls that twisted and turned like an enclosed waterslide at midnight.

A light dawned from below and M tumbled out of the tunnel into a blisteringly bright, open space. An unflinching floor caught her in a dazed heap, knocking the wind out of her on impact. Bruised and gasping for air, she tried to stand up and refocus her blurry eyes in the intense white light of the room. She stood, then fell back down, unsure of where she was now.

"Made it, huh?" came Vivian's indifferent voice from the far corner of the room. "Noles, the subject has completed the mission. What's her next step?"

Keyshawn's response crackled through a speaker. "Remark-able," he said. "That's a run for the record books! The others are nowhere near completion."

"Protocol, Noles," demanded Vivian as M's lungs fought to breathe. "I don't care about the others or about the records. Just tell me what I need to do next. This test was supposed to take all day and I don't care to babysit."

"Sorry, sorry," said Keyshawn. "Her suit tells me that she could use some rest. Take her back to the rec room and let her lie down. I'll come get her as soon as the others finish."

"Great," huffed Vivian in an annoyed tone. "Get up, Freeman. Time for some R and R."

M held out her hand, expecting Vivian to help her up, but Vivian simply turned and walked out the door, leaving M alone, slouched on the floor and wondering if the Maze was really over or if this was another part of the wretched test.

Either way, M stood up and followed Vivian into what looked like a hospital waiting room. The well-worn chairs were a throwback, orange fabric and wood. They looked out of place against the glossy environment of the academy. If anything, these chairs belonged at the Lawless School, and something about them instantly made M focus on her situation.

"Hey, is there a bathroom around here?" she asked.

"Yeah, just outside on the right," said Vivian.

"Thanks," said M with a smile. She turned right out of the rec room and made her way down the empty hall, seizing the opportunity to explore the Fulbright Academy without direct guidance. The doors on this level were all closed, but a few actually had windows, which M glanced through while walking past them, careful not to stop and stare.

Classes. The rooms were filled with Fulbright students, sometimes sitting at desks and taking notes, sometimes sparring with one another in hand-to-hand combat. The teachers all stood tall and rigid like generals.

M turned another corner only to come face-to-face with another roaming student, who barked out an order. "Pass, cadet."

Great, thought M, *a hall monitor.* She looked the boy up and down before smiling, shaking her head, and patting her uniform searching for a nonexistent pass. "Sorry, I'm in a hurry. I'm looking for Devon Zoso," she said smoothly. "Direct Downing sent me to fetch her."

"Direct Downing," repeated the monitor with a suspicious look. He pulled out a tablet and flicked through a list of names. As she waited, a bell rung like a buzzer at a sports event, and the hallway filled with Fulbright cadets moving on to their next classes. Dressed in the proper attire this time, M took her opportunity and ducked into the flowing lines while the hall monitor had his head down.

"Hey, cadet!" she heard the boy call out from somewhere behind her. "Wherever you are, whoever you are, you better hope I don't catch you again!"

M shrugged off his empty threat, marched with the crowd, and continued her search. She knew her mother wasn't going to be down this corridor. There was no way the Fulbrights would keep their prisoners so close to their trainees. Though M was here, wasn't she? But then, they thought of her as a cadet, which was a mistake.

Another buzzer rang out and the cadets neatly filed into their various classrooms, clearing the hallway for M again. Only, the hallway wasn't entirely clear. Standing right in front of her was Vivian, shaking her head slowly from side to side. "You're not as smart as they made you out to be."

"What makes you say that?" asked M defiantly.

"Well, for one, this tablet tells me everything about you," said Vivian. "Even when you have to go to the bathroom. Guess what? You didn't."

"So why did you let me go?" asked M.

"I was bored," admitted Vivian. "I figured I'd see how far

you'd take your little escapade. Maybe also see how accurate your tracker is."

Ugh, the tracker. M made a mental note to have Merlyn crack that as well.

"But then you had to go and get that poor cadet in trouble," continued Vivian. "Plus, you implicated Downing, Zoso, and myself. Come, now, Freeman. What did we ever do to you?"

"Do I really have to answer that?" asked M, who couldn't believe she was actually feeling bad for duping that half-wit hall monitor.

"Well, I hope whatever we did isn't half as bad as what I have to do now," said Vivian as she made a quick swipe on her tablet.

M's body immediately froze in place from the neck down. She felt like she was turning to stone. "What are you doing to me, Medusa?"

"Tsk, tsk, Freeman," said Vivian carelessly. "I'm not doing anything to you. You did this to yourself."

Suddenly M's suit started to constrict around her, squeezing so tight that the air was forced out of her lungs. Her head rolled around on her neck as the crushing force weighed down on her, and her vision went red, then black.

Her dreams came swiftly, like thieves in the night through open windows. She dreamed of her father, of the "whole house" games of hide-and-seek they used to play. But in her dream, her father was terribly well hidden. And as she combed through the house, searching in every closet, under every bed, she floated past familiar faces.

Her mother was seated in the room they called the once-living room, admiring a painting with a handsome, golden-hued wood frame embellished with sculpted angels and demons. M strained to see the painting, but the image was unfocused, almost like several different paintings on top of one another all at once. When she turned back, her mother had disappeared.

In the hallway, Jones knelt by the fireplace, dressed in the same disguise he'd worn at the Lawless School library. He did not look toward M at all. Instead he was tearing out yellowed pages from an ancient book with determination. Then he tossed the pages into the fire, which sparked and licked intensely at each sheet. It seemed the most natural action in the world: Fire burned the book's paper because this paper was made to be burned. Smoke fogged the room, forcing M to move on.

Ms. Watts was waiting in the kitchen, razor-sharp knife in hand, but instead of preparing a meal, she was carving out patterns in the walls, in the cabinets, and in the hardwood floor. M felt that she was seeing something that was not meant to be seen, as if Ms. Watts were slicing away at reality itself, cutting through to something primordial, long buried, and never meant to be exposed. Then the carvings began to pulse and throb, and suddenly the kitchen was breathing with mad-ness, with Ms. Watts trapped in its cold heart.

M ran to the upper level, screaming for her father. The game wasn't fun anymore. The game was sick, threatening, and unhinged. Cal stood at the top of the stairs, waving for M to hurry. Perhaps he had found her father? He pointed to an open door, and M saw Jules clinging to the doorknob, feet in the air behind her as her body throttled violently, like a rope in a tug-of-war over a black hole that ate away the room. M grabbed Jules and pulled her with all her might, screaming for Cal to help her, but Cal had vanished. When she turned back to Jules, M discovered that she wasn't gripping her friend's hand anymore, but the antique, ornate knob to a closed door.

She quickly shoved the door open, but Jules wasn't there. In her place was Devon, deviously picking a locked safe with a stream of light cracking through the seams in the steel. M rushed over and threw Devon down to keep her from seeing what was inside the safe as the latch flew open and radiance erupted into the room. But Devon fought back. Her hands, black with soot, pushed against M's face, leaving fingerprints all over M's cheeks and throat. They tumbled out of the white room and into a bathroom across the hall, where a masked Fulbright snatched Devon up and tossed her into a bathtub filled with water. As Devon struggled to breach the surface, the Fulbright faced M and yelled, *"DON'T RUN!"*

Terrified, M backed out of the room, then bolted downstairs and through the front door, trying to escape the Fulbright from the bathroom. But beyond the porch, Professor Bandit stood in the yard, poised with a shovel caked in wet mud. With his sharp shoes and pant cuffs stained with grass, Bandit scooped a mound of dirt back into a crudely dug, chilling hole of exposed earth. His stormy eyes met hers with a mixture of sadness, exhaustion, and apology. Whatever he was doing, he did not want to do it, but he did so out of obligation. As he returned to his task, the floorboards beneath M gave way and she tumbled through the deck into the basement.

The darkness consumed her. She quickly stood and ran her hands along the crumbling walls, trying to find her father's flashlight, but it wasn't where it should have been, by the other hanging tools. Then there was a click as a small light shined behind M and cast her shadow on the cracked hairline fault working up the wall. *"Who's there?"* asked M as she tried to see past the bouncing glow that moved toward her. *"Who's there?"* she called again.

"Who's there?!" M screamed aloud as she launched out of the orange chair and tackled a very surprised Merlyn.

"M! It's Merlyn!" he hollered as she held him down. "Wake up and snap out of it before you really hurt me!"

"I told you not to wake her up," said Cal with a snort. "You never wake someone who's in a sleep that deep."

"Merlyn, geez!" snapped M. "You freaked me out!"

"I freaked you out?" Merlyn replied incredulously. "If *I* freaked *you* out, then why am I the one scared for my life?"

M looked around the room to see Cal and Vivian regarding her, wide-eyed, as she pinned Merlyn to the floor with a fist raised in the air, ready to strike.

"Now that's the M I expected to see in the hallway," said Vivian.

Ignoring her roommate's comment, M unclenched her fist and helped Merlyn back up. "Sorry. I wasn't myself, I guess."

"No, that was the same M I remember," said a worn-out-looking Jules, leaning against the doorway as if her life depended upon it.

"Finally," exhaled Cal. "We've been waiting forever for you to get through that Maze."

"Wait," said M. "How long have I been back here?"

As if in answer to her question, the white walls dimmed.

"That's the cue for lights-out, everyone," announced Keyshawn as he stormed into the room like an angry teacher annoyed by misbehaving students. "I wish I could say that this has been a great day for all of you, but it looks like we've got our work cut out for us. Get some sleep, and we'll gather back in the lab tomorrow."

Devon drifted into the room soundlessly to collect Jules, as if she had been waiting just outside, while Keyshawn motioned for Merlyn to follow him.

"Let's go, Freeman," Vivian said as she stood up. "Or do I need to make you strike another pose?"

M got to her feet and turned to Cal. "What about you? Is your direct coming?"

"I'm sure he's on his way," said Cal. "He's pretty reliable when he wants to be. You go and get some more rest. And have good dreams this time, okay?"

M smiled at the thought. Good dreams. What would that be like? "I'll try" was all she said as she walked into the hallway after Vivian, following her up the first staircase M had seen since coming to the Fulbright Academy, which only led to another dimming path.

CHAPTER 5
MASK

Hours. That's how long it had taken the others to complete their personal Mazes. M wondered how she could have gotten through her challenge so much faster than her friends. Sure, everyone experienced a different Maze, according to Keyshawn, but that hardly explained why Jules, the most fit person M had ever met, came out last and looking like she'd just run two triathlons.

Vivian remained her usual robotic self on the walk back. It had been a poor effort on M's part to assume she could give Vivian the slip with a simple lie. Especially when her clothes were monitoring her every biorhythm. If M was going to make any headway with her direct, it was up to her to break the ice that surrounded Vivian.

"So," M started when they were in their room, "I don't suppose you've ever had to use that stonewalling technique on another Fulbright before, have you?"

"First time for everything," answered Vivian, nonplussed. "Nifty suits Keyshawn tailored for you."

"Yeah, fits like a straitjacket," said M as she loosely swung her arms around, trying to lose the tiny pins-and-needles feeling at the tip of her fingers. "It hurt, you know. Could you seriously not do that again?"

"Let's make a deal. Don't run away and I won't stop you from running away," said Vivian.

"That doesn't sound like much of a deal to me," M said as she undid the back of her suit. It wasn't clenching tightly around her at the moment, but still, she felt better with the magnetized latch open. Then in an effort to keep the chitchat civil despite her hurt pride, she switched conversational gears. "So, the Maze, huh? It's sure something else."

"That's what they say," answered Vivian absently.

Getting Vivian to talk was like pulling teeth, but since M had been put in a full-body sleeper hold for most of the day, she was anything but tired now.

"But you've run it, right?" she asked. "Like, it must be standard training around here."

"Standardish," said Vivian, disappearing behind a partition wall to prepare for bed.

M sat on her bunk, still dressed in her Fulbright suit. Looking at the black webbing and wires, she felt like an off-duty superhero who hadn't changed back into her secret identity yet.

In a pair of light and airy pajamas, Vivian breezed across the floor and into bed. Her hair was neatly combed and draped loose around her shoulders. M was suddenly ashamed of her rugged wear and rat's-nest hair in a way that she'd never been at the Lawless School. *Pretty* wasn't something the students did there. No, there was always another safe to crack or trophy to steal. Plus, coiffed hair and painted fingernails rarely survived the Box. Still, the allure of soft pajamas was a siren song to M. "Do I have a pair of pj's, too?"

"You'll find everything you need in your closet," answered Vivian, who had picked up a book by her bedside.

M stood up clumsily and stepped behind the partition. Through her open closet door, she saw an empty hanger on the rack. Pausing, she stole a glance at Vivian's closet to see her roommate's lone Fulbright suit hung there, mask and all. The mask sat motionless and empty, and M couldn't help thinking of the discarded mask she'd found months ago on the crash-landed plane to Lawless. The hollow eyes, the green webwork of wires — that mask had been a very unsettling sight. "Ugh, still a creep factor nine," she whispered to herself and shuddered.

Peeking from behind the partition, M saw that Vivian was engrossed in her book. Without a sound, she slipped over to her roommate's chest of drawers. She needed to get her hands on Vivian's tablet. That thing was M's control board, and M didn't like being controlled. Vivian had the tablet when she'd come back here, but not when she came out. It must be in the drawers, reasoned M. But she froze as she was about to pull open the top drawer. Taped across all five drawers were tiny strands of blond hair: Vivian's hair. This was an old and effective security trick. The hair was difficult to see if you weren't looking for it. Once broken, the hair would prove that someone had gone through Vivian's property. A trap like this had to be reset every day, assuming Vivian wanted to get into her drawers, which meant using a new strand of hair each time.

"Paranoid much?" M whispered to herself, but then she

realized that Vivian had a very good reason to be paranoid. She was M's roommate, after all. M pieced together a scenario in which she swung for the fences tonight, breaking into Vivian's dresser, cracking the tablet, and bolting to find her mom. But no, it was too much for right now. She needed a little more time to gather intel. When she had it, Vivian's bombshell blond strands wouldn't stand in her way.

M slid back over to her assigned set of drawers and found pajamas and a brush neatly displayed in the top drawer. So, following Vivian's example, M quickly hung up her suit and changed. The new clothes were heavenly, but brushing her hair for the first time in what seemed like months yanked her back down to earth by the roots.

"There," M said as she walked out from behind the partition. She presented herself as a model on the runway, hoping to get a smile out of Vivian. "Now I feel at least a little more human and a little less like a cyborg."

Vivian looked up from her book, unfazed, and nodded. "Indeed. And please stay out of my personal things. I'll give you a warning this time."

"How in the world did you know?" asked M, looking behind her for a well-placed mirror that might have broadcasted her every move.

"I didn't know. I was just guessing. You've got to work on your poker face, Freeman."

"So," M continued casually, even though she was totally aggravated at herself for stumbling yet again, "are you going to tell me why you haven't been in the Maze?"

If she surprised Vivian with her question, her roommate hid it well. "Who says I haven't?"

"You say it," said M. "It's written all over you. Avoiding the conversation, not answering questions, and that suit in your closet looks brand-new, while mine is already beaten down from a single run in the Maze. Now, are you going to tell me or are you going to make me guess?"

Vivian closed her book and sat up straight. She appeared to be keeping her composure, but M knew that there was a quiet pride behind Vivian's steely eyes. And pride can be a dangerous thing when bruised, as her father used to tell her.

"The Maze," responded Vivian, "is the Keyshawn Noles show, a carnival ride that's virtually untested. He found it in a pile of other scrapped projects built by some Fulbright old-timer. Since he fixed it up, only a few recruits have been asked to run the course, and I wasn't chosen for the program."

"But you put in for it, didn't you?" asked M with a smile.

"Of course I did." Vivian yawned as if the conversation were boring her to sleep. "Even though Keyshawn is a divisive person at the academy, I like to try every test available to push me."

"Push you to what?"

"To be the best."

"Wait, you're telling me that Keyshawn, little old dorky Keyshawn, is divisive here?" asked M. "He's just a science nerd."

"There's a saying around here," said Vivian. "Keyshawn Noles everything or Keyshawn Noles nothing. And only time will tell."

"What's that supposed to mean?" asked M.

"It means that your lab partner has some crazy ideas about how science works and he's been given a short leash to prove his theories," said Vivian. "When his concepts work, they're brilliant."

"And when they don't?"

"When they don't," admitted Vivian, "bad things happen."

"And that's why he's on a short leash," concluded M. "And that's one of the reasons we're working with him now. Beta testing."

"It's not for me to involve myself in your issues," Vivian told M coldly. "Now, if you don't mind, it's been a long day." Then, like flipping a switch, Vivian laid her head down and fell instantly asleep.

She's like a robot powering down, thought M as she watched her roommate slumber. Lying back in her own bed, M ran through her Fulbright experience so far, processing this new information. The thoughts scrambled in her head as she tried putting everything together, but the big picture was elusive.

She remembered her father's video. It had been so strange to see him again, to hear him say her name one last time. She smiled at how nice it made her feel even though he was warning her. But what specifically was he trying to warn her about? Was he honestly telling her that the Fulbrights needed her help, or was that a ploy to get them to show her the video? Maybe he'd planted another message in the film somehow. She shut her eyes and replayed her father's words and images over and over again.

Two things stood out immediately. The first was the other voice outside of the booth, but that felt too random, too unrehearsed, and too out of her father's control to have been a coded message. But one thing every filmmaker controls is the camera. So why did the video begin with her father out of the frame? Perhaps because he was showing her the bench . . . the bench covered with initials! Then M remembered her father's closing words: *Always remember that you are greater than the sum of the parts your mother and I gave you.* It didn't sound like something he would say at all. It was too clunky and more than a little hokey. M culled together all the initials from memory, which were linked with plus signs, then added up the *sum* . . . and decoded her father's true statement.

Do as they say, not as they do.

Tracing the slight bump on her left wrist, where her tracker was buried inside her, M realized that she was already following her father's secret instructions. She was playing along with the Fulbrights but hadn't believed for a moment that she was one of them.

Periodically through the night, M got out of bed and paced around the room, looking for any sign that her activity was waking up sleeping beauty, but Vivian remained recklessly asleep. It was a small victory. Her roommate was confident in the power of the tracker and the suit, and that reliance was something M could exploit once Merlyn found a way to rewire their outfits. But where would they go once they had their freedom? M crawled back into bed and riffled through every fact and fable she had ever learned about the Fulbright Academy.

And somehow, at some late hour, amid a swarm of schemes, M finally dozed off, too.

The next morning M climbed back into her suit and followed Vivian to a cafeteria that buzzed quietly with scripted activity. The students moved in concert, like honeybees diligently building their hive. The lines to receive food were straight and orderly, and there might as well have been assigned seating — once each student had his meal, he walked single file to the next open seat without hesitation. The calmness of it gave M the creeps. Mealtime at Lawless had been a free-for-all, so this well-behaved performance felt forced and unnatural. But what really gave her the creeps were the dagger stares that each Fulbright aimed directly on her and her friends.

Seated at their own table, Merlyn, Jules, and M were castaways on an abandoned island. An island surrounded by molten lava that wanted nothing more than to destroy that island and everything it stood for. Clearly they were not welcome here.

"I feel like a gazelle locked in a lion's cage," said Jules.

"Ignore them," said Merlyn, pushing a fork through the gelatinous substance on his tray. "Pretend they're jealous of our delicious-looking food."

Their trays sat in front of them with a tidy smattering of unearthly-looking grub. On M's tray, bright red pudding stayed firmly in its assigned section alongside a black-and-white-striped cake and green, licoricelike cords.

"It's not that the food is bad," continued Merlyn, "but the presentation is just bizarre! I mean, if you wanted to make the food of the future, can't you just make it into a pill that we take with water?"

Shrugging, M crunched into the green cords, which turned out to be an incredibly rich version of pesto bacon. The cake was a buttery marble-rye French toast with a honey glaze, and the red pudding was apple-fried grits with melted cheese.

"Ugh," muttered Jules in frustration. "I hate that this ugly stuff is so delicious. I can't get used to my eyes and my taste buds disagreeing."

"Where's Cal?" asked Merlyn with a mouthful of cake.

"Yeah, he'd have a lot to say about this stuff," added Jules, absently stirring her yellow pudding.

"Guys," said M in a hushed voice, "we need to talk about yesterday."

"I don't want to talk about it," said Jules sternly. "Not my shining moment in the Maze."

"I'm not talking about the Maze," said M. "I'm talking about our suits. While you guys were still in there, I ran a quick recon, but Vivian was able to track me down. Not only that, she used the suit against me, just like we thought they would. She completely shut me down with the touch of a button."

"Geez," said Merlyn. "Keyshawn certainly didn't intend for the suits to be used that way."

"Didn't he, Merlyn?" asked M. "Listen, yes, Keyshawn is a brainiac, but you need to pull him down off whatever pedestal you've put him on, because he's not on our side — the same as all these cadets around us now that have an urge to arrest us. We need to outsmart his design or else we're walking around in handcuffs for the rest of our lives."

"I'll see what I can do," said Merlyn reluctantly. "I took a closer look at my suit last night. This stuff is beyond my expertise, to be honest. It's less of a computer and more like a spaceship."

"Merlyn, I have faith in you," said M. "Even spaceships run on computer programs, right? And you've never met a computer program you couldn't hack. I guarantee there's a back door for you to exploit somewhere. Keep looking." She gazed around the cafeteria at the silent eaters, almost taking their bites in unison. "Before we end up like them."

As breakfast ended, the students placed their empty trays on a conveyor belt and left the cafeteria as spotless as it had been before they arrived. The Lawless crew stayed seated and waited for their summons to Keyshawn's lab, which didn't happen until every last Fulbright had exited. *We're on display,* thought M. *They want us to be seen, to prove that the Lawless School is nothing but a bunch of kids. To prove that the Lawless School can be tamed.*

When they finally reached Keyshawn's lab, Cal was already there, but Keyshawn was missing. Cal answered M's curious look by motioning to the door across from the Maze entrance. It was halfway open and M could hear Keyshawn muttering to himself on the other side.

"I don't think we're doing the Maze today," said Cal. "He's been in that room since I got here and he's showing no signs of coming up for air."

A poor choice of words, thought M. "So, seriously, why did it take you all so long to get out of that Maze?"

"The better question is why did it *not* take you so long?" quipped Jules, whose ego was obviously bruised.

"Jules is just mad because she actually didn't finish the course," said Cal.

"You didn't?" M was dumbfounded. For Jules to not finish a physical task was just plain unthinkable.

"Ex-tract-ed," said Cal, slowly stressing each syllable of the word, which must have felt like the twisting of a knife in Jules's back. "She had to be extracted from the Maze after a panic attack."

"Seriously, M, how'd you do it?" continued Jules, paying no attention to Cal's comments.

"I wish I knew," said M. "I followed a random path that popped into my head. Just sort of pretended I was in my basement back home. I mean, it was a place I never really went, but for some reason, it made sense . . . up to a point."

"What do you mean, *up to a point*?" Merlyn chimed in.

"I mean," recalled M, "the layout seemed familiar to me, but it led to a dead end. I couldn't go any farther. Then the walls closed in around me, so I broke through the floor."

"Sounds like dumb luck to me," said Jules with a hint of relief in her voice. "Like, if we did it again, you'd probably be as lost as we were."

"I'm not so sure," admitted M.

"But you're not going to find out today," announced Keyshawn, who had silently slipped back into the lab. "No, today we have a group project for you. I wouldn't want to rush back into anything too stressful too soon." His eyes flicked over to Jules. "Follow me."

Keyshawn walked through the mysterious third door in his lab, opposite from the Maze entrance. On the other side was a room with an exceptionally high ceiling — perhaps no ceiling at all, as far as M could tell. Looking up at the space, she could see that there was a lone rope, which hung from the deep darkness above. Whatever was beyond that point was a mystery. But it wasn't the lack of ceiling that had M brimming with an awkward energy. It was the Fulbright mask that Keyshawn held in his hands. "This, I assume, you have all seen before, but I doubt you ever imagined wearing one."

He tossed them each a mask. It was soft to the touch, like a well-worn T-shirt but with a sturdiness to it at the same time. M flipped the mask over in her hands and marveled at the circuitry. Wires spired, spiraled, and laced in and out of every inch of the mask, creating a gaunt silhouette that didn't seem like it should be solid to the touch. She was reminded of Peter Pan's shadow, lost until Wendy stitched it back onto the ever-young boy. The mask folded delicately over her hands and through her fingers like some fine silk fabric. Even the lifeless green-tone goggles were so paper thin, they seemed to ripple as she bent the mask back and forth. True, she'd held an empty mask in her hands before, but this mask was different.

This mask was hers.

"Okay, everybody," said Keyshawn with a smile. "Try them on!"

M slowly slid the mask over her head, adjusting the goggles slightly to fit along the bridge of her nose, and that's when she felt it: an easy snap — once again, like magnets gently pulling together to create an invisible seam when the mask latched on to her suit. Then it powered up. A humming droned around M's face as the mask settled into position. She felt the ear cups cover her ears as gently as a butterfly landing on a leaf. The goggles repositioned themselves again, this time automatically, wrapping around her face to the perfect fit. Through the lenses, everything and everyone in the room became visibly ... well, more visible. It was like M had graduated to 30/30 vision. Instantly the others' voices were audible in her head as well, as Merlyn let out a "Holy smokes, Batman!"

Looking at her friends, M saw a red glow pulsing through their masks.

"The masks," she began. "The ones I've seen before, they glowed bright green, but these are red."

"Yes!" exclaimed Keyshawn. "Good observation. That is exactly right."

"Are we color coordinating or something?" asked Cal as he stared at his hands.

"Remember, your masks, your entire uniforms are totally different," answered Keyshawn with pride. "Over time, we've learned a thing or two from the Lawless School, believe it or not. And one of the more baffling technologies has been your gas."

"My what?" laughed Cal.

"Gas, chemical agent, whatever you call it," responded Keyshawn, flustered. "The mind-altering substance that Lawless uses." He probably hated not knowing the official name of something scientific. M had noticed a pattern through-out her science class studies growing up at home. Newton's laws, Darwinism, Heisenberg's uncertainty principle, the Higgs boson, and even new elements like flerovium — scientists loved to name things.

"Anyway," Keyshawn continued, "some time ago the Fulbrights figured out the formula for the gas and they've used it since for the same effect, but I think it's meant for a higher purpose."

"Which is?" asked Jules.

"I'm calling it Total Persona," Keyshawn whispered as though if anyone else heard it, they'd steal his idea.

"Which is?" echoed Merlyn.

"The person you most want to be!" he answered them ani-matedly. "This chemical agent has the potential to make you your best, whole self. M, you're scared of heights, correct?"

"Yeah," she replied nervously.

"Then look up," Keyshawn told her.

When M turned toward the dark ceiling again, the room was lit up as if by magic. She saw clearly what was waiting for their next challenge. It started with a death-defying vertical climb to a course filled with ropes, ladders, and bridges, before reaching a series of platform ledges that rose like a giant ladder, presumably to a top-level finish line. Even her new mask couldn't see that far up. M began to hyperventilate at the thought of climbing this dizzying behemoth. Her heart dropped and her knees buckled as she staggered back and whispered, "No way." But then, to her surprise, a sense of calmness came over her like a wave. Suddenly the height seemed less severe. After a few deep breaths, M looked at the course and felt a surge of adrenaline at the chance to climb it. *This must be how Jules feels all the time!* she thought.

"That's not funny, dude," said Cal. "M, are you all right?"

"Better than all right, Cal," she said with a confident laugh. "I'm ready to conquer this thing!"

"And that's how your masks work," said Keyshawn. He was bubbling over with enthusiasm. "Your masks, your suits are working in conjunction with the key elements of the Lawless gas."

"I don't see any delivery mechanism," noted Merlyn as he patted his suit from top to bottom as best he could. "Where's the gas coming from?"

"It's inside us, isn't it?" said M, still staring at the course. "That shot you gave us, it had the Lawless chemicals in there, too, right? And now the chemicals are part of us, waiting to activate at the suit's command. We're like hybrid soldiers."

Keyshawn clapped his hands and bounced, looking more like a toddler than a brilliant scientist. "On the nose, M! On the nose!"

"Good," said M. "Then can we climb this beast already?"

CHAPTER 6
HANDS OFF

The course looked twelve floors high at least and twisted into the empty air. It was a tower of traps, with gravity on its side, but it beckoned M. She tapped the cold, hard floor under her feet . . . definitely not a net. Still, she felt no fear at all. Sprinting forward, she pushed up off the opposing wall and caught the rope, pulling herself up without anyone else's help. "Who's with me?"

Jules and Cal jumped next and were quickly behind M.

"Brilliant," said Merlyn before following their lead. "I guess we're doing this."

"You'll need to work together." Keyshawn's voice vibrated through their earpieces. It sounded as if he were standing right next to them. "There are levels for each of you to solve, so don't leave anyone behind."

But no one replied. They were too busy racing across rope bridges, which swayed with their every step, until they reached the first platform. There the team was stopped short by a new challenge. The only way to reach the next level was through a power-locked manhole built into the ceiling. An LCD panel stretched around the circular vault door and blinked a multidigit code at random intervals. The numbers flashed so fast that the effect was mesmerizing and dizzying all at once.

"Oh, come on," huffed Cal. "When are we ever going to come across a lock like this?"

Merlyn stepped forward. "My turn?" he asked ironically. "Cal, break into that box on the wall."

Cal peeled open a small control panel like it was a can of dog food — his new strength in the suit surprised them all — and a nest of colored wires tussled out. Merlyn peered back and forth between the flashing numbers and the multicolored wires, mumbling a litany of pronouns under his breath. *This there, that here, you belong to you, he fits him, but what about her.* It was Merlyn's problem-solving language. M knew it from her long nights cramming with him for Code's unthinkable exams. It made no sense to anybody else, but to Merlyn, this was his Zen, a calming step that helped him see through the problem and find the solution.

Then, as a butcher carves a cow or a painter colors a canvas, Merlyn effortlessly picked the wires apart one by one and repatched them into the system's motherboard. And one by one, the flashing numbers along the circular path fell into place like a massive, silent slot machine. When the final number held, the metal door let out a magnificent hiss and loosened its locked grip. Merlyn eased himself through the hatch and held out his hands to boost the others to the next level. "Ladies first."

They could hear a wild ticking sound before even peeking up to the second level. M popped her head through and was met with a wall crammed with clicking cuckoo clocks hung side by side.

"Sweet grandmother's house!" cried Cal.

M eyed the wall before them. It seemed solid and showed no signs of a hidden door. "Jules, check the ceiling for an exit."

While Jules gingerly climbed the clocks and began combing the ceiling, M stood back and looked at the wall of timepieces. She didn't know why, but she had a strong gut feeling that this level was meant for her. There were over one hundred clocks in the room, each set to a different time. Scanning the clock faces, she quickly went through all the possible connections she could imagine. Time zones, no. Opposite times, nothing. Sequential times, nada. There was no rhyme or reason to the clock settings that sprang to her immediate attention.

"Got something," called Jules from above. She motioned at a corner of the ceiling, where a tiny fissure was barely visible. "We've got the keyhole . . . now we just need the key."

As Jules said this, one of the clocks struck the top of the hour, and a small yellow bird jumped from behind the wood-crafted door, tweeting and bouncing on its spring-loaded podium. Flitting in and out of its home, the tiny bird seemed almost to be mocking M, laughing at her inability to solve the problem. Behind her mask, M secretly stuck her tongue out at the bird.

"Hey!" said Cal. "There's a key on the end of that bird!"

"Cal, no!" M shouted, but it was too late.

He snatched the key quickly from the canary and the room started to shake. With a hideous crack, part of the floor crumbled away. The crew scrambled to firm footing against the wall as the once-solid floor crashed through the previous level, snapping the rope bridges in a concrete avalanche on its way to the unrelenting ground below.

"Keep your hands to yourself, Cal!" scolded M. "That mistake destroyed our only safe way down, so it's a good time to realize that this course will fight back if we make the wrong moves. From here on out, everyone keep cool and don't jump at the easiest answer."

"Sorry, guys," Cal said with remorse. "Do we at least want to try this key?"

"No!" the other three said in unison.

Looking back to the clocks, M was at a loss for a link that might lead them to the correct key. "Merlyn, thoughts?" she asked.

"Hey, I hot-wire computers, not handcrafted clocks."

Handcrafted, thought M. These clocks weren't merely made to keep time; they were artistic. M stepped back carefully to study the clock designs. Some had sloping roofs, some had giant leaf designs, and some had barnyard animals etched into a scene. Each was woodcut. What did her father used to say? *Never discount an obvious answer.* Then she found her first match: two clocks, hung clear across the wall from each other, had the same sculpted deer's head.

"That's it!" cried M. "Each clock has a twin on this wall that matches it. I'll bet there's an odd one out somewhere. We find that, we find the key."

The crew quickly connected each clock with its partner

until they found the clock, shaped like a woodsman's cabin set in the midst of tiny, ornate falling leaves. The clock's hands were thick, hardy, crisscrossing axes, which were designed to tumble over each other as time moved on.

"This is the one, guys," said M. "Are we in agreement?"

Inching back from the crumbled edge, the rest of the crew nodded their masked heads in approval. "So where's the key?" asked Jules.

"Inside the house," said M as she slowly eased the longer axe to the 12, making it two o'clock. With a shuddering cough, the clock released a small wolf, which sprung from behind its closed doors, gripping a strikingly shiny key in its worn, sculpted teeth.

"Bingo," said M, palming the small-toothed secret. She handed Jules the key and, with Cal's help to balance, Jules twisted the mysterious lock.

The ceiling quaked to life and dragged itself open like a retractable sunroof, but instead of revealing a blue sky on a summer day, a long stretch of wall riddled with holes faced down at the crew. Just above the top line of clocks were eight metal pegs pointing jaggedly outward like knives stuck into the wall.

"It looks like a giant cheese grater," said Cal.

"That must be, like, seven more stories right there." Merlyn gulped. "And no stairs in sight."

"Who needs stairs when you've got these?" said Jules with a laugh as she leapt up and grabbed hold of two of the metal pegs. Then, swinging back and forth, she worked one of the pegs out of the wall and slotted it back into the empty hole just above her head. She pulled herself up a little higher as she loosened the second peg and made the same motion again. Continuing this over and over, Jules finally made it to the top. When her voice came through the earpiece, she wasn't even winded. "Okay, this one's a breeze. It's like building your own ladder as you climb."

"Yeah, a real breeze," Merlyn repeated nervously.

"No worries, Merlyn," said Cal. "I got your back." Without warning, he picked up Merlyn and heaved him to the nearest set of pegs. "Now you climb and keep your feet on my shoulders the whole time."

"Seriously?" asked Merlyn.

"Leave no man behind, that's what Keyshawn wants," said Cal as he gripped his own pair of pegs. "Besides, this looks too easy for me. Let's make it a *real* challenge."

As the boys started the climb, M waited below. There was no getting around it — the height made her pause. She could never figure out why people decided that climbing walls was a good idea. Sure, it helped people train to climb mountains, but then again, who were these people who thought climbing mountains was a good idea? But as her deeper fears set upon her, the suit reacted. Suddenly her legs were buoyant and her arms — previously happy to be crossed in front of her chest — yearned for the strain of burning muscles. Her whole body clenched and released at the thought of the wild climb. Before M knew it, she had climbed the clocks, and her hands had clasped around the pegs while she swung her body side to side like a pendulum, shinnying up the wall one swift reach at a time. Once at the top, she snuck a peek back down the sheer drop. Below them, Keyshawn had become a miniature version of himself and the narrow room converged down to the size of a credit card. She tried hard not to imagine how quickly they would both become life-sized if she fell.

"What next, Jules?" Cal strained, obviously beginning to feel Merlyn's shaky weight sinking into his shoulders.

"See the marked holes in the wall?" prompted Jules. "Everyone, place a peg in each slot and I think that will open the ceiling."

As directed, M plunged her pegs into the slots, leaving Merlyn and Cal to add theirs.

"Cal, I can hang on by myself if you help me to the top," said Merlyn. He clearly hated admitting that he wasn't strong enough for the climb, but M knew better.

"Use the suit, Merlyn. You can do it."

But Merlyn stayed frozen on Cal's shoulders.

"Hey," said Cal as he swung out from underneath Merlyn. "If M believes in you, you should, too."

"No!" screamed Merlyn, kicking his feet wildly. But instead of falling, every muscle in his body suddenly flexed and the computer geek quickly and acrobatically scaled the remaining rows as easy as a spider climbing a wall. "Whoa . . . the suit works!"

Cal pulled himself next to Merlyn and winked before lancing the pegs into the last spots. Once again the ceiling above them retracted, and once again they saw that the course kept going up. "Ladies first," Cal said to Merlyn with a sly smile.

If Merlyn was upset, he didn't show it. Instead he laughed and scrambled over Cal.

The next level was nothing but net. Literally. Above them a giant web of rope flapped to and fro in a light breeze.

"Ugh, now I know how Mario felt in *Donkey Kong*," said Merlyn.

"Is that anything like Super Mario Brothers?" asked Cal. "'Cause I could sure use a leaf now to get that raccoon flight power."

"You guys are speaking a foreign language to me," said Jules. "Let's just climb this thing. It looks reasonable enough."

But when Jules gripped a higher rung of rope, the oversized net suddenly spun around end over end, sweeping up the others.

M's feet dangled off the rope, kicking and trying to touch solid ground, but there was none to be found. Merlyn wound himself tightly against the rope into a human knot, but the more he squirmed, the more unstable the course became until Jules lost her grip and flipped backward, barely holding on with her legs.

"Worst hammock ride ever!" screamed Merlyn as the twisting picked up speed.

But Cal calmly climbed from the edge of the web to the center. "Balance the weight to keep the net from spinning! M, move to the left edge. Jules, take the right edge. Merlyn, join me toward the middle!"

When they each scrambled to their assigned places, the net actually held still, balanced with the ballast of their bodies, just as Cal had suggested. Satisfied that the net wasn't going to whip around again, the crew climbed in tandem toward the next level. On the way up, M couldn't help staring at Cal. His third-grade jokes with Merlyn and idiocy with the cuckoo clocks didn't match up with his quick thinking on the ropes or his selflessness on the peg wall. He was hard to get a handle on, and that bothered M. But what bothered her more was that she ultimately didn't care how unpredictable he was; she still wanted him on her side.

At the top was a set of latches that clipped the net in place and prevented it from spinning again, allowing the climbers to access the opening in the overhanging platform off to one side. Wordlessly the crew shuffled toward the exit. Their heads were dizzy, their hearts were beating out of their chests, and their hands ached from holding on so tightly.

M was the first to lift herself to the final platform that overlooked the drastic drop. She lay down on the ground and stared over the edge at the distant sections they had completed below by all working together. *Take a photo for the scrapbook,* she thought. *How many more of these tests do we have left?* But she realized that she probably didn't want to know the answer to that question.

As she rolled over, something caught her eye. Across the gap, there was a frosted glass window. Someone was watching them.

"Who's that?" asked Jules as she popped up through the floor.

"Judges," answered M, getting to her feet. She focused harder on the window and, as if on command, her mask worked to sharpen the outlines of people. The haze from the glass began to lift and the shadows became more defined. Finally M could just barely make out four people behind the glass: three adults she didn't recognize and one unmistakable cadet . . . Devon Zoso. M eyed her old sparring partner and gave her a knowing wave to say that two could play at the staring game, but then Devon turned and said something to the others, and whatever she said, it wasn't good.

M's vision went black and a blaring static hissed into her earpiece. She lost her balance and came crashing to her knees, then ripped off her mask to clear the biting noise from her head and to regain her vision. Her friends rushed to her side.

Waving the crew off, M said, "I'm fine, I'm fine," but the words caught in her throat when she saw the full height that she had climbed. Her world started to wobble and gravity tugged at the back of her neck, sending her tipping helplessly over the edge of the platform. M could see it all: the ropes course zipping by, the open peg holes gasping like onlookers as she plummeted, and the cuckoo clocks tweeting and singing out that her time had come.

But that didn't happen at all. Because Cal's firm hands grabbed the back of her suit. Dangling there above the abyss, M wished above all else that she could be invisible, even if only for a moment. But it didn't work. The window held her hanging reflection high above the ground.

"Should I still keep my hands to myself, M?" he asked with a heavy laugh that sounded more like a sigh. "Now get your mask back on. Audience or no audience, we've still got to find a safe way back down this thing."

CHAPTER 7
MAGNETIC PERSONALITIES

Two steps forward, one step back. That should have been the motto for M's training. It didn't matter if she was at the Lawless School or the Fulbright Academy; whenever she made giant leaps, she almost always followed them up with giant mistakes.

The climb down was long and quiet. M's strength held up, but her confidence had been rattled by Devon and her shadowy cohorts. M had shown fear, let it slip through her cracks to surface like a geyser, and that had led to her suspended above the free-fall drop. Shame and anger shot through her like a bolt of lightning as her feet finally touched the base level's solid ground. She was incredibly mad at the Fulbrights and even incredibly mad at Cal, though he had saved her life. But, if she was being honest, the person she was most frustrated with was herself. The suit had lured her into thinking that she was indestructible, when in fact she wasn't. She hadn't conquered her fear of heights; she'd masked it. M vowed that the next time, mask or no mask, she wouldn't be afraid.

To add insult to injury, Ben was waiting for them at the bottom of the course. With his ramrod posture and hands clasped behind his back, he stood miles taller than Keyshawn at his side, who held his head down like a scolded dog. What-ever came next, M knew it wouldn't be a pat-on-the-back, mission-accomplished speech.

"Masks off now," ordered Ben, and the crew obliged.

"I'd really like to say, *Great job, everyone*, but we had a big snafu at the finish line, didn't we?" he said. His voice was quiet and controlled, but his eyes seethed with frustration. "First, look at the masks in your hands. *Never lose your mask in the field*, that's a big rule to remember. Your mask is your identity now. It's your new face. The you underneath the mask, *that's* your disguise. That's the boring person who walks unnoticed on the sidewalk and blends into the wallpaper."

"Like ghosts," said Merlyn, rolling his eyes. "We heard the same spiel at Lawless."

"No," barked Ben as his calm demeanor suddenly snapped. "Nothing like ghosts. I don't care what you learned at Lawless. You're Fulbrights now. A Lawless ghost is a coward, meant to disappear and never be seen. Fulbrights are meant to be seen by everyone as a warning."

"A warning about what?" prodded Cal.

"That justice is coming and it cannot be stopped." It was a cold line matched by the icy glare that Ben shot Cal. But Cal didn't avert his eyes. Instead he stared down the direct with a snarled smile that could only mean trouble.

M could imagine how Ben's words might be awe inspiring to other, more rule-abiding Fulbright cadets. How his speech might stir their blood and fire up a new recruit. But here, to this crew, his words were a threat. He wasn't calling on them to defend the world from evil. He was calling on them to eradicate evil from the world by any means necessary. He was daring them to prove their allegiance.

"And, of course, secondly, let me remind you that curiosity killed the cadet," said Ben as he zeroed in on M.

M clenched her mask deep into her fists, channeling all of her frustration there so as not to snap back at the direct. But she couldn't help herself.

"What was Zoso doing up in the skybox?" she asked. "I thought she was your subordinate. Or does unleashing a devastating weapon get you promoted around here?"

Ben swiped Keyshawn's tablet and tapped it harshly, unleashing the Medusa effect on all the Lawless cadets. It was a milder setting than M had previously been subjected to, but terror stretched across the others' faces as they felt the constriction for the first time.

"Ours is not to reason why. Ours is but to do and die," ground out Ben. "Do you really think that the Lawless School wasn't planning to use the *umbra mortis* themselves? We simply beat them to the punch."

"Liar!" yelled M. "Yes, Fox Lawless is a crazy man, but he gave the meteorite to me without using it. The game was over when you came crashing in. Nobody had to get hurt! Nothing bad was going to happen until Zoso came along."

"You can't be sure of that, Freeman," said Ben. "This is a war, a war between the Fulbrights and Lawless that has been raging for lifetimes before you or me or Zoso or even your own father came along. We needed a victory that day, so we took one."

And you call yourselves the good guys, thought M. She may have been disavowed by Dr. Lawless, and she may have turned her back on what the Lawless School stood for, but this mindless belief that violent means could lead to a *good-guy* ending, it was crazy. How could her father have ever associated with such a cult?

There was one explanation. Maybe her father hadn't been a true Fulbright, the same way he hadn't been a true Lawless Master. Was it possible he was playing both sides? Was it possible that he himself was doing as the Fulbrights said but not as they did?

Ben turned his attention to Keyshawn and asked, "Noles, can I assume that these cadets have not been trained in the art of Magblast?"

"No, sir," answered Keyshawn, snapping to attention. "Magblast training has been set for day four, sir, and given the cadets' reaction times to the Maze, I advise against moving them along any faster."

"Oh, I didn't know it was your job to advise me, Noles," said Ben with a venomous sneer. "Or perhaps I didn't hear you correctly."

"True, sir," said Keyshawn. "You must have misheard me because I said that we could begin Magblast training whenever you see fit, sir."

It was a bald-faced lie, but M could see the concern in Keyshawn's eyes even through her own arrested frustration. The concern wasn't for himself or for the cadets, though. No, it was for his precious inventions. *What are these things to*

Keyshawn? she wondered. At first she'd assumed he was after the bragging rights to a great creation, but now she was beginning to think there was something bigger at stake for him. And whatever it was, it was more important than anyone else in this room . . . himself included.

"Excellent!" said Ben with a skip in his step and a tap of his finger on the tablet, which released the cadets from their frozen states. "Then let's have some fun now, shall we?"

Keyshawn escorted the quieted crew back through his lab and into yet another door, which led to a long and narrow room. Everyone seemed shell-shocked by Ben's antics and the further insight into the Fulbright mind that he'd provided. If Merlyn wasn't convinced that he needed to jailbreak their uniforms now, he was never going to be.

The new room looked like a car-crash test facility, complete with disturbingly well-dented and scratched gray walls. It was every bit as bruised a room as the mountain-pass runway that M had shredded up during an emergency landing on her first day at Lawless. Then M noticed a dark silhouette in the far corner of the room, standing silent as the deadened echo of the crew's footsteps ricocheted off the crooked walls.

"Ooh, shadowy stranger. So *this* is where you keep John Doe?" joked Cal. But he didn't have much time to appreciate his wit before he was unexpectedly thrust against the wall by an invisible force.

No, not quite invisible, M realized. She had seen a slight rippling effect, as if the air itself had been disturbed. And the disturbance had originated from behind her.

She whirled to see Ben standing in the doorway. He held up an ungloved, clenched fist, showing off the same thin silver ring M had noticed him wearing in the Glass House. "The Magblast," he began, "is a simple mechanism that's been amplified. Remember when your parents put your report cards on the refrigerator? What did they use? Anyone?"

The group was in shock at the swift and mysterious violence that had just sprung on one of their own. M tensed, preparing for an attack, and watched as Cal shook the cobwebs from his head.

"I take it from your silence that you all meant to say *magnets*," said Ben with a smile. "And you'd be right. Keyshawn, tell the ladies and gentlemen what they've won."

Picking up the lesson in earnest, Keyshawn explained, "The ring Direct Downing is wearing is what we refer to as a Magblast. This is, as mentioned, a modified magnet. What that means is that the ring is designed to emit a wave of energy that pummels whatever is in its path. Case in point, Cadet Fence.

"Now, these are powerful weapons. We do not allow most cadets to use these, as they are still, technically, in the experimental stage. The Magblast is difficult to aim and it carries a massive kick, so target practice is a must. We need you to hit the bad guys, after all, not each other."

Hit the bad *guys,* M mused, nodding along with the others as Keyshawn approached Merlyn. When the time was right, that's exactly what she intended to do.

"Now, if I may," said Keyshawn as he lifted Merlyn's left hand and tapped his gloved knuckles. "Your Magblast is located here. Well, technically it's in the right glove for the rest of you. I've integrated the device into your suits, as just one of many upgrades. Until now, authorized Fulbrights wore rings like Direct Downing's. The difference might seem minimal, but it means that you won't ever lose yours in the field."

"How does it work?" asked Merlyn.

"It's a feat of concentration, aim, and muscle coordination," answered Keyshawn. "Just like everything else in your suit, the Magblast is an extension of you, your will, your strength, perhaps even your emotions, if that's where you choose to draw your power."

"Enough of the Zen speak, Noles," interrupted Ben. "I think it's time to line up the targets and give the cadets something to channel their emotions toward."

Keyshawn walked toward the shadowy figure on the other side of the room. It was only a mannequin, which he dragged slowly toward them. The scrape of the wheels across the floor reminded M of the School of Seven Bells, the ratty old mannequin that Lawless students used to master the art of picking pockets. But this poor mannequin was worn down not by time, but by pure aggression.

"Noles, isn't this target a little below standard for our fine new recruits?" asked Ben. "Given the limited training time we have together, why don't we throw them into the deep end of the pool with a good old-fashioned duel?"

"Duel with who?" demanded M.

"With each other, of course," answered Ben. "Eaves and Freeman, you're up first."

Merlyn and M instantly protested in unison. "No way!"

"I can always bring well-trained Fulbrights in for the duel, then," Ben offered. "Would that address your rather delicate objection to sparring with an equally matched opponent?"

"Yeah, right," said M. "This magnetic toy of yours obviously did a number on these walls. And now you want us to turn it on each other?"

"If I may," Keyshawn interjected, "Direct Downing does have a point. As beginners, you see, you won't be able to achieve the full power of the Magblast. And since we know there's a limited time for your training, the duel would create a more . . . *engaging* situation, greater incentive for you to master the tool quickly."

"Dude, we don't need Devon coming in here and whipping us with waves of magnetic force," said Cal, rubbing his head where it had hit the wall. "Let's just get this over with so we can learn our lesson."

The blast may have rattled his brain, but Cal had a point. There was safety in fighting one another. *Better the devil you know than the devil you don't.* That was another Dad-ism that had stuck with M over the years, even though it had taken her a while to understand it fully. In hindsight, she wished she had remembered it when joining the Masters and leaving her friends behind. But the good devils, apparently, had a way of catching back up to you. In Germany, in London, and in the grip of the Fulbrights, M's friends had always found a way back to her.

"Merlyn, I challenge thee to a duel," declared M in her worst British accent — half to be funny and half to rub it in Ben's face.

Following standard duel rules, M and Merlyn stood back-to-back with their hands at their sides and their masks in place. Then they walked ten paces away from each other. M could hear each of Merlyn's footsteps striking a half second behind hers. She wiggled her fingers, trying to feel for any sign of the Magblast in her gloves, but like everything Keyshawn had worked into the suit, it was next to impossible to know it was there until you experienced it.

Ten.

M whirled to her left, hoping to dodge Merlyn's left-handed attack, and swung her right fist in a violent, uppercut arc. The room remained absolutely silent, but the air itself erupted in a gust of throbbing waves visibly parting the once-static particles of dust that hung around them. Her left arm was clipped with a stinging blast, but poor Merlyn took M's attack on the chin and was knocked flat on his back.

"Say you're okay, Merlyn!" yelled M, running to him.

"Ugh, if I say it, do I have to mean it?" asked Merlyn, who groggily sat up and massaged his jaw. "Kidding, M, kidding. I'm okay. Good shot."

"Score one for Freeman," cheered Ben. "Let's see what kind of trouble Fence and Byrd can start together."

Jules and Cal reluctantly joined each other back-to-back and counted off their ten paces. Jules had a good jump on Cal and let out a whirlwind burst that scribbled a trail across the room, but missed her target. Cal ducked the blow and threw back a rippling attack that started thin and spread out like the beam of a flashlight as it traveled. It scraped the walls and forced M and Merlyn to the ground in order to dodge the blast from the sidelines. Jules leapt over the wave of force just in time, but Cal had already sent another pulse that worked its way into a small webwork pattern, catching Jules before she landed. The blow popped her up and away, carrying her kicking and screaming into the wall.

"I'm okay," said Jules, sprawled on the floor.

"No fair," said Merlyn. "Cal's clearly done this before. Look at the sophistication of his attacks. That can't be beginner's luck."

"I swear, Merlyn, I've never done this before in my life," promised Cal.

"He's telling the truth," said Keyshawn. "While showing alarmingly good skill, he could not have touched this tech until now."

"How do you know?" asked Merlyn. "Maybe his dad trained him on it before Cal shipped off to Lawless?"

"Impossible," announced Ben. "Fence's father is unauthorized to use this tech, given his dubious relationship with Lady Watts. If anything, M should know the tech best."

"And why's that?" asked Cal.

"Her father invented it," answered Keyshawn.

M wondered how many more times she would be tortured by hearing a new secret about her father from strangers. It's not like she'd never met her dad, but she'd known him as the person who stumbled heroically into her room at night to calm her down after a nightmare, not as an art thief who also invented high-tech magnetized weaponry. And why would he invent something like this for the Fulbrights if he wasn't really on their side? Maybe he was on their side after all. Maybe he *had* been, until something changed his mind.

"My father invented a lot of things," said M. "From fabricated stories to this weird new device. But that doesn't mean he taught me how to use them."

"Are you sure?" asked Keyshawn. "Because you did escape the Maze in no time flat."

"The Maze? My father did that?"

"None of this is more important than our current experiment," said Ben. "Freeman and Fence. Fight."

M faced Cal. "Looks like it's you and me."

As her back met his, she realized how tall Cal had grown. He must be almost a foot taller than her now. Their steps began, but M was lost in thoughts about her father. His calmness, his dopiness, his knack for always making people laugh, even at his own expense . . . those details didn't match up with this mad-scientist criminal-cum-Fulbright, who was quickly overshadowing the father she once knew. A jolt coursed over her skin as her feelings flared. She was angry about the mysteries hidden under the mysteries in her life, and the suit channeled that anger. She felt it tingling through every bone as she pivoted on her heel and released a powerful Magblast at Cal, which looped like a crushing tornado. But at the same moment, Cal fired a cometlike blast and the two attacks tussled and held in midair, pushing and pulling against each other. M held her ground, digging her heels in as her outstretched hands shook and her legs trembled. Where the attacks converged, the friction of the pulses caused actual sparks to pop in the turbulent air. The smell of burning filled the room.

Cal closed his eyes, and M thought for sure that he was about to give up. Then a final thrust burst forth from him, blowing her tornado apart. A flowing pulse descended on her, thudding against her chest. It felt like her legs and arms were being pulled apart.

Collapsing on the floor, M tried to catch her breath, but the blast had knocked the wind right out of her. The room blurred. Even through her mask, with its magic corrective lenses, the world looked like a loose watercolor painting: Everything poured into everything else. M felt someone lift her head and heard a distant sound that could have been a voice or merely the ocean crashing on the shore. When at last she regained focus, she realized that Jules was cupping her head and yelling at someone. She rolled her head to the right to see Keyshawn running out of the room. Then she picked her head up just in time to see Cal Magblast Ben with an attack that was ten times more forceful than what she had experienced. Ben crumpled and the audio finally broke through to M's ears. It was Cal.

"I don't know about you guys, but I'm getting out of here."

He bolted for the door, and something inside M clicked into place.

It was panic. It was a vision of Cal captured and never released. But more than that, it was the notion that she needed Cal to help find her mother, to help find the moon rock, and to help stop whatever their parents had set in motion. And that wasn't going to happen if he set one foot out of that door.

M jumped up and screamed, "Don't run!"

Then, effortlessly, she fired a throbbing pulse that not only cut off Cal's escape route, but tossed him clear across the room, creating a large dent in the wall where he impacted. He lay helpless there, like a bird stunned by a window in its flight path.

As quickly as the energy had surged into her, it flushed out, leaving M shaking and feeling hollow. Something horrible had happened. But what horrified her wasn't the sight of unconscious Cal or barely-there Ben. It wasn't the appearance of several Fulbrights rushing in to secure the area. It wasn't even the empty looks that Jules and Merlyn's masks were casting on her. No, M's horror was a sense of déjà vu. She had run screaming from this situation before in her fever dream. From the Fulbright who had held Devon coldly underwater. The Fulbright who screamed, *"Don't run."* The very Fulbright who M had just become.

CHAPTER 8

BE A HERO

The Fulbright guards were not gentle. In fact they were exactly as rough as M remembered from her last time being caught, at Lawless. Ben led the way as the guards marched M and Cal through the illuminated hall. And even though M and Cal weren't struggling against their captors, the Fulbrights still forced them along angrily until they came to a dead end. It was the first time M had seen evidence that the endless twisting hallways weren't literally endless, and she didn't like the looks of it. Ben faced the wall, which seemed monolithic and impassable, like the final turn in the wrong path of a maze. But instead of retracing their steps to find another way out, they watched as the wall slid open. It was a secret entrance . . . and now she and Cal were being ushered inside.

The room was crisp. White walls ran to a black ceiling and black floor, making the space feel as if it constricted around them, like a living beast. The rigid furniture was all right angles, and behind a stark, monstrous black desk sat the first adult M had met since arriving. His blond hair was groomed carefully to create a helmetlike style that gale-force winds wouldn't muss up. Refusing to stand, the man directed them wordlessly to the straight-backed glass seats opposite the desk. As M came closer, his eyes, his high cheekbones, and his strong build gave him away. He was one of the men who'd been watching them from behind the glass on the vertical course. And more than that, he was . . .

"Mr. Fence?" asked M.

"Ms. Freeman," he replied curtly. "I do not like having to do this."

"What?" spat Cal. "See your son?"

"Enforce Fulbright standards on cadets who cannot behave themselves," Mr. Fence answered firmly and without any emotion. "Downing, what happened here? Are you unable to manage the task given to you?"

Ben snapped to attention. "No, sir, I had things under control until —"

But Mr. Fence interrupted him. "Until you didn't. Guards, please escort Downing to one of the Glass Houses. We will continue our discussion there, but know that you've earned a demerit."

The same guards who had marched M and Cal here on Ben's orders promptly turned on the direct, and Ben's eyes exploded like flares sending an SOS in the deep night sky. The very threat of the demerit instilled terror in this hardened teenager. M almost couldn't believe that this was how the Fulbrights treated their own, but it made sense. Fear was a surefire way to keep each recruit on the straight and narrow. Ben was being turned into an example, just as he had tried to turn her crew into examples by forcing them to duel each other.

"Don't take it out on him, Dad," said Cal. "He's a jerk, but all he did was get blasted by me."

Ignoring his son, Mr. Fence said, "Freeman."

The way he used her name was totally devoid of personality, as if he were naming an inanimate object. *Freeman. Cup. Table. Doorknob.* M stiffened in her seat, wrapping her feet around the glass chair's legs, determined not to be dragged to a third location like Ben.

"Don't be a hero yet. There will be plenty of time for you to prove your bravery. I appreciate," Mr. Fence said, swallowing hard after the word, as if it had been a foreign object lodged in his throat, "your efforts to keep Calvin in line and protect him from his own delusional ideas of escape. As you surely know, Calvin has not always proved the best at making the right decisions, but I am content that your paths have crossed. You brought him home and we don't intend to lose him again."

It was apparently the closest Mr. Fence could come to saying, *Thank you for returning my son,* though he said it with all the emotion of an empty packing box. And maybe that was how he saw himself, thought M. His love for Cal was a job. It was up to him to protect his son, to shield Cal from the harmful outside world. If anything could hurt the implacable Mr. Fence, it was probably Cal choosing the Lawless School over the Fulbright Academy. As if suddenly the prized package he had carried all those years turned out to be damaged.

"Both of you," he continued, "focus on your training. You are safest there."

"What do you mean, safest?" asked M.

"Ms. Freeman, please escort Calvin to the infirmary," Mr. Fence ordered, as if she were one of his personal guards. "That cut on his head will require stitches."

Indeed, a wet patch of red had matted into Cal's blond hair.

"Cal! Your head!" exclaimed M as a fresh set of Fulbrights pulled him to his feet. They guided them both out of the room.

"That will be all," they heard Mr. Fence announce as the door shut behind them.

Six stitches later, Cal lay behind a white curtain. His father hadn't said a word to him, had hardly acknowledged him aside from mentioning the laceration. If their situations were reversed, if it had been M's father behind that grim wall, he wouldn't have been able to shut up. M's father had always been a talker, especially with M. He would lead her down bizarre paths, taking unexpected twists in conversations about anything and everything, making connections between subjects where M wouldn't have seen them. A meal he ate in San Jose would transport him to a mountaintop monastery where he'd been hired to clean some ancient painting and where they had fed him a similar tortilla soup. As easily as that, he would make connections in his life and share tales of those experiences with M. She used to dream of a day when she would travel the world and make her own connections. And now she was, only instead of eating another amazing meal, she was in yet another infirmary, listening to Cal breathing deeply as the stitches wove through him.

At least it wasn't her who required medical attention this time.

Wanting to avoid the gory details, M hovered outside of Cal's closed curtain as the doctor sewed him back together. The rest of the room was cloaked in darkness, cold and alienating, just like everything else at the academy. *How was anyone supposed to get better in a place like this?* wondered M. The concrete floor was smooth and tilted downward just slightly, hardly noticeable, but it made her gag to feel the lean. Because the slant, she knew, led to a drain at the far side of the floor, designed to drain people's insides.

"Hey, where'd you go?" Cal called out from his bed. "The stitches are done, you big baby. You can come back now."

"Yeah," she responded. "Like I'm falling for that old trick."

"Scout's honor, M," said Cal. "I swear it's all done."

Pulling back the curtain, M saw Cal sitting on his cot, suddenly smaller, like an actual kid, instead of a master criminal turned supercop. "It's not the stitches," she said. "It's the hospital. I'm not a fan of these places since, well, you know."

"Oh yeah, that," said Cal. M's time in the Lawless sick bay had marked a turning point in their relationship. Not because Cal had anything to do with putting M there — but because he had taken it upon himself to avenge her against the person who had by subjecting Devon Zoso to a surge of electric shocks. Devon still had her hair cut short as a result. It made M queasy to remember that side of him. That darkness.

Anxious to change the subject, M took control of the conversation as Cal's doctor exited into the hallway, leaving them alone in the large room. "So, I've met the whole Fence family now. Your father seems nice."

"Yeah, if by nice, you mean he hasn't tried to harm you yet," said Cal with an attempted laugh that sounded more like a staccato cough.

"Can I ask . . . well, what was it like, growing up with them?"

"Well, it mostly wasn't a *them* household," answered Cal. "My mom split when I was little, like, too little to remember her, really. My father raised me himself."

"Wait, if you were raised by a Fulbright, then why would you ever choose to go to Lawless?" M asked, but what she really wanted to ask was, *Why were you given a choice?*

"It's a twelve-year story," Cal said as he absently massaged the white gauze around his new stitches. He looked like an amnesiac struggling to remember the truths in his life, but M sensed that the truths were closer to the surface than Cal was comfortable acknowledging. "My dad, he meant well, but he set me up, you know? Not as in setting me up to get caught for a crime, but, like, for, I don't know, failure at everything I tried. I was a late bloomer in school. Teachers wanted to hold me back, but he wouldn't let them. He couldn't imagine that his son was having trouble reading, having trouble making friends, or having trouble following the rules. I was supposed to be his 'good soldier.' That's what he called me all the time. *Morning, good soldier. These poor grades are perplexing, good soldier. Good soldier, we need to discuss the phone call I received today from your school.*"

Cal's tone, when he impersonated his father, was spot on at recalling the man she'd just met. Direct, orderly, and demeaning.

"I mean, there wasn't anything I did that he didn't take the opportunity to correct. And his worst threat, the worst future he could ever imagine for me was that I'd grow up to be like my mother. *Study harder, good soldier. You don't want to end up like her.* That's all he would ever call her. *Her.*"

"Geez, how did they ever meet in the first place?" asked M, though as soon as the question fell from her lips, she wished she could take it back. "No, wait, you don't have to tell me that. I'm sorry. It's hard for me to think of them as your parents, is all. It's hard to wrap my head around Ms. Watts as a mom."

"No," started Cal. "I mean, it's okay. I ask myself the same question. It's always weird when parents divorce, but my mom, she, like, disappeared. Pictures of her, pictures of us together, they didn't exist, so it really was like she didn't exist, either. All I knew about her was whatever my dad let slip, and he didn't have a very high opinion of *her.*"

M's bedroom at home had been filled with pictures of her father. She cherished them after he passed. They were a part of him that stayed behind to be with her. It would have destroyed her if those old photos had been taken away.

"So, then, one day, I got in a fight at school," continued Cal, "with this kid who had lied about me. He told the teacher I had cheated on a test, but I hadn't. . . . I mean, I got a C on the test, for crying out loud, but the teacher believed this other kid. So I found him and, I don't know, I just lost it. My dad had to pick me up from the principal's office and that's when we had the talk.

"He told me that it was very important that I tell him the

truth. Was I mad at this kid because I was caught cheating or because I was wrongly accused? I told him that I was innocent, and that it tore me up inside to know that this kid was getting away with a lie and I was getting punished when I hadn't done anything wrong. That's when he told me about the Fulbright Academy and the Lawless School."

M smiled. "Hey, at least you got that much. I didn't know anything about the Lawless School when I signed on. And I'd never heard of the Fulbrights before they tried to kidnap me."

"Hmm, I may not have come from the most honest family, but I guess I got the truth eventually. He finally told me about my mom as part of the talk." Cal shook his head. "Long story short, he'd had no idea who she really was until, one day, a fellow Fulbright told my father that he'd been compromised by his wife. By the time he got home, she was gone and I was alone, asleep in the bassinet."

"Whoa, no wonder he dislikes her," said M. "But then, why'd you choose the Lawless School over the academy?"

"To find my mother," admitted Cal with a steely look in his eyes. "And make her pay for what she did."

As he sat on the hospital cot, Cal's whole body tensed like it had just been pulled out of the freezing waters of Hamburg.

"Why did you chase that painting onto the frozen river, Cal?" asked M. "You were on thin ice and we had already discovered the hidden message about Wild and the Black Museum."

"Because she wanted it so badly," he said coldly. "I wanted to be the one who destroyed it and I wanted her to watch me do it."

Being here, so close to Cal again, like that night under the icy waters, M realized something. Despite the darkness in him, she would dive into anything to save him again if she had the chance.

She looked around to make sure they were alone. "Cal, I'm sorry I took you out with the Magblast, but I need your help. There's another moon rock out there, and your mom is after it. If we don't get out of here soon, well, we all know what she's capable of. And I think that's exactly what the Fulbrights are training us for. We need to play along for a bit while I figure out a plan and Merlyn figures out how to hack our suits. Will you help us out, for old time's sake?"

If M expected Cal to be taken off guard by her hastily explained, secret mission, he didn't deliver. Instead he smiled so wide, it looked like he'd just won the lottery.

"I should have known you were up to something, M. Well, that's the best news I've heard all day," he whispered. "I'm in."

Almost on cue, a set of Fulbright escorts arrived to collect Cal. He slid off the gurney, and the masked men clamped his hands tightly behind his back with luminescent white cuffs.

"Hey," said M sharply. "Why are you treating him like that? He's wounded and he's on your side, you know!"

But if the handcuffs surprised Cal, he didn't show it. Instead he remained calm and allowed the Fulbrights to lead him away.

"Cal, I don't get it," said M. "What's going on? Who's your direct?"

He just smiled and repeated, "I'm in," and his voice sounded tiny but brave in the overwhelming silence of the sick bay. The Fulbrights pulled him out of the room and into the hallway.

M tried to follow them but was met at the exit by two more Fulbright sentries. "Your direct will gather you shortly, Cadet Freeman," a gruff voice announced from under the mask as M watched Cal being shoved along on his way.

Once she was alone, the sick bay took on an even more unsettling atmosphere. She didn't like suddenly having all these guards looking over her — dealing with the directs had been troublesome enough. M gazed over the medical land-scape, searching for another way out. The Fulbrights had placed her in handcuffs once, and she didn't feel like waiting around to let them do it again — she could find her own way back to her room.

Where the large bay had once been dark, a murky light now shined at the far end. The slanted floor pulled her toward the mysterious glow. It felt as if the empty cots and silent machines were tombstones in a graveyard and M were hunting ghosts. But what kind of Fulbright ghosts lived here?

Up close, the dim light cast a quiet shadow as a respirator's clicking sigh sounded, a sign of plugged-in life.

"Hello?" M asked as she pulled back the curtain.

There, lying in bed, was Foley.

Why was he in here? Cal had made it sound like he was a

prisoner, but it was worse than that — he was in a coma. No, not just a coma. At a second glance, M could see wires wrapping in and out of him like he was a robot ready for reboot.

This must have been the Fulbrights' "heavy surveillance." They were keeping him unconscious, medicated and strapped to a cot. M shuddered over the prone body of her old... friend? Had Foley and M ever been friends, really? Either way, he didn't deserve this kind of punishment. No one did.

A camera lens whirred above her, signaling that Foley was being monitored, which meant she was being watched, too. Oh, how she hated those cameras. The infirmary trip had been a setup. Someone at the academy *wanted* her to find Foley, to face the likely future of her crew if it didn't fall in line soon. This wasn't a discovery. It was a lesson.

Closing Foley's curtain, M looked directly at the camera to show whoever was watching that she knew the play. With a deep breath, she added Foley's name to her ever-growing need-to-save list.

Then, as she turned, M accidentally bashed her knee into a nurse's cart, which crashed into a cabinet door, popping it open. The sound should have woken the dead, but when the metal instruments ceased their angry rattles, Foley's steady clicking continued in concert with the silence. M tried to replace everything just as she had found it, but the stubborn cabinet door refused to shut. Opening it wide, she found a small fiberglass orb wedged in the corner. She plucked it out — and retched at what she held. It was an eyeball. Slick and colorless, it slipped from her fingers and rolled into her palm. The black iris tumbled and held in place, staring deeper into the cabinet of what ended up being very disturbing curiosities.

It must be fake, M thought. Then, regaining her composure, she let the ball roll freely around in her hand as she studied it. It was fake, all right, but it wasn't a standard glass eye. It had a port on its backside, meant to connect to a computer. Looking into the cabinet, M found the bin of other eyeballs and tossed it back on top. But the eyeballs weren't the only bionic body parts inside. Artificial lungs, hearts, ropes of silicon arteries, kidneys, and stomachs were all carefully wrapped, cataloged, and stored here.

What kind of roughhousing do these Fulbrights get into if they need extra spleens? wondered M as she closed the cabinet. She briskly walked away from what felt like the scene of a grisly crime.

Retracing her steps to the front of the room, she heard a commotion coming from the hallway. She sat back on the cot, behind the curtain that had obscured Cal from her view, and listened to the ruckus unfold.

"Sir, we can't leave. We have orders to watch over the Lawless kid," said one of the Fulbright sentries.

"I don't care about your orders, cadets," yelled the same doctor who had patched up Cal's wound. "I need you now!" M heard him storm into the sick bay and rummage violently through drawers, which slid open and slammed shut with the sharp sounds of glass beakers and metal instruments clanging against one another. "Or do you want to explain why our mentor died on your watch?"

The curtain before M tore open and the doctor urgently shoved her aside as if she were another cot. "Out of the way!" he commanded as his white coat floated past, heading directly to the very cabinet M had just discovered. She watched as the doctor pulled out some squishy object wrapped in plastic, then ran past her again and through the door. The Fulbrights at the doorway looked at one another and shrugged before turning and following the doctor, leaving M all alone.

Whatever was going on, it was deadly serious. And it afforded M a unique opportunity. Chasing after them, M snaked through the halls, trying to keep a safe distance from her marks so as to not be spotted. Not that it mattered, because the doctor and the Fulbrights were only concerned about what they were running toward, not who was running after them.

Suddenly they veered left around a corner and out of M's sight, and she turned the same corner only to find a dead end. It had to be another secret entrance. Stepping forward, she pulled her mask down over her face. Whatever was behind that wall was something she wasn't supposed to see, so it might be better to make sure whatever was behind that wall didn't see *her*. As the mask settled onto her face, nothing but dead air hissed through her headset. M flexed her hands in her gloves, making sure the Magblast was still at the ready, then she ran her hands over the wall until she found a small latch. Pressing it, the dead end opened to an empty stairway.

Darting up the stairs, M burst onto the next level to find herself adrift in a sea of dimly lit Glass Houses. The clear walls blended together to create a deep blue hue, which made M feel like she was trapped in the middle of the ocean, only nothing was wet or liquid or living in these dark waters. Instead everything had been frozen solid. Heavy footsteps fell to her left as a hazy set of shadows moved away from her. M took her chances and raced in the same direction. A beacon of light shined in the murky distance, making the shadowed figures she was trailing grow taller and taller as they approached it. But instead of stopping at the light, the shadows ran past it, deeper into the maze of glass.

M had also intended to run past the light, but when she reached the intersection, her heart stopped. Under the pale blue light was Cal, sitting on a glass bed all by himself. His hands were still latched and his eyes stared lifelessly out into the hall, watching and waiting for the Fulbrights to return. But when he saw M's black-and-red mask, his eyes widened and his nonsmile turned into an all-out frown.

"Cal!" whispered M as she banged on the glass wall with her fist. "What are you doing here?"

He jumped up and shook his head like a mime, mouthing, "Get out of here!"

M waved him back and considered the glass. What would happen if she used her Magblast now? The glass wall would shatter, an alarm would go off, but maybe they'd have time to find her mother before escaping? Although that would mean leaving Merlyn and Jules behind. As she weighed her options and strategized an endgame in which everyone came out alive, Cal suddenly leapt forward to get M's attention, but it was too late. She felt the suit's familiar seizing around her body, tightening its grip like quick-drying cement. M tried to turn her head, but her mask locked in the forward position. Frantically she looked into the glass wall and saw Vivian's reflection emerge from the darkness behind her.

"You're wanted, you're found" was all Vivian said.

"Stupid tracker," gasped M. "I'm beginning to think you like using my suit against me."

"People who live in Glass Houses shouldn't use Magblasts," Vivian said flatly as she walked away, unconcerned that M couldn't follow her. "Noles needs to see you now."

The suit released her and M felt the blood rushing back into her arms and legs. She hit the cell wall one more time and looked at Cal through the glass. They were both exhausted, but he motioned for her to go. Wherever she was, it wasn't safe here. M suddenly got the feeling that Vivian had perhaps saved her from making a big mistake.

She waved good-bye to Cal and left him behind in his lonely crystal castle. And even though she hated following Vivian like a lost puppy dog, she was more than ready to leave this new, strange place . . . counting her steps the whole way, for when she needed to return.

CHAPTER 9

UNLOCKED

"Are we going to talk about what just happened?" M asked Vivian as they returned to the regular cadet level.

"Noles wanted you; I retrieved you," Vivian stated. "As far as I'm concerned, that's all that happened."

Getting Vivian to open up was a tall order. She surrounded herself with a force field of indifference, but M had cracked those types of shells once or twice.

"And the fact that Cal's being held in a detention center, does that matter to anyone here?" pushed M.

"I suppose it matters to Cal," said Vivian. "No more questions, Freeman. You're annoying my knee again."

M was surprised at how relieved she was to finally reach Keyshawn's door, which somehow she instinctively recognized this time. *The suit must be working,* she thought.

"I'll wait out here," said Vivian.

"You sure I can't interest you in a quick lap around the Maze?" snapped M, but Vivian returned only a blank stare. Happy to have the last word, M made her way inside.

Keyshawn's lab was as cluttered as ever, but he was nowhere to be found. M noticed Keyshawn's bookshelves.

Most of the texts were exactly what she had expected to find: a collection of science-based, quadratically hard-to-read books filled with more numbers and solve-for-x quotients than actual words. She walked along the four oversized bookcases, tracing her finger up and down the rows, looking for something that might give her a deeper insight about Keyshawn, about his research, or about what the Fulbrights really had in store for M and her friends. That's when she noticed that there were books on the back sides of the bookshelves as well.

Squeezing through an almost nonexistent gap between cases, M found herself in a hidden section of Keyshawn's library. Entering this area gave her the same feeling as when she'd walked through the false fireplace at the Masters' compound. This time, she'd stepped over to another side of the academy.

The books were written in Russian. And Latin. And Greek and French and Italian and Mandarin and Cherokee and even hieroglyphics. M happened upon one especially thick volume with an oxblood leather cover. Pushing against the bottom of the oversized book made it lean and tip off the shelf and into her arms, landing with a startlingly heavy thud that made M's knees buckle. The book must have weighed twenty pounds easily. Setting it down on a table, she studied the cover. The text on the spine was carefully, artistically hand etched into the taut leather and looked almost like English. But it wasn't the language that caught her eye; it was the author's name: Chaucer. As in Geoffrey Chaucer, medieval poet and revered father of English literature.

Gently opening the book, M was shocked to find herself holding what must have been an original edition of one of Chaucer's texts. The yellowed pages felt like canvas, strong and barely bending to her touch. Detailed artwork sprang from those pages' every corner and flourished in the margins as leaves and vines wrapped into pillars, framing the interior text, which was hand-written in richly roping, impeccably crafted calligraphy. M could even see the ghosted baseline traced lightly on the page to keep the writing straight and orderly.

Suddenly aware of the rarity that she had in her posses-sion, M cautiously turned to the title page. The Middle English meant nothing to her, but the art on the page was breathtak-ing. It was a collection of ornate circles and symbols overlapping in seemingly random ways. The effect of circles within circles was almost hypnotizing, and the crisscrossing grid of curving lines looked like a drawing of a tornado or a hurricane, with arcs and rays spinning off in all directions. Roman numerals ran around the outermost circle like numbers on a clock. Near the bottom, at what would be six o'clock, was the image of a dog's head. There were birds at other points around that outer circle, beyond which a blast of rays stretched out like snakes reaching to the edge of the paper, changing colors gradually from yellow to orange to red to black with white dots that almost looked like stars.

"What kind of crazy stuff are you into, Keyshawn?" M whis-pered as she heard footsteps coming from the other side of the bookshelves.

Delicately shutting the book as if she were closing a coffin, she peered through and saw Keyshawn dressed in a filthy jumpsuit with stains on top of its stains. He paced back and forth in the lab, slipping between stacks of books and doubling back to scribble notes on a smart board. M tried to decipher his notes, but his handwriting was as abysmal and hectic as chicken scratch. He could have been writing Middle English for all she could make out.

Turning from the smart board, Keyshawn tapped his tablet, and an incredible sight flickered onto the wall across the room. It was a video of the Box in action. The scene made M automatically clench with preparation, as if the room around her were about to transform the way the Box always had. Perhaps the bookshelves would become tidal waves, or the floor would drop out and send her cascading down the side of a cliff. But thankfully the only thing that happened was a video played, showing a Lawless student slinking through an ornate room with marble statues lining the walls.

Keyshawn walked over to the wall and hung a Fulbright outfit under the projection. But M's attention was on the playback. Whenever she had been in the Box herself, she'd been too focused on the scenario she faced to give much thought to how the Box did what it did, creating realistic simulations of settings and movement and even adversaries. And when she'd stood and watched the Box from the observation room above, all her focus had been on studying the other students and how they escaped from their assigned situations. But now, from a distance, the way the Box worked seemed surreal. The walls of the room were alive, rippling in waves of endless fluctuating motion, changing form seamlessly from buildings to mountains to water. It was like watching a nightmare forming around someone else and having no way of stopping it from happening. Maybe that's how Cal had felt just now, watching M get ambushed by Vivian.

As the video continued, though, something even more fascinating happened. The suit that Keyshawn had placed under the projection started to morph, matching the devious variations of the Box. Hanging there on its peg, the suit became the woods, the sky, the Taj Mahal at night, blending into every scenario the video showed.

Suddenly M realized that with Vivian waiting for her outside, she was going to be found hiding in Keyshawn's lab sooner or later. So it would be best if she kept the upper hand. While Keyshawn was mesmerized by the camouflaging suit, M put the Chaucer book back, slid through the bookshelves, and walked up quietly behind him.

"You rang?" she said, and Keyshawn nearly jumped out of his skin.

"Where did you ..." he blurted out before scrambling to shut down the projection.

"So where'd you get the video?" M asked. "Looks like it was filmed up in the control room at the Lawless School. Can I assume this is Devon's handiwork?"

"How long —" Keyshawn started. "You should, I mean, how long have you been there? What did you see?"

Ignoring him, she continued, "I've experienced the Box firsthand, but I never learned how it works. What's the secret?"

"Forget you saw that, okay?" said Keyshawn with a hint of true fear in his voice. "This could get us both in serious trouble."

"So you don't know the secret," guessed M. "But you're close to figuring it out, aren't you?"

"Oh, I know the secret, all right," he huffed.

Ah, vanity can be an amazing weapon if used correctly, thought M. "Prove it," she challenged him.

"If you promise to keep your mouth shut about this video . . ." he started.

"I promise, Keyshawn, geez," said M.

The look in his eyes as he stared at her told her that there was more at stake here than a stern warning from the powers that be, which made M even more curious to know what he was up to.

"It's programmable matter," whispered Keyshawn.

"Sure, yeah, programmable matter." M nodded. "Obviously. But here's my next question. What's programmable matter?"

Keyshawn sighed. "This isn't why I wanted to see you, you know. Okay, programmable matter is a material that can be controlled and manipulated to become something else . . . *anything* else. The walls of the Box, in my estimation, must be made up of millions of tiny, programmable nanocomputers that respond to the control room's request. The wall essentially remolds itself to create any programmable, three-dimensional situation imaginable."

"This matter, umm, morphs into whatever it's told to become?" asked M.

"Exactly," answered Keyshawn. "But here's the thing. This tech, we're years away from this level of expertise. The network connections alone to coordinate this many hundreds of thousands, maybe millions of tiny computers . . . it's daunting to even imagine how it works so fluidly."

"So the Lawless School beat you to the punch and won first place at the science fair," said M. "Wait, my dad didn't invent this, too, did he?"

"Don't know," admitted Keyshawn. "Whoever it was, I thought I was the closest to figuring it out, but there's the truth."

"But you took the same tech and developed it into the suits, didn't you?" asked M.

Keyshawn cringed at the suggestion. M could tell that he was on the verge of retreating back into his science headspace, so she tried to keep him in the here and now. "But none of this is why you needed to see me, correct?"

"Right, of course," he said. "Is Vivian waiting outside? Ugh, we've already taken too long, then."

Flustered, Keyshawn shuffled across the room to the front door and listened for a second. Then, satisfied, he walked back over to M. "I'm double-checking everyone's suits and trackers. Can you roll up your left sleeve?"

M eased her sleeve up as Keyshawn took her arm. He held his tablet over the tracking nodule and clicked his tongue. "Yep, all checks out okay."

"I could have told you that," said M, remembering how Vivian had found her near the Glass Houses. "What happened?"

"You mean besides Fence turning his Magblast on a superior?" asked Keyshawn. "That was the icing on the cake to a totally wasted day. But listen . . . the suits, the Magblasts, these are all highly unstable and unproven techs. We need to know that everything is still intact after taking such vicious hits. Magblasts can pack quite a punch. They could potentially short out your tracker, distort your headgear, or wipe out your suit's functions completely. It was a stupid idea, anyway, to pit you against each other."

"You didn't seem to think it was a bad enough idea to argue with Ben," said M.

"Yeah, well, his orders outrank my opinions," answered Keyshawn. "That's a lesson for you to learn if you're going to survive around here."

"I think I've proven otherwise," said M with a smirk.

Ignoring her comment, Keyshawn continued his calibrations. "I checked Merlyn and Jules already and their equipment was operational. Now I just need to check out Cal and we should be in order again. How is he, by the way?"

"Fine," M answered, "if you're fine with being shackled and locked away in a Glass House. What's going on there, Keyshawn?"

"How exactly did you figure that out?"

"Saw him with my own two eyes," she said.

Keyshawn's jaw dropped. "Did anybody see you? Does anybody else know you made it up to the Glass City?"

"No," said M. "I mean, just Cal. Oh, and Vivian."

"Vivian!" he choked.

"Yeah, she dragged me back down here to see you before I could Magblast the glass wall and save him," said M. "What do you think that means?"

"I think it means you're lucky to be alive," Keyshawn exclaimed. He looked around the room again, making sure that they were alone. "I don't know what game Vivian's playing, but protocol demands that you should have been turned over to the authorities for leaving the cadet floor. That's grounds for early dismissal and could make you a Ronin. And is that what you want? To be kicked back into the real world? To live the rest of your life knowing that, at any second, either the Lawless School or the Fulbrights could show up at your doorstep and do you in?"

"Okay, so it was a big deal," said M. "I'll be more careful next time. But regardless of my actions, Cal doesn't deserve to be treated any worse than the rest of us."

"Like it or not, according to the Fulbrights, Cal made the wrong decision by choosing the Lawless School."

"That's not fair," said M.

"Who said Fulbrights were fair?" asked Keyshawn. "Now, can I please check your suit and get you out of here before you somehow get us all in trouble?"

It was true. M was a purebred troublemaker, but she'd never realized she was so talented at fanning the flames from spark to inferno until joining up with the Lawless School. Her father had taught her to question everything, to see a problem from every angle before attempting to solve the issue at hand. His voice popped in her head again: *An answer today doesn't mean a solution tomorrow.*

"What happens if this little suit study of yours goes according to plan?" she asked Keyshawn. "If we pass the tests and complete whatever assignment John Doe has in store for us, what then?"

"Well," said Keyshawn, "then they would start a mass production of the suit and equip every Fulbright with one as a standard issue."

"And what do you get out of that?" asked M pointedly.

"Bragging rights, I guess," he said absently as he gazed into his tablet. His brown eyes reflected the flashing lights from his screen, but they were searching for something deeper than the function of M's suit. There was more hinging on his success than the prestige of equipping an army of Fulbrights. M recognized that faraway stare. She'd had it herself whenever she thought about her fallen father or her imprisoned mother. Keyshawn had skin in the game, so to speak. And the suits were his way out.

"You loaded the Magblast into our suits," continued M, trying to parse out what other motives Keyshawn may have hidden, "but why didn't you add the tracker in there, too?"

"Because the suit can come off," he said.

"And you want tabs on Fulbrights at all times."

"Geez, is everything a conspiracy with you, Freeman?" asked Keyshawn. "You assume the tracker is meant to keep cadets under control, but really it's designed to help you. If you were ever in trouble, we could find you."

"Am I going to need help on the base?" asked M. "And are you going to help me?"

"It's not for the base; it's for the field," said Keyshawn. "That's where the real danger lies. But, technically speaking, if we lost contact with anyone in a place like the Maze, it would be very worrisome. We wouldn't be able to pull back the walls or adjust the course based on their progress because we wouldn't know where they were. And without that knowledge, a recruit could be crushed or mauled before we could extract them."

"Ouch," came a familiar, sharp-edged voice from behind M and Keyshawn. "Wouldn't want new recruits to go splat during the training, now would we?" Devon sharked through the door with Vivian in tow. "Look who I stumbled across in the hall. Figured I'd stop in to see how our VIP is doing. Rumor has it that you're a natch with the Magblast, M. Too bad you're still afraid of heights, though."

"Our time here is up," said Keyshawn in a very clinical tone. "Freeman is approved to continue. Now, if you'll excuse me, I have to prep for tomorrow."

"When are you going to make me one of those choice suits, Noles?" asked Devon, her voice uncoiling like a loose whip. The extra suit hanging on the wall suddenly looked very suspicious. Like any good artist, M realized, Keyshawn wasn't working on just one idea at a time. Her suit was one work in progress, but there were other ongoing experiments that she wasn't a part of.

"Once we've passed the beta stage," said Keyshawn, putting on a brave face against Devon's unsaid accusations. "Until then, the suits are for test subjects only."

"Did you hear that, M?" asked Devon. "You beat me to the dance again. Bet that makes you happy."

"Not really," said M coolly. "I'm good to go, Keyshawn?"

"Yes, of course," he said. "Thanks for coming in."

As M and Vivian made for the door, Devon spoke up again. "Hey, Ware, word of advice for you: Don't underestimate Freeman. Leaving her alone with Noles wasn't a smart move. I'm sure you, of all people, should be able to feel Freeman's Lawless background in your bones . . . or should I say, knees?"

"I'm *shocked* to hear you, of all people, say that, Zoso," sniped Vivian with ease. "Or did you mean to get that haircut? As far as I'm concerned, Freeman is fine. She checks out, she follows orders, and most importantly, last I was told, she's not your recruit. So save the dossier for someone who wants your opinion."

Vivian's barb wasn't necessarily a resounding vote of confidence in her relationship with M, but it spoke volumes about her relationship with Devon. And apparently M and Vivian were on the same page there.

As they left, M wished again that it were easier to talk to Vivian. She had a feeling now that, under different circumstances, they might have been friends. But likable or not, Vivian still stood between M and her mother, which is to say she stood between M and potentially saving lives from another black hole. No, friends come and go, but the end of the world is forever. That's why tonight M was going on a reconnaissance mission after lights-out. She needed to solve at least a few of her new mysteries by finding out exactly who her Fulbright directs really were. *There's always a reason a team is put together,* she thought. Why were Ben, Vivian, Devon, and Keyshawn tapped for this mission?

Maybe their pasts could tell M more about her future. Because threat of Ronin or not, her time was running out.

CHAPTER 10
HUNTED AND GATHERED

As the walls dimmed, M visited her closet to put on her pajamas. Vivian had proven to have an uncanny ability to fall asleep at precisely the same time each night. Not only that, but she was a healthy sleeper. Tonight M hoped to use that to her advantage.

M shifted over to Vivian's closet and tugged at her booby-trapped top drawer. The newly taped strand of hair broke soundlessly, and inside lay Vivian's tablet, as well as her brush, tufted with blond hairs. M snatched up the tablet, turned it off, then set it back and closed the drawer, carefully replacing the broken tripwire with a new strand of Vivian's own hair.

By the time M stepped out from behind the partition, Vivian was already snoring. Still, M was careful not to let the sleeves of her Fulbright suit show under the soft edges of her pajamas as she climbed into bed.

M forced herself to lie still, but her heart jumped against her chest and it was hard to keep her breathing calm. This was a reckless and dangerous experiment she was about to try. Vivian had caught her the past few times. If someone else crossed her path tonight, she didn't know if she could talk her way out of real trouble.

Looking at the closed door to the hallway, M began to review the long list of unknowns about the academy at night. Were there monitors roaming the halls like they had during the day? Students were supposed to report to their rooms at lights-out, but that didn't mean the Fulbrights didn't assign night patrols to ensure that all stayed safe, and more important, stayed put. Were there cameras? The only ones M had seen here were inside particular rooms, like the first Glass House or the infirmary — but those were cameras that they'd wanted her to see. The halls always seemed clear, but there was no way of knowing for sure.

She was going on a gut feeling. The gut feeling that said that the Fulbrights didn't expect trouble from their cadets. There was bound to be heavy security elsewhere, but if they thought the dormitory level was sheltered and protected, and their cadets were perfectly disciplined, well, then when M slipped into the hallway, there should be nothing waiting for her except hundreds of closed doors.

A half hour passed. Then another. Finally, when Vivian's breaths became deeper and her snores settled into one repeating tone, M silently slipped out of her bed, now dressed only in her uniform. As she pulled on her mask, the room brightened, and M froze, thinking she had been caught. She peered down at her slumbering roommate, who usually awoke at the slightest introduction of morning light, but Vivian continued to saw logs in her sleep. Peeling back the mask revealed that the room was still dark. It was the mask that had made the space appear illuminated. M made a mental note to prepare for more surprises from the uniform. There was so much more to learn about this tech, and M felt suddenly justified for taking a nighttime stroll. It was time to take the suit on her own personal test run.

With her mask back on, the room lit up again, but this time M was expecting it. She could see everything as if it were daylight. With one last, deep breath, she opened the door and stepped into the empty hallway.

No alarms went off, which was always a good sign. But that was only the first challenge. Now she needed to find the computer room situated underneath the Glass House where she first met Ben. Knowing that the Glass City, as Keyshawn called it, sat right above the cadet section, M guessed that the control room, filled with flashing computers, had to be on this floor. She retraced her steps through the halls, passing door after door after door, looking for another apparent dead end like the ones that led to Mr. Fence's office and the stairwell. She couldn't help but recall something Zara told her once. *Too much watching and not enough doing leads a Lawless student down a dead end.* But at the academy M had seen the Fulbright dead ends lead to hidden secrets.

When she reached the edge of her previously traveled routes, M took the next turn and found herself in an expansive hallway that looked like everywhere else she'd been in the academy. Yet she had never been this way before; she felt it in her bones. As she walked, the rows of doors echoed like a house of mirrors, twisting the single image into a relentlessly repeating reflection without end . . . until she noticed an anomaly. There was a door missing along the wall, a break in the monotonous pattern. It wasn't a dead end, but the blank wall raised a red flag. If something looked out of place at the academy, there was probably a reason.

Putting her ear against the wall, M listened carefully, trying to register any murmuring, shuffling, or even breaths, but whatever waited on the other side, it sounded empty. She found the hidden latch and the wall opened onto a computer lab. The place was a ghost town. She pulled off her mask and walked into the middle of the room. Above her, M could make out the smooth floor of a Glass House, but it was dark. The lights were out and she hoped they stayed that way.

Before sidling up to one of the smaller screens, M accessed her own mental database on Code's old classes and wished that Merlyn was there to help her. Hacking into a system was one thing, but not having your own secure computer and attacking the system face-first through its own hardware was quite another. But Code's class hadn't been a waste of time. Almost on autopilot, she dove into the Fulbright system, flitting through password-protected security as easily as a bird flies between international borders.

First she pulled up Vivian Ware. Born in Des Moines and raised in Chicago, she was the only child of a single Fulbright parent. After years of private school, Vivian joined the Fulbright Academy to follow in her father's footsteps. She accelerated through the ranks during her first year, but in her second year, something horrible happened. She met M. According to the file, after she failed to capture one M Freeman and returned to the academy wounded, Vivian was assigned to be a desk jockey for the rest of her life. The administrative role did not come easily to her, though. Her temper flared over the simplest data-collection assignments. She claimed to see conspiracies in throwaway news reports, and when confronted about her overblown theories, Vivian refused to accept that she was mistaken. She began to break down, detached from her colleagues completely, and rarely talked to anyone. Instead she split her time between data mining and the gym, to build back the strength in her knee.

Then M found the single word that makes every Lawless student salivate:

CONFIDENTIAL

Apparently Vivian had been given several psych evaluations during the past year. Each one suggested that she had renegade tendencies, fueled by a hard-nosed drive to accomplish her goals at any cost. Because of that, she had been tagged as a possible Ronin dismissal if her defiance led her to be deemed unfit for a nonfield Fulbright role.

This was where Vivian's report ended. There was no mention of her assignment as M's roommate or her working with Ben, Keyshawn, and Devon. Maybe the files hadn't been updated recently, but it felt to M like something was missing. Or being left out on purpose. She moved on to another record.

Benjamin Downing was born and raised in Brighton, England, as a picture-perfect Fulbright recruit. His parents were both Fulbrights, his test scores and field scores were off the charts, and he was at the top of his class. There was no dirt to dig up in his file at all, leading M to believe that he may be a little too good to be true. *Perfection is a special sort of weakness all its own,* she thought. *The higher your pedestal, the harder the fall . . . ergo the greater your fear of falling grows.*

Again, there was no mention of M's crew or any of the others who now reported to Ben. Surely his file would have reflected that sort of promotion.

"Fool me once, shame on you," said M under her breath. "Fool me twice, shame on me. Something's not right."

She set her sights on Keyshawn Noles. An Atlanta native from a large family, Keyshawn was an oddity at the academy, which his file explicitly stated: Neither of his parents were Fulbrights. In fact, no one from his family had ever been associated with the Fulbrights or the Lawless School. There was no history of his previous schooling, but as soon as Keyshawn joined the academy, he had been asked to pursue nothing other than his own scientific studies. "All brain, no brawn," M said to herself. "Ms. Frank would eat you alive in the Box," she added, remembering the Lawless gym teacher.

A fringe cadet at best, Keyshawn shied away from other recruits and buried himself in his work. He had zero field skills and zero hand-to-hand fighting experience. As far as M could read, he wouldn't know a con if it confessed itself right to his face.

So why was Captain Perfect teamed up with Miss Unstable and Sir Scientific Weakling? There had to be a connection.

Deep in thought, M typed in the next name with determination. *Devon Zoso.*

FILE DELETED.

"That's weird," said M. "Now, why would you be outside of the system, Devon?" As she sat and waited for an answer to her own question, the silence of the room gave her the creeps. "Were they protecting you from Lawless, or did you do something crazy enough to require a clean slate?"

M stood up from the computer and put her mask back on. Every second away from her bed was a further risk she was taking, but then another question made her stop in her tracks. If the Fulbright files had information on cadets, perhaps there was information on the higher-ups as well. She quickly sat back down and typed in *John Doe* to see if these files went all the way to the top.

NO SUCH NAME EXISTS.

Not surprising. Cal had told her that Doe was a big secret around here. So she tried another name, her father's: *M Freeman.*

As soon as she pressed enter, a piercing alarm sounded off, blasting in her ears. Shocked, M tumbled back from the computer, tripping over her chair, and bracing against the wall.

M burst out of the computer room and rushed down the

hallway. Footsteps were gaining on her. She didn't dare stop to look over her shoulder. Corner after corner, it seemed like her pursuers would be upon her at any moment, so in an act of desperation, M pushed against a random door. Luckily it gave way and she ducked inside as the footsteps clattered almost on top of her.

The room was crowded with six huge, unplugged medical machines that were part gurney, part tanning booth, part casket, all pushed against a wall. The rest of the place was filled with rows of oversized canisters, shaped like torpedoes, silently huddled together. The canisters all displayed a chemical formula, too long and involved to make sense to M. But this strange collection of objects wasn't what held her attention. It was the glass ceiling above her that froze her in place as she stared up into another floor. There was someone in the room, sleeping on a glass bed. Then the door to the cell above slowly opened and M shrank low to the ground, hiding herself in the shadows of the machinery.

Two sets of Fulbright boots stepped into the room above her. Suddenly her mask audio kicked in as the soldiers' voices came through loud and clear over the sharp alarm.

"She's still here, safe and sound."

"You better hope that alarm is just a test. Why did you leave your post? You know this is a high-security prisoner."

"I swear I heard footsteps. Maybe someone is trying to break in from below?"

One Fulbright flashed a light down, and the room M was

hiding in exploded in illumination. She crouched tighter in the shadows.

"Nothing there but tech."

"I'd feel better if we checked the recruit trackers and made sure everyone is where they should be. I hear they have her daughter on the floor below, too. Training her, even."

"Okay, but you stay put outside. I'll finish my rounds first, then go back to base to review the trackers. Our primary concern is this floor, this prisoner, not what's happening beneath us."

The two soldiers left the room and M could hear a set of footsteps march off into the distance above her. As she crawled out from under the machine, she let out the deep breath she had been holding the entire time the Fulbrights were hovering. Looking back up, she could see exactly who was above her, exactly who the Fulbrights were guarding — her mother, Beatrice Freeman.

M pulled off her mask and stared up at her sleeping mother. With the mask off, though, both rooms were pitch-black — and the blaring alarm was gone. She put the mask back on and the alarm raged at full blast again. "The alarm is in my mask, not down here," she said with a sigh of relief. Her mask must have flipped to the emergency channel automatically when the alarm had been tripped. But tripped by what? Had entering her father's name — *her* name — into the computer set it off?

Despite the chaos of the floor above, M's mother didn't stir. It was completely unlike Beatrice's sleeping habits at home.

This was a woman who woke up as soon as the birds chirped in the morning and would stir at the sound of footsteps on carpet. M walked underneath her mother and could barely believe it was actually her. Her hair was a mess, her shirt was wrinkled, and her shoes were badly scuffed . . . all inexcusable lapses in her mother's eyes. Beatrice Freeman was always pressed and dressed for success. This slump of a person floating in the air above M, she looked like a lost cause.

"Get your rest now, Mom," said M. "I'll be back soon."

She ducked into the hallway, praying that it took the Fulbright longer to finish his rounds upstairs than it did for her to make it back to her room. Thankfully, when she got there, Vivian was still in sleep mode and didn't appear to have stirred at all while M was out. Her covers were crisply pressed around her, without any sign of jostling, tugging, or kicking, as if Vivian were an inanimate body pillow, lying perfectly, peacefully still. Slinking into bed, M pulled off her mask, pulled on her pajamas, and waited. Waited for the Fulbrights to crash open her door, waited for Vivian to catch her red-handed by saying something droll like *Someone's been out past curfew*, waited for sleep, or whichever of those three options came first.

CHAPTER 11
JAILBROKEN

By morning, it seemed that sleep had won out, as M rubbed her eyes and yawned in the brightness of the sunlike walls. Her arms weren't in shackles and Vivian didn't let on if she suspected anything. Instead her roommate leaned over her and jerked back the covers, letting out all of the warmth M had collected during her sleep.

"Up and at 'em," said Vivian with zero gusto in her voice. Her unexcitement made M's heart pang for Zara and her wicked zingers. Somehow M had come to enjoy their verbal sparring and sisterly roommate relationship. While Zara had given M a spark every morning, Vivian was as ire raising as a houseplant.

But M couldn't help wondering where that defiant version of Vivian, highlighted in her permanent record, was hiding. Sure, she had pulled some vicious Medusa action on M, but only when M had forced her hand. It almost felt like she'd been saving M from doing something stupid each time, rather than punishing her.

No, there was more to her boring direct than met the eye. M knew a play when she saw one, and the report she'd hacked was all the confirmation she needed.

Unfortunately whatever Vivian was up to would remain a mystery. Tonight, M was going to save her mother. There was no turning back. There was also no denying that for the rest of the day, M was most likely stuck training with Keyshawn. But when she and Vivian arrived at the lab to see Devon standing alongside M's crew, she realized her day was going to be worse than she first thought.

Ben was back from his night of lockup and refused to make eye contact with her. Instead his intense gaze swept over the room, as if he were about to address a legion of soldiers. Keyshawn's eyes were glued to his tablet. Devon, on the other hand, unleashed a cold stare that honed in on M like an arrow.

"Mind if I play?" Devon asked.

Ignoring Devon's remark, Ben spoke with an authoritatively venomous tone. "There have been orders to speed up your training process. We do not know why, and we will not question why, but today, we will ramp things up. Noles?"

"Thank you, sir," said Keyshawn, before turning to address the cadets. "You will be running the Maze again today, but this time you will have company."

"You're not all going to chase us through the Maze, are you?" asked Jules.

"No," barked Ben. "You're not the criminals; you're the Fulbrights."

"Meaning it will be you chasing the more experienced directs," continued Keyshawn. "The goal is to keep us from escaping the Maze by any means necessary."

"By any means?" repeated Cal, with a wink at Jules.

"But remember that we will be armed and dangerous," said Ben. "You may be chasing us, but that doesn't mean we won't fight back."

"I like those odds," said Cal. "When can we get this show rolling?"

"Ground rules first," said Keyshawn. "Almost anything goes in the Maze during this exercise. Magblasts, hand-to-hand combat, it's all allowable. When you are in the field against a Lawless rogue, they will stoop to the lowest level to escape justice."

"What is that supposed to mean?" asked M.

"It means, watch your back when we're in there," said Devon with a crooked smile.

"How will we know if we win?" asked Merlyn.

"You win after you capture your target," said Keyshawn. "If you lose, well, it will be painfully obvious if you lose. Now take a minute to prepare, though there's not a lot of planning involved. This is a test of instincts, stamina, and street smarts."

The crew walked into the Maze room as Devon, Vivian, Ben, and Keyshawn huddled together and spoke in low voices, despite Keyshawn's claim that no planning was necessary.

"Not good," said Merlyn. "How did I get stuck having to capture the creator of our tech *and* the Maze course?"

"At least you're not chasing after a trigger-happy psycho," said Jules. "You remember, the one who put M in the deep freeze."

"Hey, you should have seen the hole my dad ripped in Ben's still-beating heart the other night," said Cal. "Plus, Devon wants payback for what I did to her hair. I think I've got it the worst. How about you, M?"

"Me?" asked M, who hadn't been paying attention to them. She was more focused on how to access the upper level and find her mom without getting caught.

"Yeah, did you do anything to earn the righteous fury of Miss Personality over there?" asked Merlyn.

"Um, I shattered her knee once," answered M, "but it was a long time ago. She seems okay with me now."

"Wait, what?" snapped Jules.

"Long story," said M. "Listen, Merlyn, any luck with what we discussed earlier . . . about the suits?"

Merlyn's eyes shot at her, then quickly scanned the room. "This is a risky time to bring up such a sensitive subject, but, yeah, I think I've got something you're going to like."

"What are we talking about here?" asked Cal.

"No way," whispered Jules admiringly. "You hacked your suit, didn't you?"

"Not only that, I can rewire the comm links to give us our own private channel." Merlyn chuckled. "I mean, I kind of can't believe it, but there was an opening in the suit's configuration that allows for a bypass thread. It's so small that it's almost imperceptible."

"In English, please," said Cal.

"It's like the exhaust vent of the Death Star, a tiny flaw that makes the whole system vulnerable."

"How do you know if works?" asked Jules.

"I tried it out yesterday while Keyshawn was in the lab," answered Merlyn. "It works and I can adjust your suits, too, if we can grab five minutes alone."

"Good luck there," said Cal.

M smiled. "We'll find five minutes."

"What makes you so sure?" asked Jules.

"Let's just say I'm feeling lucky," said M. "Now, what are you guys doing tonight?"

"I was going to see a movie, maybe," joked Cal. "Why? What did you have in mind?"

"I'll tell you after we kick these Fulbrights' butts in the Maze," said M.

"Hello, old mysterious M," said Jules. "It's good to have you back!"

The huddle of directs opened up and gave a resounding clap that echoed in the empty chamber. Then they each positioned themselves, spreading evenly across the width of the room.

"Okay, our team will have a five-minute head start on you," said Keyshawn. "Remember, you must stop us from escaping . . . in three, two, one."

With a crash, walls blinked shut and swallowed the four directs, who were now officially the targets. The Maze race was on.

"And there's your time frame, Merlyn," said M excitedly. "Get us in control of these suits."

Merlyn pulled down the top of his suit and motioned to a

small circuit board at the base of the neck. "Here's what we're looking for. This is the central nervous system of the suit. It connects your mask to the rest of your body."

The others peeled down their suits, revealing their bright white Fulbright-issued undershirts. The circuit board was a microscopically tiny city of connecting tracks that bent and folded as effortlessly as cotton cloth. M had actually mistaken it for a button that clasped the suit together. She never would have found it.

"Now," Merlyn continued, "one of these little wires is all you need to be free." He held up a plastic tube filled with what looked to be metal shavings.

"I'm going to need a hand with this," said Cal.

Merlyn ran and grabbed a soldering iron from Keyshawn's lab, and within two minutes he'd successfully implanted everyone's new insert. "You see, this little piece acts as a bridge, allowing us to bypass outside commands. If anyone tries to Medusa us, the signal gets rerouted over the bridge. You get it?"

"Not really," admitted Jules. "But you swear it works?"

"On Albert Einstein's grave," said Merlyn.

"Good enough for me," said M, readjusting her collar. "How do we lose the trackers?"

"Um." Merlyn paused. "That's something I couldn't quite figure out."

"Okay," said M. "But we can secure our own comm-link connection?"

"Yeah, just tap here," Merlyn said, pointing to the right ear of his mask.

It was all coming together. M decided now was the perfect time to spring another surprise on the crew. "Great. So last night I snuck out and found my mother."

"You *what*?" asked Merlyn, mouth agape.

"I'll show you tonight, when we all sneak out to save her," said M.

"Sure, I'll just sneak past Devon, the roommate who sleeps with both eyes open, waiting for me to step out of line so she can report me to whoever it is that you report people to around here," said Jules.

"John Doe," said Cal.

"Yeah, this Doe dude," said Jules. "And I personally don't want to meet him."

"Look, we can do this. Trust me," said M. "Have I ever led you wrong before?"

It was the last thing M said to her friends' faces before the walls erupted around them. She pulled on her mask and peered forward, looking for any sign of Vivian, but the coast was clear. The head start meant that Vivian would be totally far ahead in any other race, but in the Maze, M wasn't worried. She plowed forward through the shifting walls and in no time she found a target. Unfortunately it wasn't hers. A few yards to her left, Ben knelt down, facing the opposite direction, with his arm extended and Magblast ready.

Tapping her mask to switch channels, M heard an audible click, followed by the others' slow breathing. "Cal," she whispered, "you've got an ambush waiting ahead. Ben is hiding low, waiting for you to turn the right corner."

"Thanks, M," came Cal's response. "On it."

She slid in the other direction, unnoticed, and continued her chase. As she turned a sharp corner, a blast rang out, sending her sliding backward to avoid the attack. The singed wall hissed where the blast had just narrowly missed connecting. Someone had aimed for her head.

"Jules, I've got Devon this way," said M. "Err, well, she's actually got me, so please swing around and give me some help."

"Always here to bail you out," said Jules.

As she stayed sheltered, M watched the walls shift again and again, slight movements that made her feel like she was at sea, the ocean lifting the world up and down at its own lumbering pace. But by staying in one place, M realized that the walls were doing a great bit of talking. She saw Vivian settled in for a surprise attack down a side path, before the path shunted from view. A minute later, she spotted Keyshawn on his stomach, slithering along a stretch of wall, ready to trip up any would-be pursuer.

"Attention, everyone!" said M. "It's a trap. None of the targets are trying to escape. They are all prepping ambushes. And it looks like they know where we all are."

"How are they doing that?" asked Jules.

"It's our trackers," said Merlyn. "They're tapped into our trackers. This is a stacked playing field."

"That's okay," M said confidently. "We can stack the field back in our favor. Everyone, Magblast your own arms just above the tracker."

"Are you crazy?" Jules said.

"Probably, but what other choice do we have?" said M. "Keyshawn told me that the Magblasts might have an effect on the trackers. That's why he checked us all the other day after our training session."

"Good enough for me," said Cal. "Everyone fire on three, two, one. . . ."

M grimaced as she took aim and blasted her own arm. She felt a vibration surge through her suit. It was like a force field had enveloped her.

Suddenly Vivian screamed, "Keyshawn! What just happened? They disappeared. They all disappeared!"

"Noles, scrub the exercise," called out Ben. "Use the Medusa effect on the Lawless cadets, now."

"It's not working!" hollered Keyshawn. "The suits aren't responding."

Merlyn's patch had worked!

What happened next happened fast. Cal must have rushed Ben because there was a surprised shout from behind M. Confirming his target, Cal said, "Downing down. Coming to help you guys." But as he stepped closer to M, Devon let out a blast that knocked him back with enough force to crack the wall behind him. It shattered into particles of glass and dust.

"What just happened?" yelled Keyshawn, which gave away his location as easily as Devon's blast had given away hers. Seizing the opportunity, M ran safely between them and hustled after Vivian, who had broken into a full gallop through the Maze. M could only catch glimpses of her target throughout the moving room. She struggled to follow until two walls parted and she darted down the new path. Suddenly M was on top of a very surprised Vivian, who crashed down underneath her.

"White flag?" asked M as she pinned Vivian against the ground.

A light flicked on in Vivian's eyes, casting pure anger over M. It seemed she had finally woken Vivian's slumbering Fulbright beast. With a surprising amount of power, Vivian swept her legs up and around M's torso to flip her into the distance.

Smashing against a corner, M looked up just in time to see Vivian's vicious karate kick aimed at her skull. She rolled, and the kick landed low on her shoulder instead, but the pain was intense. With an audible crack, her shoulder was knocked out of its joint. No sooner had the bones popped out, though, than the suit shoved them back into place with a second, more sickeningly audible pop, which burned as M parried Vivian's follow-up attack. The two Fulbrights pushed and shoved each other into the walls, stumbling over themselves along the path until M finally landed a square shot to Vivian's chest and sent her reeling backward. That gave M just enough time to fire a Magblast, which knocked Vivian's legs out from underneath her. Both out of breath, they looked up and were shocked to find the Maze walls had shifted, revealing a way out.

But standing in the way was a shadowed figure leaning on a cane, which he clutched with an ashen gray hand. Wheezing, the man croaked with a British accent, "Both so close, eh? To winning. To losing. There's a lesson here if you chose to learn it, I'd gather. For now, let's call it a draw, shall we?"

M braced herself for the mystery man to cross the threshold into the Maze or for the light to reveal his face, but he simply hobbled out of sight with a *click-tap* from his cane and one shoe scuffing slightly behind the next. M stood and held out her hand to help Vivian up, but Vivian remained down.

"What have you done?" she whispered through her mask.

"Me?" said M, surprised at Vivian's unmistakable trembling. "Hey, I just did what Keyshawn told me to do and caught you. Game over, I win. Now, who was that old geezer?"

"John Doe," said Vivian, as if the name itself were cursed. "And now you've dragged me onto his radar."

"Isn't that a good thing?" asked M. "Like, isn't it your job to be noticed by the top brass?"

"Not by him, not like this" was all Vivian said before the walls started to buckle. Quickly and violently, the Maze walls retreated to reveal the others, frozen in place around the room like statues locked in epic battle poses, stunned by the sudden dismissal of the tight quarters around them.

"Did we win?" asked Cal, who pulled at Ben's jacket.

"You cheated!" yelled Devon.

"Didn't think you'd mind, Devon," said Jules. "Isn't cheating your bread and butter?"

"They couldn't have cheated," called out Keyshawn. "It must be a glitch in the suits. Everyone, give 'em over. I'll take a look at them while your directs take you for the day."

No! thought M. Keyshawn would definitely notice Merlyn's handiwork. Underneath her mask, the blood drained from her face.

"What's wrong with her?" Devon asked, motioning toward Vivian on the ground.

Forcing herself to act natural, M quipped, "She doesn't like getting beaten by a rookie." The others hadn't seen Doe, and from the severity of Vivian's reaction, M figured his presence and comments were best kept secret.

As the targets and chasers eased back into being directs and cadets, the crew begrudgingly handed its uniforms over to Keyshawn and left to do whatever it was the rest of the Fulbrights did during the day.

CHAPTER 12

GLITCH

Data, data, data. Piles of data. Spreadsheets about spreadsheets of data neatly tucked into a folder marked DATA. This was apparently how Vivian Ware spent her days, in a sea of information, fishing for clues that might uncover a Lawless crime. Emails, newspaper clippings, phone call transcripts, social media sites, or photos from public cameras, the data piled higher and higher around M as she helped comb through paper after paper. For the first time she wished she were back in Keyshawn's lab, ducking under Magblast fire or even back in the Box, jumping off a speeding locomotive. Anything beat sitting at this desk and sieving through random reports.

"Aren't there computers that do this stuff now?" M asked Vivian.

"It's our job to double-check the computer's findings," she answered civilly, but the cut above her lip reminded M of everything that had just happened between them in the Maze. "Computers miss things all the time. And computers can't see the kind of crime we're looking for."

Leaning towers of paper from the FBI, CIA, MI6, Interpol, even old KGB files rose from M's desk. She picked through pages on everything from missing paintings to bank robberies to jewelry heists to traffic violations and major contraband leads. "Lawless would have loved to have this much access to the good guys' files. I guess it pays to be on the same team."

"Same team?" laughed Vivian. "Freeman, Fulbrights work alone. These agencies, they only represent the law. We *are* the law."

M didn't like the sound of that one bit. "Wait, so you pull these reports without their permission?"

"Ugh, we have to. They're worse than the computers, as far as paying attention for Lawless discrepancies. We have to keep an eye on everything."

But who keeps an eye on you? thought M. She decided to steer the conversation back toward Vivian. "So this is what you do all day?"

"Don't look so excited," said Vivian. "It's not all as glamorous as this."

"Well, not that it's any of my business," said M, "but they should send you back out in the field. It felt like you pulled the muscles from my bones in the Maze. My shoulder and ribs are still angry at me for chasing you down."

Vivian smiled, obviously pleased at her performance and to hear M admit that she still had what it took to take down an opponent. "In a few more weeks, I'll be cleared for duty."

"A few more weeks, eh," said M. "That's just enough time for you to finish being my babysitter. Coincidence?"

"That's the deal," said Vivian.

She doesn't know, thought M. According to her file, Vivian was never going back into the field.

"And since we're being honest," Vivian continued, "how did you all disappear at the same time in the Maze?"

"Lucky, I guess," M lied.

She looked up to see Vivian giving her a determined stare. Vivian seemed to study M's every word, searching each one for a sign of truth. "I don't believe in luck."

"Maybe you just never had any," said M as she parsed through another binder of the world's most mundane papers.

Several mind-numbing hours and thirty paper cuts later, M went back to reclaim her suit from Keyshawn. Vivian stayed behind to finish documenting some extra reports, which M guessed was code for "reports that M did incorrectly." Roaming the halls freely as herself, without a mask or uniform, made her feel incredibly out of sorts. It was like walking through a prison, only she wasn't sure if she was one of the guards or one of the prisoners. Her entire time at the academy had been spent trying to see through everyone else's motivations and agendas, instead of considering what *she* was doing here — and whether maybe she belonged.

The Lawless School had taught her that the Fulbrights were evil barbarians, but wasn't the Lawless education actually training her to be evil? She thought back to the Black Museum, with its exhibits on criminals and their ghastly crimes. She remembered the hallowed halls of the Masters' dorm, set up like a shrine to the school's most infamous alumni, with portraits of truly bad people who had done really bad things. And that's not who M wanted to become.

But everything M had experienced with the Fulbrights proved them to be an overly aggressive group of vigilantes willing to go too far for justice. They'd kidnapped her mother, torched thousands of priceless paintings, spied on the spies of the world, and continuously threatened M and her friends. These were supposed to be the good guys, but they didn't play that role at all. Morals weren't part of their "good guy" code. Their real goal was to defeat the Lawless School at any cost, no matter how deadly or destructive their actions.

Yet her father had been a Fulbright, a double agent, no less, and he had recruited M without her consent and without explaining the rules of this bizarre world. Running over everything in her mind, she should logically harbor a deep-seated mistrust of her father, who had withheld the truth from her and taken countless secrets to his grave. But he was her father. Good or bad, he had loved M and she had loved him. The same went for her mother. If her parents had kept the truth from her, there must have been a reason. The truth was probably uglier than she could imagine.

Keyshawn's lab was much harder to find without her suit, but M was apparently the first one there. The four suits hung against the wall, empty skins under Keyshawn's lock and key.

"Oh hey, just finishing up here," said Keyshawn. "The suits were fine after all. Give me a second and I'll get yours."

"Can I ask you a question first?" asked M, willing to risk a hunch.

"Sure," he answered with his back to her as he tapped something into his computer.

"So, I know why I lied back in the Maze," said M. "But why are *you* lying about the glitch?"

Keyshawn looked up without facing M, as if he were searching the far wall for an answer, but ultimately he just shook his head. "I don't know what you're talking about. I looked for a glitch, combed over every suit, but everything looks normal to me."

M didn't believe him. There was no way Keyshawn could search those suits without pinpointing Merlyn's handiwork.

"Wait. What did you lie about?" asked Keyshawn as he took M's suit down from the wall.

"Why do you think the Maze drill ended?" asked M.

"Because you won," said Keyshawn.

"Hardly. Vivian almost had me beat," admitted M, "when John Doe showed up. He was there, watching us. And why would that be? Why would Devon, Vivian, and Ben put up with us all? I think I know the answer. You're grooming us for John Doe's army, aren't you?"

"Every Fulbright is in John Doe's army," said Keyshawn. "That's nothing new."

"Oh no," replied M with confidence. "This is new. We're training to be a whole different strand of Fulbrights, aren't we? You gave us the shot. You gave us the tech. You gave us the Magblast. And you've kept us separate from the other Fulbright classes. We're Doe's very own black ops team. That's why he's watching us. That's why you're so nervous, isn't it?"

"Here's your suit," Keyshawn snapped as he shoved the folded fabric into her hands. "Wear it in good health."

She'd struck a nerve. She was on a hot streak for getting under people's skin today.

"So you don't deny it," said M smugly.

"You know what your problem is, Freeman?" said Keyshawn. "You think you've got this all figured out, but you don't. How could you? It's not done yet."

"What's not done, Keyshawn?" asked Merlyn, who walked into the room and nervously added, "Um, the suits, uh, did you fix the glitch?"

"Oh, he fixed a lot of things, Merlyn," said M. "Didn't you, 'Keyshawn Noles it all'?"

Tucking the suit under her arm, M stormed out of the lab. There was no reason why Keyshawn should let her, of all people, in on his plan, but it irked her that he ended up being exactly what she thought he'd be: a dishonest, scientific snake in the grass. She hated being right about people all the time. Just once she'd love for someone to surprise her in a good way.

Surprises or not, tonight M was going AWOL with her mother, who had to be the key to whatever came next. Why else would Lawless be after her? Why else would the Fulbrights hold on to her? Even Zara had told her that her mother was a small-time crook before meeting her father. Hopefully Beatrice would lead M to the moon rock and together they could destroy it once and for all, just like her father had planned. That was the only assignment M needed to complete, as far as she cared. *Fox Lawless and his Masters want to cook up another plan to ruin the world, go ahead.* The Fulbrights could handle it. They'd gotten this far without her help, right?

M marched into the cafeteria and grabbed her allotted meal, a drastic-looking purple blob with white stripes and puffy pink circles on the side. Before she could sit down, another student nudged her from behind.

"Excuse you," he said. It was the hall monitor M had ditched during her first unaccompanied excursion.

"Excuse me?" she asked, flustered. "Are you seriously going to try to bully me? All I'm doing is eating my purple slop. Can I do it in peace?"

"No, you can't," said another Fulbright student, who stood up and smacked the tray back into M's chest, smothering her with the hypercolored meal. "You're not wanted here, you know. And you're not safe."

"None of us are safe, since we're all being trained for combat. So first, there's that," M fired back. "And for your information, I'd rather be somewhere else, too. Just about anywhere else, actually. You don't get to be the only one mad at this situation."

As the rest of the tables emptied and stone-faced Fulbright students encircled her, M wished she had been more careful with her words. Why did she have to make such a scene everywhere she went? She was angry at a lot of things, but not at all these kids around her now. How could she dislike them? They were sheep following orders. They'd been trained to hate people like M, because to them, she looked like a wolf. She howled like a wolf, snarled like a wolf, and made a pack with other wolves. These kids were just doing their jobs and M was the only business in the room.

As the flock of Fulbrights was about to fall on its prey, the lights in the walls flickered. The aggro kids who had been ready to skin M alive stopped in their tracks and looked around the room, confused. A change in routine was obviously rare enough around here to steal the show from M's big breakdown.

"Cadets, return to your rooms," a voice rang out over an intercom. "We are implementing an early lights-out tonight."

The spell of anger and frustration broke as the cadets' training took over and they left the dining area in an orderly fashion, bussing their tables as they went. M followed suit, cleaning up as much of her mess as she could before hustling back to her room.

She arrived to find that Vivian was gone, probably still tied up with paperwork. M couldn't have asked for a better set of circumstances. After quickly changing her clothes and putting on her uniform, she spoke softly through the comm link. "Hey, guys, you there? I think our mission is a go."

CHAPTER 13

LIGHTS-OUT

"Finally," Merlyn said, his voice tinny and nervous in her earbud. "M, we've been waiting for you. Everyone's on the line. What's the next move?"

"Are you free to leave your dorms?" asked M.

"Keyshawn's back in the lab, so I'm clear," said Merlyn.

"Devon's gone, so I'm good," said Jules.

"Cal, you're probably in the hardest situation," said M. "We can come get you, but you'll have to be ready to book it."

"No, that's the weird thing," responded Cal. "My guards deserted me when I was picking up my suit. I think this early lights-out thing is more than a technical difficulty. I'm out in the halls now."

"Merlyn, you're sure we'll be able to control these suits?" asked M. "'Cause if not, then I'll go this alone. It's my mother out there."

"My modifications still work," said Merlyn. "I checked. Keyshawn didn't catch the bypass."

"Guys, this feels like a setup; I'm not going to lie," admitted M. "But I'll take any opportunity they give me. You don't have to come if you don't want."

"You think we're going to let you do this by yourself?" said Jules. "She may be your mother, but you're our friend."

M smiled and was filled with a new confidence by the fact that whatever was waiting for her in the hallway, maybe even in her whole life, her friends would have her back. "Then let's meet by the dining commons in five."

Minutes later the whole crew had regrouped. Quietly, they drifted single file down the dimmed halls, looking in all directions, waiting for a guard to turn the corner or a door to burst open — waiting to be caught. But nothing of the sort happened. They were alone with the flickering lights, which were especially annoying with their masks on. The goggles were constantly trying to adjust for the flickering, and the flaring visual corrections made M's eyes ache. "I feel like I'm at the world's worst dance party," said Cal, covering his masked eyes for some relief against the exaggerated strobe-light effect.

Finally they reached the door M was looking for, but this time it was already open. M rushed inside with her Magblast at the ready. The room looked undisturbed, and just as creepy as it had been the previous night. The coffinlike machinery, the chemical tanks, they were all still in place.

"You gonna tell us what that first-through-the-door tough-girl act is about?" Jules asked M once they were all inside.

"Someone else has been here," said M as she looked up to the Glass House. But it was empty. "That's where my mother was last night."

"They moved her," said Cal. "It's too dangerous to keep a prisoner in one place. I'll bet they're moving her around every few days, like a shell game. As soon as you think you know where she is, she's not there. That's what they did to me."

Then Merlyn interrupted their conversation by running past them and over to the rows of cylindrical tanks. "Whoa, do you guys know what's in these?" He passed his hands carefully over the spigots.

"Oxygen? Hydrogen? Helium?" guessed Cal.

"It's *the gas*," said Merlyn, astonished. "The special Lawless brew. Guys, this is enough gas to hypnotize the whole academy."

"Then what are these?" asked Jules, pointing to the casket-like contraptions.

"Don't know," said Merlyn. "Looks like an oxygen chamber or a sensory deprivation tank, maybe?"

"Okay, guys, back to the issue at hand, please," said M, redirecting their attention to the glass ceiling above. "My mom's up there somewhere. How do we break through the glass ceiling?"

"Why not take the stairs?" Cal asked. "Too old fashioned?"

M shook her head. "They'll be watching the stairs."

"Anybody got a diamond?" asked Jules.

"I think I've got one better," said Merlyn with a smirk. He pulled out a stone that looked like a diamond to M. "WBN, my friends."

"What's a pretty little rock like this going to do against reinforced glass like that?" asked M.

"Wurtzite boron nitride," said Merlyn, "will slice that glass like butter. Observe." Then, standing on one of the large machines, he took the rock and scratched a circle in the glass.

"Where did you get WBN?" asked Jules.

"Perks of being roommates with Keyshawn," answered Merlyn. "He has so much cool stuff in his room — you wouldn't believe it. There. Now, Cal, would you do the honors?"

Cal jumped up and dislodged the glass disk with a gentle, precisely measured Magblast. Then he slid it over like it was a manhole cover. The whole group was impressed. "Guess I'm getting the hang of this thing."

"Okay, everyone," said M as she climbed. "The easy part's over. We have no idea what's up there, so be prepared for anything."

Finding the exit from the Glass House wouldn't have been easy if M hadn't seen the guards come through it the night before. It definitely wasn't a room designed with a quick exit in mind. Jules found the sliding panel and grabbed the wurtzite from Merlyn. Slicing down the seam, she unsealed the glass door and slid it open carefully. The hallway beyond shimmered endlessly, like a mirage. As they crept along, each wall looked into another empty room — all Glass Houses that reflected the Lawless crew and their movements. There wasn't another soul in sight.

"So far this actually seems pretty easy," said Cal.

"She's got to be here," said M. This was it. This was her big plan. But as they turned the first corner, then the second, then the third, they were met with consistently empty rooms. She started to doubt herself.

"Maybe they moved everyone off this floor?" suggested Merlyn. "As a precaution because of the lighting issues below?"

"Oh no, the lights are flickering. Guess this calls for a mass evacuation of high-security prisoners," mocked Cal. "No, I'm with M. Her mom's here, but there's something going on."

Suddenly there was a distant boom that stopped the group in its tracks.

"What was that?" asked Jules.

M scanned the glass rooms until she found one in the distance that was very different from all of the others. The room was filled with an impenetrable darkness, a black cube nested in the midst of this glass city. "It's a smoke bomb. But why would someone set it off in a sealed room?"

M ran up to the wall and tried to see inside, but the deep blackness blocked out even her mask-enhanced vision. Looking down, she saw the outside door had an etched handle. She motioned to the others that she was going in. Everyone braced and gripped their Magblasts tightly. She slowly touched the handle and then counted to herself. One . . . two . . . but on three, the door ripped open inward, pulled clean off its track, and the black smoke flooded into the hallway. She could barely make out the two masked Fulbrights in full uniform who stepped out into the growing darkness. It was over. They'd been caught. But instead of stopping to apprehend M, the Fulbrights shoved past them, launching out of the cloud of smoke and down the hall.

Alarms pounded over the loudspeakers, echoing shrilly through the air, as M sorted out what had just happened. It was obvious now. The smoke bomb, a man with the strength to rip the door off its track, and most important, the sight of an old friend in a Fulbright uniform, like she'd seen on the plane to the Lawless School. M wasn't the only one coming to save her mother.

Jones, the family butler, was here, too!

"After them!" screamed M over the mind-numbing noise. "That's my mother! If we follow them, they'll get us out of here!"

The crew hauled tail down the hall, following the false Fulbrights. M's mother and Jones ran with determination; they must have known exactly where they were going. They sped past room after room until they reached an open hatch in the ceiling. M's mother leapt up gracefully through the opening. Then before Jones followed, he threw a hockey puck–sized object that skated across the floor toward M.

"Take cover!" yelled M, but it was too late. Another blast went off, releasing an inky darkness that swelled around them. The gloom was incredibly dense; M couldn't see anything. Stumbling forward, she finally found her way out the other side of the murky cloud, but the hatch was closed — clamped shut by the very same vault door they had faced back on the vertical course.

"Come on!" Cal yelled with aggravation as he stumbled into the light to see the familiar lock.

"When are we ever going to come across a safe like this?" Merlyn screeched sarcastically in a high-pitched voice.

"How was I supposed to know we'd ever see something like this again?" complained Cal. "Where's the control box for this one?"

"There," cried M, pointing. "Hurry up. They're getting away."

Merlyn worked his magic quickly, but M couldn't stop counting the seconds tick off the clock. Who knew where that passageway led? They could end up in another labyrinth and have lost her mother forever.

In no time, Merlyn cracked the code and the vault door swung open, unleashing a blast of cold air. Behind them, a group of real Fulbrights burst into the hallway and pointed at the crew through the glass rooms.

"Jump!" she screamed. Then, leaping, she pulled herself up into an alien world. The ground was cold and hard, and the bright light of day shocked her mask's visual system. Slowly everything came back into focus and M realized that she wasn't inside the academy anymore. The sun hung broken just above the horizon as if the very clockwork of the Earth were jammed. The bright star beamed unfiltered light down upon the surrounding landscape, which was covered in snow and ice. Nearby there were several high-powered helicopters. M was standing on a tarmac. Then a giant unlatching sound rattled through her skull, and the world suddenly cracked open. No, it wasn't the world — it was a humongous glass dome that enveloped the space, designed to keep the helicopters sheltered from the brutal elements outside. Wherever they were, it wasn't a place people naturally called home.

As the dome slid down into the earth and the others climbed through the hatch, M heard an engine roar to life. The slow swoop of helicopter blades cut the air, faster and faster and faster until she could see one of the great machines begin to lift off the ground. Without thinking, she raced toward the copter and launched herself into the air, grabbing hold of the landing skids. Her legs kicked against the ground and she pulled against the skids, trying feebly to tug or will the helicopter back down, but there was only one direction that this whirlybird was headed now. Up.

M clutched the skids and pulled herself up as the others watched helplessly below. The helicopter tilted forward and bounced against the bone-chilling wind, which whipped over the frozen scenery. As the machine jerked and jumped, M seized her opportunity to climb. Maybe she could still convince her mother to turn around and save the others. Her arms burned as she reached forward and tugged herself into a standing position. When she knocked against the window, she startled her mother, who had just pulled off her mask. Jones grabbed the controls and motioned violently toward M. Beatrice turned to face her daughter and M smiled with relief. They were finally face-to-face, closer than they had been even in the restaurant back in London.

"Open up!" yelled M over the coughing revolutions of the giant whirring blades above. "It's me, Mom! It's M! It's M Freeman, your daughter!"

But then M saw herself in the glass door just as her mother must have seen her: the last remaining Fulbright, masked and clinging to the side of her getaway helicopter, while hammering against the window. Before her mother could react, M ripped her mask off. The chill of the air bit her exposed flesh, and her hair flipped wildly out of control. She stared into her mother's eyes and screamed again, "It's me! It's me!"

Beatrice froze in place, watching her daughter hanging on for dear life. Time stopped as M let out a relieved, if bitterly icy breath. She'd done it: She had found her mother and now they were escaping together. All Beatrice had to do was open the door and let M climb aboard. But then her mother's eyes hardened with a look that M had never seen before. It was a mixture of disbelief, anger, and sadness.

"It's me, Mom," M repeated as the helicopter lifted higher and higher into the air.

Then, swiftly and violently, her mother kicked the door open with both legs. The blow knocked the door sharply into M, smacking her directly in the jaw. Her body went limp as the helicopter lifted effortlessly away, and M Freeman tumbled helplessly toward the ice-covered world below.

CHAPTER 14
CATCH AND RELEASE

The helicopter lifted higher into the snowy sky as M toppled through the open air, end over end. It was like a nightmare, but her eyes were wide open, watching the blisteringly white ground swap places with the clouds and back again. It was a long way down.

Then her training kicked in. M clipped her arms and legs together to stop rolling uncontrollably through the sky. Aiming her straightened body like an arrow, she focused on the tarmac, which was sprinting toward her with an unforgiving force. *Better to crash-land closer to the others,* she thought. Once she was above her target, M pulled her mask back on, then spread her legs and arms wide apart to increase the air resistance, using her body as a makeshift parachute and catching the updraft to slow her fall. She went over the landing in her mind: feet first, knees slightly bent, find the softest patch of snow and roll forward on impact.

It was still going to hurt.

With her somewhat desperate plan in place, M closed her freezing eyes and thought about how the suit had pulled her bones back into place during her battle with Vivian. Would it be able to put all her pieces back together again after a fall like this one? She guessed not.

Next, M wished. She wished for wild inventions that could get her out of this situation, no matter how irrational. A time machine, an invisible jet, a jet pack, anything. *At the very least this suit should have a parachute,* thought M. And immediately she felt the back of her suit moving. No, not just moving — the suit was writhing against her back. And before she knew what was happening, she was jerked back up into the air so forcefully, she thought she might tear in half. A shadow dawned over her, and as M looked up, she was shocked to see her suit had produced an actual parachute at the very thought.

"Keyshawn!" she yelled with excitement. "I could kiss you, you mad scientist! Programmable matter! You made the suits out of programmable matter!"

But M's sweet victory was about to be squashed. Even with the parachute, she was descending too rapidly to land safely. She began to swing her body in circles, trying to cut back and forth in the sky to collect as much air as possible and slow down her death dive. Still, the ground was rushing up from below to snatch her in its frozen jaws and gnash her into oblivion.

"M!" Merlyn's fuzzed-out voice rang in her comm link. "M, fire your Magblast directly downward, now!"

M pointed her fist to the ground and blasted a furious shot that rippled the air and was met head-on by a second blast from below. She was no longer falling but found herself wobbling in place high above the earth.

"Good, now let's stop the blast on my count," came Merlyn's transmission. "Three . . . two . . . one!"

M cut her blast and resumed her descent, but this time her speed was completely manageable. She drifted down and landed softly on her feet, then toppled into the waiting arms of her crew.

"How did you . . . ?" began M to Merlyn. "I could have been —"

"A frozen pancake, yeah," interrupted Merlyn. "I guessed that if we set our blasts against each other, the end result would be like matching opposite poles of a magnet."

"You repelled me," said M. "Brilliant, Merlyn. That saved my neck."

"He couldn't have done it without your parachute," said Jules. "Where in the world did that come from?"

"Oh, that," said M, shaking her head in disbelief. "These suits are wired to do some outrageous tricks."

"Wait, are you telling me that these suits have parachutes?" asked Cal.

"Better!" shouted Merlyn now that he got a closer look at M's suit reconfiguring itself as the parachute twisted back into place. "This is programmable matter, isn't it?"

"Let's discuss it later," said M. "We have company to deal with first." She motioned to a flock of Fulbrights racing through the snow toward them.

"Do we need to get our stories straight?" asked Jules.

"No," said M. "I think they owe *us* some explanations."

M stood up and finally saw the scope of the academy's complex, which spread miles in every direction. At least half a dozen other domes dotted the polar landscape in the distance, forming a massive circle on the ice. She could now envision the contours of the hallways snaking beneath her feet — the labyrinth that had driven her crazy earlier was even more massive than she'd guessed.

"Stay close, everyone," M tried to say, but all sound in her mask had gone dead. She couldn't even hear her own voice. She moved her lips and felt the words in her mouth, but a bleak silence filled her ears as the crew all stared at one another noiselessly.

Quickly the Fulbrights surrounded them. Holding batons, the agents looked like a SWAT team ready to break down doors and ransack secrets. The quiet held M and her friends in a suspension that was almost worse than being in the Glass House. In the Glass House M had at least been allowed to keep all five of her senses.

Then a surprising pop erupted in M's ears, followed by a scratching buzz that bled into an adult's voice, cutting through the static.

"Put down your weapons now!"

Our entire suits are weapons, thought M, but then she realized they must be referring to their Magblasts. She lifted her hands in the air slowly and removed her Magblast glove, showing the encircling Fulbrights that she was on their side, or at the very least, that she was obeying. The others followed her lead and the Fulbrights seemed satisfied because they lowered their batons.

"Masks off!"

Again the crew complied with the order, baring their unprotected faces to the viciously cold terrain. The wind stung their noses numb in no time while snowflakes landed frozen on their faces, but at least they could hear again. M's teeth began to throb and even the water in her eyes felt iced over in the subzero temperatures. White smoke wafted with her every breath, like smoke signals in the morning air. A few more minutes like this and they would suffer frostbite, possibly even lose an ear. By the trajectory of the sun, M made an educated guess that they were stationed above the Arctic Circle. And she would have happily told the others, if she could get her teeth to stop chattering.

Despite her discomfort, she stood her ground in front of the Fulbrights. She was shivering, sure, but she shivered stoically until the Fulbright leader spoke.

"Confirmed, it's the Lawless team. What are our orders?"

M and the others stood with their arms limply up in the air, waiting for what would happen next. When the Fulbrights broke into motion, though, it was without any verbal acknowledgment of the crew's fate. The agents remained silent as they put M and her friends in handcuffs. Then, hands secured behind them, the crew was marched back toward the open dome. Back toward the very facility they had just escaped.

As they stepped onto the tarmac, there was a hissing click of hydraulics, and the dome began to close around them like a giant mouth. The row of helicopters looked sharp and rigid, like black teeth against the glaring white outside, with a gap where the stolen helicopter used to be. The crew was led forward to a hidden set of bay doors in the floor, which spread slowly open. An oversized elevator rose up from the ground, and M and her friends were forced inside.

The sunlight squinted as the bay doors above them slid shut and they were pulled back underground. M took deep breaths as she tried to keep calm and take stock of what had just unfolded. Her mother had escaped and left her to rot with the Fulbrights. The moon rock was still hidden, but Ms. Watts had a better chance of finding it first purely because she was out there while M and her friends were trapped in this subterranean world. Not to mention that M's face hurt bad where the helicopter door had smacked her. But what hurt her the most wasn't the strike or the fall or her landing. It was her mother's sudden betrayal.

The elevator arrived at the final destination and the door opened up to a large room filled with Fulbrights standing at attention.

"Bring them in," commanded a hoarse voice with an English accent.

The Fulbrights in the elevator obliged, pushing the crew forward and through the throng of masked soldiers. At the front of the room sat Mr. Fence and the gray man who M had glimpsed before in the shadows of the Maze: John Doe.

The most striking thing about Doe was his ashen skin tone. It looked as if the life had been washed out of him. His brownish-black eyes sunk into his gaunt face, and his long black hair, which was probably dyed, tumbled around his slumped shoulders. He seemed ancient and yet the thin skin that wrapped his features looked like it had been pulled taut.

"Sit," commanded Doe, and everyone sat except for the Lawless crew — they didn't have chairs. The tribunal had begun and they were on the stand. "I want to know what happened."

M spoke up first. "It's all my fault."

"It is, is it?" he answered. "Then tell me why."

"My mother had been . . ." M paused to find the perfect word. ". . . *held* here, and I needed to talk to her."

"What about?"

"Family stuff," M said. "Anyway my friends offered to help, so we snuck out after curfew to the floor above ours, where my mother was . . . being held."

"And how did you know this?" asked Doe.

"Intuition," said M. "When we reached her room, someone else was already there. Two Fulbrights —"

"Two people in Fulbright uniforms," corrected Mr. Fence.

"Er, yes, two people in Fulbright uniforms," M agreed, "jumped us as they were trying to escape. One of them was my mother."

"How did you know it was your mother if she was wearing a mask?" asked Doe.

"Honestly, when the Fulbrights —"

"People in Fulbright uniforms," corrected Mr. Fence again.

"Right, when the *people in Fulbright uniforms* didn't stop us, I knew that they weren't real soldiers," said M. "I'm sure any soldier in this room would have held us for being in a restricted area. So we chased after them. And I just . . . I just had a feeling that it was her."

"And you were right," acknowledged John Doe. "Now, why didn't your mother take you with her?"

"She didn't know it was me, sir," M lied. "I was wearing my mask the whole time. There was no way she could have known it was me."

"And how did you end up so far from the dome?"

"I jumped onto the helicopter, sir," said M. "I tried to . . . I tried to go with them."

"With them, eh?" said Doe. "I appreciate your candor, Cadet Freeman." He nodded slowly before addressing the rest of the room. "Troops, you should be ashamed of yourselves. These cadets did more to stop the intruder and interrupt this escape than all of you combined."

"But, sir, all signs pointed us to the lower levels," said a Fulbright from the audience.

"Then you were following the wrong signs," said Doe with a winded rattle in his raspy voice. "And these children followed the right ones."

"They stumbled into a crime scene," argued another Fulbright. "It was a total mistake."

"There are no mistakes in life," said Doe. "Everything follows a design in the end; believe me, it does." He held M in his stare and then smiled a disgustingly white smile. It looked as if his teeth were made of polished ivory. "And I'll prove it," he continued. "Bring in the others."

A door in the side of the room opened and in marched Ben, Keyshawn, Vivian, and Devon. They looked completely caught off guard by the situation.

"Directs, you are here because you have failed to manage your cadets," said John Doe.

"What!" screamed Vivian. "We were under orders to prepare the next test for the recruits in Keyshawn's lab. We tried to leave when the alarm sounded, but were told to stay in place!" Before she could continue, Ben nudged her hard in the back and motioned that she should keep her mouth shut.

"But," continued Doe, "I would like to give you a second chance. Your cadets outperformed our entire Fulbright team tonight, therefore you must be doing something right with them."

M noticed Ben's eyes narrow in relief at hearing John Doe's compliment.

"So, Cadet Freeman," said Doe as he returned his attention to her. "You wanted to find your mother, did you?"

"That was the plan," answered M.

"Brilliant. Then you'll have your chance," said Doe. "Along with your directs, you are tasked with capturing your mother and bringing her to justice. You must leave tonight. She has a head start, but we know where she's going."

"And where is that?" asked Cal, attracting his father's glare.

"That's for us to know and for you to find out," chided Mr. Fence, which caused a chilling hush in the room broken only by Doe himself.

"Fulbrights, activated and dismissed for duty."

With that the Fulbrights returned to a bustle of activity, one group escorting the Lawless crew and their directs out through the side door. But M was stunned to silence at the familiar wording of John Doe's command. Could he possibly have gotten that from Professor Bandit? Or could Professor Bandit have picked it up from John Doe? Either way, the similarity didn't sit well with her.

Mr. Fence came up behind her, cutting her line of thought short.

"Okay, soldiers, we have an assignment. Directs, you are to change into uniforms immediately and meet us at bay three. Cadets, follow me. We're embarking on perhaps the most dangerous journey of your lives; there's no getting around it. And it would be prudent to give you more time to train for this, but maniacs wait for no one. We need to stop Beatrice Freeman before she destroys this world as we know it." He turned his bright eyes on M. "I trust that won't be a problem for you, Freeman."

"No, sir," M responded. She had a lot of problems to deal with, but if she were being honest, hunting down her mother was something she looked forward to. "It isn't a problem at all."

CHAPTER 15
FOLLOWING ORDERS

M followed Mr. Fence through a series of winding tunnels and up an elevator to what was presumably bay three, another glass dome canopy bubbling up from the iced earth. The sight of rows of jets made M's stomach lurch with a nervousness she hadn't expected. Jets had come to represent a bridge to her, always leading her to another level of life, each more difficult than the last. Just once, she wished she were boarding a plane to return to somewhere familiar or someone happily expecting her.

"It's gonna be okay, M," comforted Merlyn. "I'm sure these jets are the safest in the world."

"It's not the jet," she said. "It's everything on the other side of the jet that scares me. Let's get this over with."

M climbed into the black plane to find a slender, window-less tube with seats bolted to the walls like benches, and seat belts dangling limply from the ceiling. She slid down and took the last space on the right, latching her buckles into place for safety's sake, but also to keep her from escaping before lift-off. The lack of windows was a blessing, since the last plane window M gazed out of had given her a bird's-eye view of destruction on a scale she had never imagined.

The directs loaded in shortly after, dressed in their uniforms and quickly taking their seats. Keyshawn, whose Fulbright suit looked brand-new, sat opposite M. His knees would not stop bouncing and he stared beyond her as if he were trying to bore a hole into the side of the plane. Ben looked relaxed, as did Devon, both leaning back with their eyes closed. Vivian, though, displayed a wide smile and a spark in her eyes that M could read from across the cabin. This was the action she had been waiting for. She'd shown the same eagerness in the Maze and now her knee brace couldn't stop bouncing up and down, too.

"All go!" announced Mr. Fence, who lowered himself into the copilot's seat in the front of the plane after giving a smile and a wink to Cal, who sat nearest him. *How strange it must be for them,* thought M. Here was a father so excited to take his son on their first adventure together, but Cal sat as lifeless as a statue carved from a chunk of limestone rock. The contrast was shocking, how different the smooth-cornered statue of Cal was from the sharp-edged slab of his father. It was hard to believe they were made out of the same substance.

Merlyn and Jules kept their eyes on M, looking for signs of a freak-out, but she did a good job keeping it together. The jet had become the last thing on her mind. Mysteries were piling up around her faster than she could count. *How do you eat an elephant?* her father used to ask her teasingly. *One bite at a time.* Maybe he'd been trying to tell her something.

Rockets from underneath propelled the jet straight upward like a helicopter, but faster, and the sudden movement pressed

M down against her seat. Once the jet was airborne and gliding forward, the ride was no smoother. Gusts of wind rocked the cabin in pockets of turbulence, nudging the passengers to remind them who or what was in charge. M gripped her harness and leaned forward.

"Where are we going?" she asked Keyshawn.

"Don't know," he said blankly.

"You all right?" she pressed.

"Don't know," he answered.

"Well, everybody has to know something, Keyshawn," said M. "What *do* you know?"

"We're following orders," said Keyshawn. "That's all I know." He slipped out of his thousand-yard stare and met M's gaze. She saw fear in his eyes. But fear of what?

"Okay, so what are our orders, then?" she asked. "Besides finding my mom."

"Don't know," said Keyshawn, like a sound bite stuck on repeat.

"How does Doe know where my mom's going?" she asked.

"I presume she revealed something during interrogation," he answered, exasperated. "Look, I'm being honest with you: I don't know much of what's going on. I don't know where we're going or what we're after, but I know it's a major prize."

"What do you mean, *major prize*?" asked M.

"I mean that your mother won't be the only person searching for it," Keyshawn said with certainty. "There's been chatter on the wires. Others are close to finding whatever it is, and we need to keep that from happening."

The rock, thought M. What else could it be? She had wished for a light at the end of this darkening tunnel and maybe she'd stumbled onto her wish. Could she really be on her way to kill two birds with one stone? Find her mother, find the rock, and stop Ms. Watts *and* the Fulbrights from endangering the world.

"I think I know what we're going after," said M.

Glancing around, Keyshawn made sure the others weren't paying attention to their conversation. He leaned closer to M and whispered, "No matter what you think you know, keep it to yourself for now. Your mother's escape ... it was an inside job. I mean, come on, the timing didn't seem suspicious to you? Conveniently all your directs are absent, the halls are emptied of cadets, and the Fulbright soldiers don't get their man? No way. You were set up. *We* were set up. But I bet you weren't supposed to get that close to her. I bet you weren't supposed to almost get away."

M listened as the plane rushed through the unseen sky to their unknown destination. Could he be right? Could it be that she was conned by Doe, led directly to her mother's staged escape, and given just enough rope to trap herself with?

Of course, she never would have attempted it if Merlyn hadn't cracked Keyshawn's coding. . . .

"You were lying," she said. "You knew all along that Merlyn hacked the suits, didn't you?"

"Just following orders," admitted Keyshawn. "Why else would I give him so much free time away from oversight? And the Maze match, that was my idea. I needed to give him time with all of you away from your directs. He did a great patch job, for what it's worth. I didn't make it *too* easy for him."

"You used us," M whispered harshly.

"We're all using one another, M," said Keyshawn. "The sooner you get that through your head, the sooner you'll appreciate the magnitude of this situation."

"Big words coming from someone who doesn't even belong here," she answered. They locked in a death stare. "I've seen your file. You're not one of us and you're not one of them. So what is John Doe holding over you to make you do his bidding?"

"More than you'll ever know," he said as the corners of his lips turned down. M saw clearly that an awful truth was hidden behind his eyes. It was something he wasn't ready to admit, or didn't know how to admit, and it meant the end of the discussion for now. Keyshawn kicked against her bench and pushed himself as far away from her as possible.

Fine, M thought. She leaned back and felt her eyelids grow heavy. It was, after all, nighttime in the underworld of the academy and she hadn't slept in some time. In the end, as she closed her eyes "for just a minute," sleep overtook her.

She awoke when the plane touched down hours later. Silently Mr. Fence guided the directs and the cadets out of the plane and onto a dark field surrounded by empty bleachers, which stretched up into the night sky.

"Are we in a soccer stadium?" asked Jules.

"More like six football fields wrapped in one stadium," said Ben, looking around.

"It's a Communist-era sports complex called Strahov Stadium, to be exact," said Mr. Fence. "Excellent cover for an unlisted jet landing. This way, Fulbrights."

As he led them across the overgrown grass, crisp with frost, M could see that Mr. Fence loved being out in the field. If his confident steps and blithe tone weren't enough of a tell, then not reprimanding Ben for speaking out of turn was a dead giveaway. They walked into a set of open gates and through the insides of the derelict stadium. The walls were covered in indecipherable graffiti, and the halls stunk of mold, rotten food, and urine. Keyshawn gagged at the smell and ran ahead to try and escape the unpleasant atmosphere. *If the poor kid wasn't ready for this kind of surprise, what will he do when the Lawless agents show up?* thought M.

"You always pick the nicest places to take me, Dad," said Cal.

Mr. Fence smiled at his son and took a deep breath as they stepped outside again. The exterior of the stadium looked even worse than the inside; the concrete façade was in utter disrepair. It made the ancient, crumbling Roman Colosseum M had seen in pictures look downright cozy. The air was cold, but nowhere near as cold as it had been outside the Fulbright Academy. Mr. Fence led them across the street, where two monolithic towers stood on the edge of a cliff. Below the cliff, a dimly lit, time-worn city unfolded before them. Instantly M knew where they were.

"Prague," said Devon. "Your parents ever steal anything from here, M?"

"All of our parents have," Cal laughed.

As the Lawless students snickered, Vivian focused intently on the city, like a cartographer sketching out newly discovered coastline. M knew that determination. It meant that nothing was going to stop her from completing this mission.

"Ah, our ride is here," said Mr. Fence as a van with dark windows crept around the corner. Its doors slid open. "Everybody, in, and I will brief you on our quick visit."

Everyone poured in, with Ben jockeying to nab the seat closest to Mr. Fence.

"Our target is in the Prague Orloj," he started. "Now, for those who are unfamiliar, the Orloj is basically a giant clock in the middle of the city. Somewhere in this structure there is a box. We must retrieve this box and return it safely to the academy. Understand?"

"Got it," chirped Cal from the back of the van. "We're looking for a box. Will any box do? 'Cause you're not telling us much about what this extremely valuable thing looks like."

"We only know the *where*," answered Mr. Fence sternly. "The rest is up to your squad."

"Oh, I get it," said Cal. "You need us to break in and steal this box. You need us to be thieves."

"Right now, we need you to shut up, cadet," snapped Devon. "You'll follow the orders given, no questions asked."

The rest of the ride remained awkwardly quiet as the van curved through the winding streets. The closer they got to the city, the narrower the roads became, until the van was practically brushing up against the buildings that lined the block. The buildings were vibrant in color even at night. Buttery yellows, bright brick reds, and picture-perfect white — these structures were a far cry from the drabness of Strahov Stadium. It was as if the squad had stepped into a fairy tale.

Finally M broke the silence. "Okay, you want that box, then you need to tell us more about this clock before we face it. What's the deal?"

"It was built in the year 1410 and was famous for being an astronomical clock," Keyshawn said, surprising M — she hadn't expected *him* to give this briefing. "But it's been through a lot."

"What do you mean by *astronomical*?" asked Jules.

"It's designed to tell more than time. It can depict the positions of the sun, the moon, the Earth, and the stars."

"How do you know so much about it?" asked M.

"It's a hobby," Keyshawn answered her flatly.

"When you say, *It's been through a lot*," said Cal, "what do you mean?"

"He means that the Orloj has had a lot of renovation done since 1410, as you can imagine," said Mr. Fence, almost like a loving father answering a son's innocent question on a sightseeing tour. "But it was also burned by Nazis at the end of World War II. Parts of the clock and its interior have since been replaced."

"But we have no idea when the box was hidden in the clock tower, right?" said M.

"Right," confirmed Mr. Fence.

"So are we sure the box still exists and that it wasn't destroyed?" asked Merlyn.

"Our intel leads us to believe that it remains hidden," said Mr. Fence.

The van slowed to a stop. "This is as far as I go," said Mr. Fence. "Move through the alleyway ahead of us to get to Old Town Square. There you will find the clock, get inside, and uncover the box."

The group exited the van and walked along a thin street lined with beautiful buildings. As they pulled on their masks, the night disappeared. In its place, an unnatural sunlight lit up the city, bathing it with otherworldly clarity. "It's just like being in a maze," said M as she passed through an open archway that led to a courtyard. Below their feet, ancient cobblestones made every step uneven. Above, M saw floor after floor of balconies with wide, arched windows and exquisitely crafted, wrought-iron railings that swirled as artistically as elegant cursive script. For a moment, she remembered the pristine handwriting in the Chaucer book from Keyshawn's hidden library lair, but that was forgotten as an even more opulent sight unfolded before her.

The courtyard opened onto a wide square that gave the city a luxurious amount of breathing room. The surrounding buildings looked majestic but tired in the darkness, leaning on one another for support, while the shops and cafes at ground level were locked behind metal gates. The picturesque streets were empty at this time of night. The tourists were all asleep, thought M, as a cold wind whipped through Old Town Square.

M found the Orloj clock right away. Truthfully it was hard to miss. The first thing she noticed was how the tower rose into the sky like a stone arm trying to snatch the moon. It cast its shadow across the square grounds even at night. M could make out the charcoal-gray stones and spire roof that seemed to whisper "haunted mansion," and, for a moment, made her feel like she was back home in upstate New York.

"That thing is awesome," announced Merlyn over their comm channel as they drew closer. And he was right. The structure was one of the oldest and most magical things M had ever seen in her life. It looked like a giant cuckoo clock, standing at least three stories high, with carved and detailed pillars on each side of two large clock faces. Statues were perched around the structure, too. Some were angels, some were people, and at least one was a skeleton holding an hourglass and a bell pull, like death personified, ready to ring in the next disaster.

"Whoa, talk about 'for whom the bell tolls,'" said Cal. "But seriously, how is anyone supposed to tell time with this thing? I don't even see a regular clock."

"The regular clocks are on the adjoining sides and high up on the tower," answered Keyshawn. "But these larger 'things,' as you refer to them, are much more interesting."

It was true. The bottom face was bright, round, and golden, its outer arc filled with a row of incredible artwork arranged in twelve circles, almost like scenes in a storybook. Farther inward toward the center of the clock face, another twelve smaller circles held what seemed to be zodiac signs. And, finally, in the center was the image of a castle surrounded by a moat of barbed crosses.

"This one is a calendar," said Merlyn. "Twelve months, twelve astronomical signs."

"That's right," confirmed Keyshawn, who sounded impressed. "Care to guess what the upper 'clock' actually is?"

"Ugh," interrupted Devon. "We're not here for Clock Watchers 101, you dweebs. How do we get inside?"

Ignoring Devon, M studied the more frenzied clock face looming above them. It held wildly structured circles criss-crossing one another like a mad Venn diagram. Letters like runes ran around the outer circle while Roman numerals lined the inner circle.

No, on second glance, the outer signs weren't runes at all, but numbers 1 through 24 written in an antiquated script. It looked startlingly like the title page of the Chaucer book. The weight of that book flashed back into M's hands and now the strange mechanism above her cast an equally enigmatic weight on her entire person. *There are no mistakes in life,* John Doe had said. She stared at the clock. "What's the connection between you and Chaucer?" she whispered to it.

Instantly Keyshawn turned toward M. Seeing the movement out of the corner of her eye, she smiled. Even a whisper over these headsets could be heard, and Keyshawn had just tipped his hand. Whatever the connection between this thing and the Chaucer book was, it was important to him.

"Seriously, snap out of it, cadets," scolded Ben. "We're not alone anymore." He pointed upward at a zip-line rope that stretched across the square from the top of a nearby building to the clock tower. M caught the high-pitched sound of sliding rope as she looked up to see several shadows floating in the sky directly into the clock's upper level.

"Follow me!" said M as she ran to the tower door. The lock was a joke; she unlatched it in no time flat. Pushing open the door, she turned to the others. "Did they see us?"

"Impossible," Keyshawn assured her. "These uniforms are cloaked. If someone walked by, all they would see is a projection of the wall behind us."

M remembered the first time she'd encountered Fulbrights, in the forest. How their uniforms had shimmered green, keeping the soldiers hidden until they'd been right on top of her.

"Good," she said. "I counted three of them, so we have the upper hand in terms of numbers, and we have the element of surprise on our side, too. Jules, can you climb this thing?"

"Definitely," she said with a smile.

"Wait, who died and made you boss, cadet?" demanded Ben. "I'll take it from here. Byrd and Zoso, shinny up to the top and we'll have them surrounded."

M was ecstatic that Devon would be preoccupied with the mysterious strangers rather than searching for the box. Fulbright or not, Devon had been skulking behind that mirror back at the academy, and M had a nasty feeling that she was up to no good.

Ben continued barking orders as Devon and Jules stepped into the shadows at the tower's base. "Cal and I will stand guard out here in case there are others coming," he said. "The box search is on the rest of you."

"Everyone else, follow me, then," said M, and she entered the building with Vivian, Keyshawn, and Merlyn behind her.

The inside of the tower was completely open; M could see all the way up to the tower's top floor. A cylindrical elevator shaft stretched the entire height, wrapped in a spiral structure that looked like a strand of DNA. Against the walls of the tower, a gated walkway also led upward.

"We're taking the walkway," said M. "Keep your eyes peeled for the box . . . and for anything else that might be lurking in here."

The crew made its way up the curving, slanted path. M tried her best to be as quiet as possible, but Vivian and Merlyn weren't the stealthiest sneaks in the world. Their footsteps were irregular and, worse, shuffling. Vivian had an excuse with her injured knee, but Merlyn should have known better.

"Keep it quiet, everyone," warned M. "Your insanely loud walking could give us away."

Scouring the walls, she searched for anything that looked out of place. With her mask, the older stones were easy to pick out from the touched-up areas. They had a darker, heavier look to them, not to mention that they were obviously fashioned with more ancient tools, giving them a more distressed shape. Still, nothing screamed *supersecret hiding place*, so she moved on.

"I don't hear anyone above us," whispered Keyshawn.

"Are we walking into a trap?" asked Vivian.

"More or less," said M. "They know we're here. Must have heard Mr. and Mrs. Bigfoot. They're waiting for us to find the box so they can steal it from us."

"That sounds like bad news," said Merlyn.

"Not at all," answered M. "It means they don't know the box's location any more than we do. Otherwise they'd grab it and go, rather than risk a confrontation. Jules and Devon will flush them out soon enough. Let's keep looking for this whatever-it-is."

M continued on and came across a closed door partway up the path. Slowly she opened it — and found twelve mysterious figures lurking in the dark. With an audible gasp she leapt back and nearly flipped over the railing before Merlyn caught her.

"It's okay!" said Keyshawn from behind her. "They're not thugs. You just found the apostle statues. Look."

M peered into the room and saw that he was right. The statues were busts of the twelve apostles, expertly crafted with a halo above each of their sculpted wooden heads.

"What are they doing here?" she asked.

"They're part of the clockwork," said Keyshawn. "Part of the show. Every hour on the hour, a gear turns, presenting each apostle out of the two closed windows there, above the clock."

"This place is too weird," replied M.

Vivian peeked in and examined the room. "No box in here. Let's keep looking."

Again they climbed the walkway, higher and higher, but there was nothing that stood out among the centuries-old architecture. M turned to Vivian and shrugged as if to ask, *Where to now?*

"Get down!" Jules's voice rang out both in the open room and over everyone's comm link. A sonic blast pulsed through the door at the top of the walkway and sent a flailing body careening down the clock tower shaft. M ran to the edge in time to see the figure's face. It was Rex Sykes, the muscle-bound Master from her Lawless past, and he shot her a chilling smile as he hurtled toward the ground. Before she could react, he released a powerful flare that lit up the tower shaft. The bright light sent her mask sensors into hypermode, leaving her temporarily blind.

M ripped off her mask and blinked rapidly until her normal sight started to return. She looked back down to find Rex, but he was gone. She looked up just in time to see another blast from her past leap lithely onto the skeletal framework of the elevator and drop down into the shadows. It was Angel Villon, another Lawless Master. Devon and Jules were in pursuit, scaling the frame in his wake.

"Cal! Ben!" M hollered. "We need you now!"

She heard the door burst open below, followed by the unmistakable sounds of fighting. The scuffling, grunts, and groans echoed off the old stone walls, and Vivian and Keyshawn ran down the path to join in the battle. M moved in the opposite direction, up the walkway to the highest point, where she rushed through the door and was met by the sight of Prague expanding for miles all around her. She had to take this opportunity to find what they'd come for. Behind her, she heard a shuffling footfall.

"Merlyn, please tell me that's you," said M, but she turned around to see none other than Adam Worth, leader of the Masters, gripping Merlyn in a sleeper hold.

"Here's Merlyn," he said as he held her friend's unconscious body against him like a shield. "You look good in black, M. I could do without the mask, though."

"But you went to jail," said M.

"Yeah, I did," confirmed Adam. "It wasn't for me. I need the open air; that's where I thrive, and quite frankly, German jail cells, well, they're just too stifling, you know?"

"What do you want?"

"Whatever it is you came here to find," said Adam. With a furious lunge, he tossed Merlyn aside and grabbed M, forcing her through a window. Her legs dangled in the open air. "Now be a good traitor and tell me where it is."

M twisted and squirmed to escape his grip, but when Adam eased his hold on her, she realized that he was the only thing keeping her from falling to the empty town square far below. She craned her neck to see if there was an awning to possibly catch her below, but the drop was sheer and unrelenting.

In the rush of fear, though, M also saw the clue they'd been looking for.

Embedded in the sidewalk below was a replica of the clock-face calendar from the tower. It was large, but unmarked with artwork: a series of empty circles within a circle. At ground level it was a flourish that people would almost never notice because they were too busy gazing up at the clock, but from up here, the design looked like the bull's-eye of a hidden target.

"It's not here," M lied. "My mom got to it first."

"Interesting," said Adam with a sneer. "Then it looks like our business transaction is over."

Callously and casually, Adam dropped M, sending her tumbling through the night . . . but that's exactly what she had wanted. With her Magblast, she shot the ground beneath her, hitting the calendar-replica stonework squarely and cracking the sidewalk, while also bouncing her into the air like a pogo stick. The speed of her fall negated, M bounded back onto the street unharmed.

Looking back up, she gave Adam a small wave and ran to the newly demolished cobblestones. The center circle was crushed into chunks, and from under those chunks M pulled out a smooth wooden box about as big as, well, the Takeaway Rembrandt. The weight felt oddly familiar in her hands. So did her urgency to escape.

From the top of the tower, Adam screamed with frustration and quickly rapelled down the side of the clock. M pulled on her mask and took off toward where the Fulbright van had been, shouting, "Target acquired; mission accomplished. Now let's all get out of here! And someone grab Merlyn — he's at the top of the tower."

"M, where are you?" called out Keyshawn.

"I'm almost at the van. . . ." answered M, but when she reached the rendezvous, the van was nowhere to be found. "Guys, we've been cut loose!"

"Well, what did you expect?" said Adam, panting from the run as he came up behind her. "The cavalry?"

M bolted in the opposite direction, deeper into the winding streets of the old city. Around a corner, she ducked into a shadowed alley and hid while Adam hurried past her. Retracing her steps, she stumbled upon a parked moped. *Bingo,* she thought as she jumped on, hot-wired the ride, and zipped back toward the clock to meet the others.

But trouble wasn't far behind her: Adam had doubled back. He lunged at the moped and grabbed hold of M's suit. She swerved violently, trying to throw the hitchhiker off, but he held tight. The box remained clutched in her right hand, pressed against her chest, but that left only one hand for her to steer with. She tried directing the moped back to the old city, but Adam had other plans. With his free hand he jerked the handlebars to the side and sent the two of them careening off in another direction.

"Heading away from you!" M calmly explained over the comm link, but there was only static in return. Adam must have disconnected her suit somehow.

As they bounced over the uneven cobblestones, M felt him clawing at her fingers, trying to strip the box away from her. She threw her head back, connecting with Adam's nose. The blow stunned him and he almost let go of her but recovered, redoubling his grasp.

"Come on!" he screamed. "Not cool, M! Not cool!"

Ignoring him, she focused on keeping the moped upright as they raced through the narrow, weaving streets until suddenly the city fell away and they found themselves streaking across a bridge. Gas lamps lined the barrier walls, casting a soft glow in the night that highlighted dark sculptures standing watch over the bridge like gargoyles. One by one the statues flew by as M and Adam raced over the bumpy, cobbled causeway, and M had an idea. It wasn't a good idea, but it was all she had.

She hit the brakes and turned the moped into a power slide. Violent sparks screeched in the darkness as the metal of the vehicle scraped against the cobblestone street. Adam was flung to the side and struck the bridge's wall solidly. M jumped clear of the bike and rolled over and over and over, crunched between the cold, hard ground and the mysterious box, which she kept tucked against her. Even when she'd come to a stop, the world spun viciously, pushing her back down to the ground when she tried to stand up. She could see Adam rise up slowly, shaking his head as he walked toward her.

"You never did play fair, did you?" he asked. "I mean, that's what I liked most about you, but it's a tough pill to swallow when you're not on my team. Now give me the box."

But as Adam reached down, a hand clutched his shoulder from behind and whipped him around. A ferocious crack echoed across the silent city and Adam collapsed to his knees and then slouched backward onto the ground.

"Maybe you didn't hear what I told you back in Hamburg, *Ross, Ross Peters*," snapped Cal as he stood over the unconscious criminal. "Remember? *If you mess with my friends again, I'll personally knock your block off.*"

CHAPTER 16

REGROUP

A bare bulb dusted off the darkness in the room, casting a grayish light on walls covered in graffiti. Adam Worth, Angel Villon, and Rex Sykes sat blank faced and bruised in the corner while Vivian stood guard. Outside of the impromptu prison cell, on the field of Strahov Stadium, Jules and M were nursing Merlyn back to health, insisting that he drink more water and eat some of the service food from the plane. They had less than an hour until sunrise, and even though the discarded Olympic stadium was a great overnight hiding place for the jet, the amount of "art" on the walls was a virtual guarantee that this place was a haven for hooligans. And hooligans meant an unwanted audience.

Ben and Devon had stepped aside to report the night's events back to base. They were tucked away behind bars in a room that must have been a concession stand at one time. It was some distance away from the janitor's closet, where they were holding the Masters captive, but M still tried to interpret Ben's and Devon's body language. Their arms would swing and their shoulders would shift up and down as they made eye contact with each other and then shook their heads as if they couldn't believe the message coming from the other side of the line. Then they paced back and forth like lions in a cage.

"You're lucky you didn't break this thing," said Keyshawn as he wrapped Cal's right hand in a bandage. "You sure you hit his face and not a brick wall?"

"Oh, I hit what I promised to hit," said Cal with a tired smile.

"What do you think they're talking about?" asked M as she shifted her attention over to Keyshawn and Cal. "All that talking they're doing with their bodies doesn't make it seem like a happy conversation. You'd think we didn't find the box and catch the bad guys."

"We achieved our primary objective, true, but it wasn't a total victory," argued Keyshawn. "Our handlers are missing, your mother is still on the loose, and Lawless has agents back in the field and after whatever is in that box."

He nodded over to the box, which sat on the dirty ground beside them. They hadn't opened it. In fact, they had been given strict orders not to. The assignment had been to retrieve the box, retrieve M's mother, and return to the academy. The Masters were never part of the plan. The Masters weren't even supposed to be operating any longer. M had a bad feeling that Keyshawn was right: The return of the Masters almost certainly meant the Lawless School was still intact and back in the game.

"We should open it," said Cal.

"Negative," said Keyshawn. "That would deviate from protocol. Now stop thinking with your muscles, Cal. You may not believe it, but you're smarter than that."

196

Cal unfixed his gaze on the box and flicked his eyes back at Keyshawn and M. It was true; he had a habit of acting on pure instinct, but Cal was very smart indeed. He always seemed to be in exactly the right place at exactly the right time. Catching M on the top of the climbing course, Magblasting Ben when he least expected it, pummeling Adam Worth . . . it didn't seem like the pure luck of someone running on instinct alone.

"You're right," Cal agreed calmly. "It's the adrenaline talking."

Keyshawn nodded. "Good to hear you come to your senses. Now we wait to see if our handlers have reported back in."

"I'm sure he's fine," added M. "From what I've seen of your father, he can handle himself."

Cal gave her a half smile and let his shoulders relax. "Thanks."

As M put her hand on his arm, Jules helped Merlyn up. He stood solidly but when he walked, he wobbled slightly, like a baby horse. Still, he looked better now than when Adam had jumped him back at the clock. Quietly M realized that this was her new family, flaws and all. Sure, Cal was acting cagey about the mysterious box and Merlyn was trying to put his head back on straight, but she was oddly happy to be on an adventure with them again.

The five of them waited silently as the late February air whistled through the empty bleachers above them. Finally Ben and Devon rejoined the group, bringing with them an aura of heavy seriousness that sizzled in the Eastern European predawn.

"Change of plans," said Ben. "The handlers are gone."

"Tell us something we don't know," said Merlyn, speaking with newfound confidence and hard-earned annoyance.

"We walked into a trap," admitted Devon. "While we tussled with your old pals, another party intercepted and detained Mr. Fence, the driver, and the pilot. The academy hadn't heard a peep from anyone until we broke radio silence."

"So what's the next move?" asked Jules. "Take these jokers back to base?"

"No," said Ben. "Time is of the essence. Whatever intel we got from M's mother, the Masters had it, too."

"That's impossible," said Cal. "You guys had her under lock and key. There's no way that information could have gotten to Lawless."

"Unless," continued Keyshawn, "there's a leak in the academy."

"Okay, listen up," Ben interrupted, obviously wanting to keep Keyshawn's words from sinking in, but it was too late. An idea, once said, can become a powerful thing. "Let's not jump to conclusions. I'm not in the bloody mood, nor do we have time to hear conspiracy theories, so let's focus on the facts. We have a box. We have the Masters. The Masters want the box, therefore this box is important. Now, as for our handlers, another Fulbright team is working diligently to find them. Our job is to keep this mission alive. We need to interrogate the Masters and find out what they know."

"I'll do it," said M.

"Not sure that's the best approach," Ben said immediately. "Given your, ahem, history with them."

"That's the point," said M. "That's what gives me the upper hand. But I'll need Devon in there, too."

"Me?" asked Devon, shocked. "I'm the last person they want to confess anything to."

"She did dismantle everything they believed in," said Jules.

"Exactly," said M. "Let's ramp up their emotions, play off their anger and egos. That's how we get them to talk."

"How do you know we can trust what they say?" asked Merlyn.

"We won't," admitted M. "At least not at first. Not until they slip up. And I know I can get them to slip up. Then we grab that little bit of truth and squeeze it."

"Careful, Freeman," Ben laughed. "You're starting to sound like a Fulbright."

Ignoring his comment, she turned to Devon. "Shall we to the interrogation?"

As the girls joined Vivian inside the small room, the Masters couldn't hide their surprise at seeing M and Devon together. Rex sneered and rattled in his seat, while Angel and Adam patiently waited for M to make the first move.

"I see you remember my new bestie, Devon Zoso," said M, hoping to capitalize on the Masters' disarmed shock.

"Gentlemen," said Devon with a wave. "Always a pleasure to meet fellow Lawless family."

But Adam wasn't ready to give them the upper hand yet.

"Give us the box and we'll let you live," he said, though his threat was undercut by a quick gasp brought on by the obvious pain in his jaw. It was swollen, probably even broken, from the disjointed look of it.

"You're not in any position to make demands or threats," said Devon as she pulled up a chair and sat across from the three prisoners. Her voice sent waves of rage through the Masters; they visibly shook with anger at hearing it. "But I'd like to talk about the box. Why do you want it?"

"Don't know and don't care," barked Rex.

"But you don't want us to have it," concluded M. "Which means you're working for someone else. Since when do the Masters work for anyone else? I don't know, Devonator; have you ever heard of that?"

"It's not their standard MO," answered Devon with a smile. "Masters are sworn to work within but without the Lawless School. It's an independent study group for scoundrels." She tapped a finger against her chin. "But now that I think about it, the Masters have danced to someone else's tune once before. . . ."

"Oh, that's right," said M with mock surprise. "That was in Hamburg with Ms. Watts, wasn't it? Well, you should know how this ends, then. I would think you'd be smarter than to go on another wild goose chase for her."

"No way we'd work with her again," spat Angel. "She ditched us in a fire, let us take the fall for her scheme, and even dunked her own son in the drink."

"Not deep enough, if you ask me," mumbled Adam as he

cut his eyes at Angel, a sign that confirmed Angel was telling the truth. Ms. Watts definitely wasn't behind the Masters' ambush.

"When we ran into you tonight, we were hoping *you* were Watts," said Rex with venom in his tone. "Wanted to say hello again for old times' sake."

"Lawless, then," stated Devon. "You're working for Fox Lawless, and this box is the key to his revenge on the Fulbrights."

"Freeman, you can't tell us you trust Devon Zoso," said Adam. "She doused you in a deep freeze and built a black hole on our front yard. Want to know more? During her first year at the school, she sent fifteen people to the infirmary, and according to the Flynn twins, it would have been double that if they hadn't intervened on many different occasions."

"Shut it, Adam," said Devon.

Fighting the pain in his jaw, he continued, "She tried to blind Professor Bandit. She broke kids' bones in the Box. She took criminal plans and twisted them into something only a maniac would dream up. When the crime called for theft, she'd add a dash of assault every time. Looks like she's got you wrapped around her finger, too. And do you actually believe she used all of the —"

"I said, *enough*," interrupted Devon, kicking Adam's chair out from underneath him. With his arms cuffed behind his back, he was unable to cushion his fall and landed face-first on the ground. A sickly smack reverberated against the concrete floor.

Rex, infuriated, shattered the back of his chair as if it were made of Popsicle sticks. He leapt to his feet and, arms still bound behind his back, rammed Devon at full speed, forcing her back and against the wall in a hysterical vertical body slam.

"You'll never get to London, Zoso!" he screamed, driving Devon harder into the unforgiving wall. "I don't care if the others do. Your ride stops here!"

M stood frozen in the sudden chaos. Adam lay on the ground bleeding while Devon's arms pawed at Rex's back like she was pinned under a boulder. How had it gone so wrong so quickly? Apparently she had underestimated the Lawless students' disdain for a traitor. Not to mention Devon's ability to get under people's skin.

Luckily Vivian took charge of the situation with quiet confidence, expertly striking Rex in the back of his neck. The big lug spasmed and toppled over. Devon sat down and cradled her arm against her chest.

"Thanks for the help, Freeman!" yelled Devon. "You good-for-nothing excuse for a soldier."

"Me? I wasn't the one who kicked the chair out from under the handcuffed guy and engaged the Rex factor!"

While they argued, Vivian picked Adam up off his face and set him back in his seat. "You're friends with a lot of hotheads, Freeman," she said.

"Yeah, I don't think any of us were ever really friends," M snapped.

Angel hadn't moved. He'd sat watching the whole show with a satisfied look on his face. The cadets had shown their cards, proven that they weren't working well as a team, and he had seen it all.

Vivian helped Devon out of the room. M smiled as they left, turning her attention back to the Masters. "This interview is over. There'll be another Fulbright team here shortly to take you away." She paused to let her words settle among the dust kicked up in the standoff. "And if the Hamburg prison didn't meet your liking, I can guarantee that the Fulbright Academy is your worst nightmare. Enjoy the ride, boys."

Vivian returned to resecure the Masters as M stepped out onto the grass. Keyshawn was bent over Devon, who lay on the ground, her breaths sounding shallow and sharp, like paper being torn in half. As he pressed gingerly around her stomach and shoulders, Devon's eyes flared with an intense discomfort. He nodded to calm her, like a coach telling a player that her time in the game was up.

"She's broken a rib, maybe two, and she has a fractured collarbone," Keyshawn said to Ben.

"Okay," he acknowledged quietly before turning to Devon. "Zoso, you are staying behind to watch over the prisoners until the second team arrives. ETA is thirty minutes. Stay true, soldier."

Devon's face fell at the order, but that was fine with M. She felt safer knowing that Devon would be miles away from the box and its contents. She waved good-bye to her, and Devon shot back a crooked smile. M swore she heard her say, in between strained breaths, "I'm not done yet."

Ben retrieved Vivian and ordered everybody back on the jet. Light was glowing over the horizon, but the interior of the stadium was still shrouded in a shadowed canopy.

Once in the jet, Ben gave a surprising order. "First things first, open that box."

"What?" M said, shocked to hear Ben, of all people, breaking protocol.

"You heard me, Freeman," he said. "Those blokes in there tried to hang Zoso like a picture, our superiors were kidnapped, and the academy has gone barmy, giving us the runaround for hours. I want to see what's so important."

The box itself was nondescript and unassuming in its design. It was smooth, polished, and completely unmarked, save for the natural knots from the tree from which it had been shaped. The box also lacked hinges or any sign of a seam. It was as if it had been carved from one solid piece of wood. Keyshawn ran his hands over it, looking for any entry point but came up empty.

"Maybe the box is the clue?" suggested Merlyn.

"No," said Cal. "Noles just can't see it. Hand it over, please."

"I just can't see what?" asked Keyshawn, reluctantly handing the box to Cal.

"How to get inside," he answered as he pushed down on a small discolored area at one corner. A hiss followed, and a distinct click, as the seamless shell of the box slid open, revealing a very old leather-bound book.

"How did you know that trigger was there, Fence?" asked Ben.

"Lucky guess," said Cal. "I've been sitting and staring at that box for the past hour outside. I kept going back to the one corner. It was too different from the rest of the box."

"He's right," agreed Keyshawn. "I should have seen it."

"What's this book about?" asked Jules.

The cover was blank, as were the spine and the back. The interior pages shined with gilded golden edges, and the thick binding had to have been done by hand. There was tremendous care and diligence put into this thin book.

"Well, it looks like a short read," said Cal as he opened it. *"Mutus Liber,"* he read off the title page. M noticed Keyshawn sat down heavily as soon as Cal said it. "Hey," Cal continued. "It's just, like, all drawings."

"What kind of drawings?" asked Jules as everyone but Keyshawn pressed in to get a good look.

"Ancient drawings," said Keyshawn. "Ancient drawings meant to unlock the key to alchemy."

"Like people-turning-lead-to-gold alchemy?" asked Merlyn.

"Like people-trying-to-create-the-philosopher's-stone alchemy," said Keyshawn. "What you're holding is the *Silent Book*, and I'm going to go out on a limb and say that this one is probably a first edition."

"Wait, what's the philosopher's stone?" asked Ben.

"It's like the Middle Ages equivalent of the Higgs boson particle," explained Merlyn.

"Meaning?" asked Jules.

"Meaning that the philosopher's stone was thought to be the magical element from which life itself sprang," said Merlyn. "Basically everyone looked for it, but they never found it. Because it didn't exist."

"But if it did exist," continued Keyshawn, "its supposed uses are endless. It could turn anything into gold. It could grant immortality. And it would probably make a powerful fuel."

"Or make a powerful weapon," added M, remembering the destructive power unleashed by the moon rock.

"I've heard enough," said Ben. "We need to get this book back to the academy immediately."

"No," said M. "The book wasn't our only assignment. We were asked to bring back my mother. I think we're missing something and I think we'll find it in London."

"Now you're just making stuff up," said Ben crossly.

"No, Freeman's right," said Vivian. "When the not-so-gentle giant attacked Devon back there, he screamed something about her not making it to London."

"He was probably setting another trap," argued Ben.

"He's too dumb to set traps," said M. "Believe me, I know from experience. Rex is all muscle, no strategy."

"Okay, let's pretend you've all convinced me to extend our mission," said Ben. "Where are we going in London? Because, in case you don't know, it's a pretty big town."

"We know," M, Merlyn, and Jules all answered in droning unison, recalling their visit to the Black Museum and subsequent race through the clogged streets.

"Here," said Vivian, flipping a tablet screen to face the others. "The British Library. They've just borrowed an original edition of the *Mutus Liber* from the University of Delaware in a good-gesture exchange. It arrives tomorrow."

"How in the world did you discover that?" asked Cal.

"Thank heaven for librarian blogs," Vivian said with a smile.

Ben stared at the others, sizing up the facts with a few heavy breaths. "Keyshawn, look through that book, and catalog everything you see. I want to know if a character's eye color so much as shifts from scene to scene. The rest of us should set our sights on London and learn everything we can about the British Library. Hours of operation, security detail, collections, maps of the building. I'll call base and tell them what's up. Which leaves one question." He rubbed his jaw. "Has anyone here ever flown a plane before?"

CHAPTER 17

THE *SILENT BOOK*

With her mask firmly in place, M felt her arms shake while she held the jet's control wheel, but unlike the last time she'd been in a cockpit, this time the shaking wasn't due to the jet crashing. This time it was M fighting her own nerves. Breathing deeply, she stared out the tinted windshield as clouds and the world rushed by. The ground beneath her was like a patchwork blanket, covering the earth with patterns of fields, forests, houses, and occasional cities. It was beautiful and still, but she knew all too well that when the ground got closer, it pulsed with life. It wouldn't seem so serene careening toward them at six hundred miles per hour.

"So, did your dad teach you how to fly?" asked Ben over the comm link.

"No, Cal's mother did, sort of," answered M.

"What do you mean, *sort of*?"

"She means, make sure you buckle up for the landing," said Merlyn. "The last time she tried this, she took out an entire airport."

"Can we talk about something else?" said M, steering the conversation away from her dubious flying skills. She had spent a good twenty minutes reviewing the jet's manual and acclimating herself to the controls. This jet was much easier to handle than her last, mostly because the takeoff and landing didn't require a runway. "What do we know about this *Silent Book*?"

"I'm connecting to everyone's visual feed in your masks now," said Keyshawn.

A small screen flashed on within M's sight line, startling her. It was small, but the idea of watching a video while flying did not appeal to her. She set the autopilot on and relaxed, happy to turn her attention away from the open air in front of her.

The video showed pages from the *Mutus Liber*, and the artwork was megacreepy. Angels, or maybe demons, hovered in the sky next to suns and moons with human faces, while the people below collected key elements and mutated them into something new and unknown.

"The *Mutus Liber* was created in 1677 in La Rochelle, France," said Keyshawn. "Before today, there were three known first editions, all identical. The book consists of fifteen plates, or artistic scenes, that many believe offer the secret to creating the philosopher's stone, though the correct order of the scenes is heavily disputed to this day. Some say once the order of the book is unlocked, so will be the path to the stone."

"Wait, people actually still believe in this?" asked Cal.

"Apparently, yes, some people do," said Keyshawn. "And given the lengths that your friends from the Lawless School went to, maybe you should believe in it, too. Now I don't want to go into the minutiae of each scene with everyone, but it would be helpful for you to exercise your fresh eyes by looking over the pages. Maybe you'll pick up something that I haven't yet."

"This is like some next-level sudoku," said Merlyn. "There's some writing here. What's it about?"

"The writing is spare," explained Keyshawn, "but the opening text announces the book as 'wordless' and the ending text claims that 'provided with eyes, thou departest.'"

From the cockpit, M shuddered at the phrase, *provided with eyes.* The box of eyeballs from the sick bay sprang to her mind, their squishy give and the watery moats that surrounded the floating irises, blankly staring in all directions. *Thou departest.* Like her father, like her mother, like the Lawless School, and almost everything else M touched.

Meanwhile, somewhere behind her, Keyshawn continued his lecture. "Some people say the book is cursed, even. As if it were a grimoire, or book of spells, but if you ask me, that kind of superstition only shows how very misunderstood alchemy was back in the day."

"Do we understand it now?" asked Jules.

"Parts of it," said Keyshawn. "Have you ever heard of chemistry? It came from alchemy, but has a more strictly scientific application. Lots of brilliant minds across all nationalities dabbled in alchemy. Robert Boyle, Sir Isaac Newton . . ."

"What about Geoffrey Chaucer?" added M sharply.

"That's right!" exclaimed Keyshawn. "Chaucer even wrote an alchemist character into his *Canterbury Tales*, but he thought them to be devious types. You know, they were humans trying to play God."

Another connection to Chaucer. M needed to have a private conversation with Keyshawn soon. He knew way more than he was letting on, but she had the sense that even he didn't know how to connect all the dots yet.

"So is this book considered religious, or is it scientific?" asked Merlyn.

"No, this book is wack," said Cal. "It looks like an ancient comic book with the most boring plot ever."

"Don't be so dismissive," said Keyshawn, sounding defensive. "There's a message here somewhere, hidden."

"A picture's worth a thousand words," added M from the cockpit.

"Exactly!" agreed Keyshawn excitedly. "Words would ruin whatever the *Silent Book* is trying to explain. And these images, they're essentially cryptograms that no one has ever cracked."

"Okay, my head's starting to hurt just listening to you guys," said Vivian. "I've got another question, though. I looked up the *Mutus Liber* online and these pictures are posted everywhere. Anyone can look these images up, so what makes these first editions so important?"

"She's right," said Merlyn. "What's so special about this copy?"

"I don't know," admitted Keyshawn sullenly. He clearly hadn't worked that out. "I'll run a scan to check if there are any discrepancies with the images online and see what I come up with."

"Ware, how's the library intel shaping up?" asked Ben.

"I've got some news," answered Vivian, "but I'm not sure you're going to like it."

"How hard can it be to get a book from a library?" asked Cal. "Isn't that, like, the whole point of their existence?"

"Well, they do things differently at the British Library," said Vivian. "First of all, their *Mutus Liber* is part of a special collection. To get near it, we'd need access to a reading room. And no one under eighteen is allowed in those rooms."

"Talk about R-rated reading!" marveled Cal.

"That's not all," continued Vivian. "Even if you were old enough, you still have to request a reader pass in advance and have proof of ID and proof of your permanent residence."

"If we knew an Ident, we could get in," said Jules.

"But you wouldn't be allowed to take the book off the premises," said Vivian. "Could we get a Fulbright team to shut the whole place down?"

"No," said Ben. "Our assignment, our problem."

As the plane flew through the clouds, a silence fell over it. "Right, then," said M at last. "So we'll have to break in. What's your take, Jules?"

"Well," started Jules. "Vivian's spot-on about everything, but there is a free tour that's open to all ages. I think that's our in."

"So we start the tour, slip into the back, and then Dewey decimal our way to the prize?" asked Merlyn. "Seems too easy."

"Oh, I can make it harder for you," groaned Vivian. "This isn't a quaint little cottage library. First of all, it's designed to keep books safe and sound for at least the next thousand years. The temperature is set at seventeen degrees Celsius, with no more than sixty-five percent humidity."

"That actually sounds rather pleasant," said Ben.

That actually sounds like the Fulbright Academy, thought M.

"Yes, well, that is the nice part," admitted Vivian. "But I wanted to lead with the good news. The bad news is that most books are shelved according to height."

"And we know exactly the right size of the book," said Keyshawn triumphantly, holding up the old text. "Unless you have another curveball, we're good to go."

Vivian sighed. "If you'll allow me to finish. The storage facility of the library extends eighty feet underground in a labyrinth of shelving to hold its in-house collection of more than thirty million titles. Not to mention that they receive newspapers and periodicals from around the globe every day, which means their collection is constantly growing at a rate of perhaps eight thousand units per day. All said and done, they probably have four hundred miles of books organized by an unfamiliar catalog system of shelf markers and grid patterns, with separate librarians for each quadrant of the collection."

Now that sounds exactly *like the Fulbright Academy,* thought M. "Ben, why don't you know this?" she asked. "Isn't this in your backyard?"

"Never been to London," he answered. "But I've found a secure meadow that we can land in. The jet should be well hidden there."

"Um, how?" asked Cal. "It's a big, space-age jet, not a horse-drawn carriage."

"Besides being a big, space-age jet," said Keyshawn, who joined M in the cockpit and began flipping switches on the control panel, "this aircraft is also equipped with noise-cancellation speakers to hush any and all flight noise to the outside world. It also has a high-tech camouflage system that allows the body of the jet to mimic the environment around it. If a helicopter pulled up next to us right now, they would have no idea we were flying beside them."

"Whoa, you hear that, M?" said Jules. "You're totally Wonder Woman flying in her invisible jet!"

Invisible or not, a voice wheezed across the pilot headphones. "Noles, come in." It was John Doe. "Are you engaging the advanced stealth mode on my plane?"

Keyshawn quickly grabbed a pair and put them on. M grabbed the other pair and listened in, too.

"Respectfully, sir, there's more to this assignment than meets the eye. And we have a lead, but time is of the essence. To get more intel, we'll need to be extra discreet."

"Are we on a secure line?"

M flashed her eyes at Keyshawn.

"Yes, sir," Keyshawn lied.

"Good. You remember our little arrangement, Noles."

"Understood, sir. I believe our current mission is too important to abandon. If need be, you can arrest me when we get back to the academy."

"You have more to lose than that," Doe threatened before cutting out completely.

Keyshawn leaned back and took a deep breath. Closing his eyes, he stayed in the front seat next to M. After a minute, she asked, "So what's Doe holding over your head? What is he threatening you with that's worse than being arrested?"

"That," said Keyshawn, without opening his eyes, "would be my entire family."

CHAPTER 18
LONDON CALLING

The flight passed quickly and the total amount of research everyone had done in that time was staggering. Vivian had memorized the British Library storage systems. Ben, Jules, and Merlyn had all studied their copy of the *Mutus Liber* so closely that M wouldn't be surprised if they were now able to draw the book themselves from memory. Cal had done some major research on the insides of his eyelids . . . but that might have had to do with the medicine Keyshawn gave him when his hand started to hurt midflight. But the most miraculous studying that had happened on the plane was M's learning how to land safely.

The meadow, it turned out, was more like a slight disturbance in a dense forest. Still, M didn't waver when the time came, and the jet touched down smoothly. As soon as the engines were quiet, she ripped off her mask, hurried outside, and dropped to her knees to kiss the cold, sweet ground.

"You were amazing," said Jules from behind her. "None of us could have flown this thing."

M rolled on her back and looked up at the sky from which

she had now descended. "Let's just not make a habit of getting around like this, okay?"

"Promise," said Jules, helping her friend back up. "Now let's get inside and change. We can't go to London dressed like this."

"Who knows," said M with a laugh. "Maybe skintight, wire-laced jumpsuits with black masks are the fashion du jour in the UK?"

Ben walked off the plane and handed out what he called street-safe garb: jeans, white T-shirts, black sweaters, and black peacoats.

"Won't it look suspicious if we're all dressed the same?" asked Merlyn.

"Nah," said Ben. "You'll just look like Brits to the tourists and you'll look like tourists to the Brits. It's a win-win wardrobe. Now let's go catch our train."

"What about this?" asked Keyshawn, holding up the book.

"Leave it here," ordered Ben. "The jet is as safe a place as we can hope for."

The walk to the train station was beautiful as the canopy of trees reached in every direction, practically blotting out the sun, even in the winter weather, where only a few leaves clung to their branches. Eventually the forest cleared and a surging intersection of traffic stood before them. Down the road, a small blue sign read, CITY CENTRE. They followed the arrow on the sign, bought tickets, and boarded a train. Destination: London. Destination: *Mutus Liber numéro deux*. And most probably, if M's hunch was correct, Destination: danger.

During the ride, M borrowed Vivian's tablet and scoured the Internet. The *Mutus Liber* was fascinating, mysterious, and a Masterful mark, but the get didn't sit right with her. And, truth be told, it was Geoffrey Chaucer, of all factors, who made her stop and think. Why *this* edition of the book? Why now? The *Mutus Liber* had been around since 1677. Seriously, there had been plenty of time to steal it. So whatever the reason for stealing the books was, M rationalized that there must have been a new discovery about these editions. And the newly unearthed fourth book must hold a special, vital clue. Why else would someone go to such lengths to hide it away from the world?

Did Dr. Lawless really want to create the philosopher's stone? Or was it John Doe who wanted the stone? Or was the stone not as important as she was led to believe it could be?

"What are you looking up?" asked Keyshawn, sliding into the seat next to her.

"Can I ask you a question?" M asked under her breath.

"You have a lot of questions, don't you?"

"Why do you have those old books hidden behind your bookshelves?"

Keyshawn's eyes betrayed him — he was obviously taken aback by M's query. "To study, of course," he said carefully. "Ancient texts can unlock a lot of secrets."

"And why would that book by Chaucer have a drawing so similar to the clock in Prague?" M asked pointedly. "What is that thing, anyway?"

"You stumble across the most interesting things, don't you, Freeman?" he asked as he let out a sigh. "That *thing* is an astrolabe."

"And what does it do?"

"It's a mapping device."

"And it maps . . ." M started his next sentence for him.

Keyshawn paused and tossed his head back. Whatever she was driving toward, it was definitely making him uncomfortable.

"The universe."

"Excuse me," she said, "but it sounded like you said that an astrolabe can map out the universe."

"Because that's what I said," he confirmed. "The astrolabe maps the sun, the moon, and the stars, all based on a person's precise location on the Earth. It's a tool that's been around for centuries, used by astronomers and astrologers."

"How does it work?" asked M.

"To understand it," said Keyshawn, falling quickly into his excited teacher voice, "you've first got to know that it was developed when people thought the Earth was the center of the universe. The astrolabe is essentially a basic model of the sky. The tool consists of three specific parts. The rete is the top piece and it corresponds to the positions of the brightest stars in the sky. The plate is the second piece and it relates to a system of coordinates. The mater is the final piece and it creates a grid and system of numbers and measurements that help compute the shifting heavens."

"And what's all that mean in English?" asked M.

"It means that the three parts together could tell people what time it was, based on the position of the stars or the sun in the sky. It could tell people what direction they were heading or sailing, and some people swear it could predict when comets enter our little corner of the universe if you had the right calculations. It's basically the world's earliest computer."

"Wow," said M.

"*Wow*'s an understatement," said Keyshawn. "And while you most certainly should never have gone through my things, the book you found must have been Chaucer's *Treatise on the Astrolabe*. He wrote it in 1391 for, it's believed, his son. It's the first technical essay on the astrolabe in the English language."

"That heavy thing was an essay!" said M.

"Yeah, they built books to last back then," said Keyshawn. "But why are you asking about astrolabes?"

"Because I don't believe in coincidences," said M. "And I don't think you do, either. Between your Chaucer book and the Prague clock, there's a bigger secret here, isn't there? What are we going to steal, Keyshawn, for real?"

"You're a Fulbright now, M," he huffed. "We don't steal; we protect. Remember that." Then he jumped up from his seat and moved to the other side of Ben. M had apparently struck a nerve again.

Stealing or protecting, she still needed to know what they were really after. She'd taken the Takeaway Rembrandt at face value and she didn't want to fall into the same trap again.

The train rolled on until they finally reached King's Cross station, where they were greeted by a massive windowed awning and a stalwart clock tower keeping careful watch over its London domain. Inside the station the crew hardly talked to one another, each walking with purpose, deep in thought, deep in their own personal spaces until the airy architecture brought them back into the moment merely because it blossomed so brilliantly. The concourse of clustered trains almost magically erupted into a wide-open area where intricate white girders rose out of the floor and lifted the older brick building into a skylike dome that was at once majestic and modern.

Somehow the room reflected how M felt. Inexplicably excited, filled up with hope, angst, confusion, and relief that if there was another plan to destroy the world, to destroy places like this that people worked so hard to build, that she was in a position to stop it from ever happening. And with that renewed vigor, M and the crew turned up Euston Road toward the British Library.

It was a quick walk, even in the face-numbing winter wind, and the library was another sight to behold. The entry gate led visitors into a low-lying courtyard that allowed the older architecture of neighboring buildings to steal the spotlight. From there, the crew entered the library and went directly to the front desk.

"Hello," said Ben cheerfully. "We're here for the tour."

"Yes, of course," said the librarian, a young man with a surprisingly punk haircut. "The tour starts at the top of the hour.

We'll meet here, but in the meantime, feel free to visit our treasures display."

Ben thanked him and led the group into another room that looked less like a library and more like a museum. Ancient books were encased in bulletproof, fireproof, and sweaty palms–proof glass. Looking through the collection, M felt ashamed that they had simply left the *Mutus Liber* sitting on the jet's seat like a well-used street map. This was how such books should be treated. A first edition of Shakespeare's plays sat next to the Gutenberg Bible, which was next to the Magna Carta, breathtakingly old . . . and valuable. Deep inside herself, M felt an unmistakable itch, a knee-jerk reaction to being surrounded by so much cultural wealth, like a hunger she didn't expect to have. The Lawless side of M had reared its ugly head, though she would never admit it to anyone. She wanted desperately to enjoy art the same way she had as a child, with a sense of wonder, not a sense of ownership. But the Lawless School had taught her well and, even in passing, she had already cased the entire room, noting camera positions, thickness of the protective glass, number of steps all the way back to King's Cross. You can take the girl out of the Lawless School, but can you take the Lawless School out of the girl? It was exactly what Ben had been trying to impress upon her about her friends. And she didn't believe him at the time, but given her own secret reaction to the treasures, she wasn't so sure now.

To M's relief the hour struck and the tour group formed around the visitors' desk. It was a big group, which was good.

As the punk librarian, Ethan, excitedly explained the history behind the library, he led the group through the building. And when the time was right, while in a back room overlooking the main reading area, M, Jules, and Cal circled behind the librarian.

"So that's where the magic happens?" asked M, stepping past Ethan to look out onto the silent floor crammed with an army of people diligently focused over their desks.

"It is?" asked Jules as she swept by Ethan's other side, holding Cal's hand and tugging him with her, which caused him to brush against the librarian.

"Excuse me," said Ethan. "I know the library is exciting, but let's all please watch out for each other. No more of this bumbling and bouncing about. This is precisely why we do not allow anyone under eighteen to enter the reading rooms without a parent or guardian present."

But Ethan's attempt at a lecture fell on deaf ears as the trio gawked out the window. So he merely continued the tour as if nothing out of the ordinary had happened at all. And as far as he knew, nothing really had.

But Ethan didn't know that Cal had just palmed the librarian's access card.

Cal slipped the card to Vivian, who had the library's catacombs memorized. Then Merlyn and Keyshawn took control of the tour with a litany of detailed questions meant to excite and engage Ethan, who was, luckily, very easy to excite and engage. Vivian and M drifted to the back of the group and retraced their steps back to a door they had passed earlier with a card lock next to it. Vivian swiped the card and the door clicked open. Everything was going according to plan.

"Find a computer," said Vivian as she and M entered a hallway that led to more doors. The third door on the left was open and M found a computer at someone's desk. They ducked inside the room, and Vivian stood guard at the closed door while M sat at the computer, ready to channel her lessons from Code. As it turned out, she didn't need world-class hacking skills to access this computer. All she had to do was notice the photographs in engraved, customized frames on the desk. SOPHIE and THOMAS — two cute kids, too easy a password.

Once in, M searched for the *Mutus Liber* and found it was being held six floors below the ground. "Got it," she exclaimed just as the door to the room creaked open. She braced herself for a flight situation, but Vivian was more prepared for a fight: She grabbed a sizable soccer trophy from the bookshelf and jumped back toward the door.

"Whoa!" said Cal as he cowered in defense. "It's me, guys. Geez."

"Sorry," said Vivian. "Couldn't take any chances."

"Vivian, would you have clocked an innocent librarian if it hadn't been Cal?" asked M, genuinely shocked.

"We'll never know," said Vivian. "Now, what the blazes are you doing here?"

"I'm your backup. Ben's suggestion," said Cal. "In case, well, in case there's more Master trouble."

"That doesn't sound like Ben," said M. "I sort of expected him to keep an eye on you."

"Desperate times," replied Cal. "What can I say?"

"Fine. Let's just get moving before someone else finds us here," said Vivian.

The elevator to the storage shelves was down a long hall, and the quiet walk was nearly interminable; they all expected to encounter staff at any minute. But the library was running at full capacity, and M supposed it was possible that everyone was busy with their everyday jobs, which apparently didn't include roaming the halls in search of twelve-year-old intruders. *Their mistake,* she thought.

They boarded the elevator and M punched the button and welcomed that slow, sinking feeling. When the doors opened six floors below, she was met with the chill of climate control. The room looked more like a computer server room than a library. The bookshelves were white monoliths crowded together side by side, without even enough space to walk between them. A three-pronged black handle at the end of each row could be turned to slide the shelving units left or right to open aisles between them.

Silently they tiptoed down the hall, afraid to make any noise that would draw attention to themselves. The librarians, however, were quite loud, which was unexpected but welcome, since M could gauge exactly where they were by the sounds of their voices and heavy footsteps. Avoiding a few close calls, eventually the crew found the correct aisle. Cal turned the handle like he was steering a ship, and the white bookshelves parted like waves in the ocean. Even before the path was fully open, M slithered inside, searching for the familiar leather binding among several racks filled with leather books with blank spines. Vivian followed suit, facing the opposite side, palming over the uniformly sized books before pulling one out. This edition of the *Mutus Liber* was in slightly worse condition than the Prague edition, but inside, the same paper and the same creepy drawings confirmed it was a match.

"Excuse me!" exclaimed a disembodied voice that echoed through the chamber. "You are most certainly not authorized to have access to this level."

Cal peered around the corner calmly and pointed into the aisle. "They're here!" he called out. "Those two kids from the tour that went missing!"

"What are you doing, Cal?!" yelled M as a female librarian shoved Cal out of the way and entered the aisle.

"I saw them," Cal continued. "They grabbed the guide's credentials and I followed them down here. They're up to no good."

"What do you have?" asked the librarian, reaching for the book that Vivian held aloft.

"Nothing that concerns you," said Vivian angrily.

"Put that down now!" demanded the librarian.

"Of course." Vivian smiled as she tossed the book to Cal.

"Wait!" yelled M, but it was too late. Despite what Vivian must have thought, Cal wasn't playing innocent to confuse the librarian. He'd actually trapped M and Vivian red-handed. And now he had the *Mutus Liber*.

"Sorry, M. Once a crook, always a crook," Cal said with a shrug of his shoulders before he turned and clamped on to the nearest fire alarm. The familiar blaring rang through the chamber and he took off in the opposite direction of the elevator.

"Out of the way!" yelled M as she tried to push past Vivian and the librarian, but both of them were stunned at what had just happened. "He's getting away!"

As Vivian's senses came back to her, the walls of books around them started to shudder and rumble.

"What's that?" asked M.

"The fire prevention process," said the librarian. "The aisles are all collapsing to protect the books!"

"Who's protecting us, then?" asked Vivian.

"This way!" yelled the librarian. She took Vivian's hand and pulled her down the narrow path as the heavy shelves slid closer and closer together. M was right behind them, but the walls were coming together too fast. She leapt forward, shoving Vivian with as much power as she could muster, and the aisle clapped closed with a nauseating crunch that clutched M's ponytail. A stinging sensation jolted through the back of her neck as she tried to move. But Cal already had a head start, so she threw her head forward and clenched through the pain that left wisps of her hair behind.

"Where's the book-delivery conveyor belt?" she demanded.

The shocked librarian was breathless and sprawled out on the floor, but she pointed in the direction Cal had run. Taking the cue, M and Vivian sprinted madly down the hall. Other librarians appeared, but the duo pushed past them until they reached a small entry, like a butler's pantry, that led to the British Library's mechanized delivery system. Vivian jumped through first and M followed, clambering up the moving conveyor belt, which was meant to carry boxes of books to and from the reading-room floor. This led to a larger conveyor belt system made of metal rolling pins that rolled along, oblivious to the chaos Cal had unleashed.

"Which way?" asked Vivian.

"Up," said M, catching her breath as boxes slid by. "He'll follow the flow of the delivery system up and out."

On their hands and knees, M and Vivian hopped onto the main belt and moved as fast as they could. M's feet kept getting snagged in between the rollers and her knees were on fire, but she kept on with the chase. They rammed boxes that were in front of them, shoving parcels full of antique texts out of their way. Finally they spotted Cal ahead of them, just as he reached the ground level and leapt out. M and Vivian did the same, totally expecting to land in a bizarre scene where hours, days, years of silent research would be curiously interrupted by kids spewing out of the delivery system. However, something more alarming had beat them to it.

"The fire alarm!" M shouted.

It was chaos. M and Vivian exited their wild ride only to slide into each other as every member of the reading room was hurriedly escaping the threat of fire. M saw a flash of Cal, but then he submerged into the crowd, mixing into the ocean of dark-colored clothes. The mass exodus carried them outside into the courtyard, where there was no further sign of Cal. He had vanished just as easily as if he had been wearing his Fulbright suit.

"M, Vivian!" cried Merlyn. "Over here!"

M tunneled through the crowd and met up with the others.

"Where's Cal?" asked Ben with a dawning suspicion in his voice.

"Turned," said Vivian, out of breath and shaking her head. "Played us. Stole the book. Pulled the alarm."

"I knew something was up when he disappeared," said Ben. "It's my fault for not keeping better tabs on him."

"No, it's my fault," said M. "I thought I could trust Cal and I thought you were crazy for not trusting him."

"Well, if it's any consolation, it's no fun being right all the time," deadpanned Ben. He pulled out his phone and studied it. "His tracker . . . it's off-line. How in the world . . ."

"He's smart," said Keyshawn. "Too smart."

"Let's get out of here," commanded Ben. "We'll radio base and take our lumps. Chin up, everyone. All's not lost, I'm sure."

Ben's optimism looked small in the London evening, like a bird with a broken wing. M wanted to pick it up and nurse it back to health, but at the same time, she was afraid that the bird might be sick and that the disease might be catching. Optimism was what got her into this situation in the first place, after all.

CHAPTER 19
BREAKING PROTOCOL

Sirens wailed across the London streets as the police halted all traffic outside of the library, dutifully interviewing any and every eyewitness they could find. The descriptions of the perps were anything but accurate. Some claimed to have seen a team of vandals, while others swore they'd seen a lone thief chased by two good Samaritans. Neither story mattered, though, as the crew had already blended into the background of lookee-loos, displaced researchers, and pedestrians trying their hardest to get home through the surge of activity. M channeled *perturbed commuter* and shouldered her way unapologetically through the King's Cross crowd.

Once inside the station, Ben decided to take advantage of the traveler mentality. "Wait here. While all these people are worried about their trains, it's probably a good time to call base."

Ben retreated to a secluded area of the grand hall and put his phone to his ear. Keyshawn followed after him. "Wait, let's talk about this," he pleaded.

"That is not going to be a fun conversation," said Merlyn. "Good day for bad news, Mr. Doe. We lost the second book, stolen by Calvin Fence, then we lost Calvin Fence, and oh yeah, his father's still missing, too. I mean, what is Doe going to do to us?"

Jules punched Merlyn lightly in the arm, though by his reaction, M figured that Jules's idea of a light punch and Merlyn's idea of a light punch were drastically different. "You're not funny," said Jules.

"I know," said Merlyn. "But somebody's got to try. It beats wondering why Cal just robbed us blind."

"It's his mother," said M. "She has him twisted in ways that we could never understand. In ways that he probably can't understand, either." She sighed. "You know, Cal told me about his life growing up with one foot in Fulbright Academy and one foot in the Lawless School. He was badgered by his father for not being good enough and he secretly longed for the mother he never knew, who he also wanted to punish for leaving him alone in such a do-right-or-else situation."

"So you think he's working for Ms. Watts?" asked Jules. "The same woman that left him at the bottom of a frozen river?"

"No," said M. "I think he's working against Ms. Watts."

"What are you saying?" asked Merlyn.

"Cal's on a dark path and nothing's going to stop him," said M. "He's out for something uglier than justice. Revenge. He's looking for a chance to make his mother finally see and appreciate everything she left behind. . . . The monster she created."

With that declaration drifting through the air, M stepped back from the group and wondered why she hadn't seen the signs earlier. Cal had basically been calling out to her from the moment he confessed to being Ms. Watts's son in a secret passage under the Lawless School. The chill of London winter wafted around M and wrapped her in an icy grip. The King's Cross station, which had seemed so majestic only a short while earlier, now seemed ominous. The open airiness felt like a vast chasm, mirroring the endless divide between the girl M had been before the Lawless School and the girl she was now. The white girder awning that appeared cloudlike before now loomed like a giant skeleton's chest cavity. M was trapped inside the beast, swallowed whole. Following the bend of the roof with her eyes, she landed on her own reflection in a distant window and was scared. Scared that she suddenly looked so small in such a big situation.

It was an audible *plop* that brought M back from her thoughts. The plop was so wet and thick that, for a moment, she thought her own heart could have slid out of her chest and hit the floor. She looked at her feet, but her heart was nowhere in sight. However, what lay in front of her definitely quickened her pulse. It was a wallet, an innocent black wallet that sat before her in a stream of rustling coats and scuffling heels, and M was certain that it hadn't been there just a moment ago.

She bent down and carefully picked it up. The leather was buttery smooth and warm in her hands. Its edges weren't worn away, the usual wear and tear of credit card outlines wasn't there, and its spine was uncracked. M quickly looked around, searching for anyone who might be combing through the crowd, searching for his legitimately lost wallet, which could have been mistakenly kicked over to her. But there was no such person. The wallet became heavy in her hands, not from the weight of money, but from the weight of knowing what it meant and who had sent it.

M opened the wallet and pulled out its only contents: a white card that read, *It's time to come home to NYC, M.*

Instantly she flashed back to her unassuming interview with Ms. Watts and Zara. *If you found a wallet near your house, what would you do?* The answer seemed obvious now. She stuffed the card in her pocket, casually trashed the wallet in a waste bin, and walked back to the group, where Ben was talking with the others.

"Good, you're back," said Ben. "I was beginning to think you ran away, too."

"No, just lost in the architecture," said M. "What's the word?"

"Keyshawn here has convinced me to give him some time," said Ben. "He's tapped into London's CCTV cameras in an effort to track Cal down, but so far he seems to have eluded them all. Shop cameras, traffic cameras, nothing's put eyes on him."

"What about the police?" asked Merlyn. "I mean, I know it's weird coming from me, but shouldn't you and Scotland Yard pool your resources?"

"Fulbrights work alone," chided Ben. "Those other agencies, FBI, Interpol, and the like, are not to be trusted. If they got things right in the first place, we wouldn't exist. We go this alone and if we come up empty, then we'll have no choice but to contact the academy and await further instructions."

"No."

The group turned in shock to hear the word so defiantly declared by the least likely person.

"No, I won't contact the academy and await further instructions," said Vivian. "I've awaited further instructions all my life and I know where that leads: down a rabbit hole filled with paperwork and desk jockeying and cross-referencing minutiae. That's not what I signed up for when I chose to become a Fulbright. There has to be a better solution, a lead that we haven't found yet. To go back empty-handed and outsmarted would guarantee that none of us would see the field again."

It might guarantee that none of them would even see the light of day again, thought M.

"Then what's our lead?" asked Ben, surprising the group a second time. "Given the urgency of this assignment and Fence's idiocy, I'm willing to strike out on our own again if we had a next step. If only to catch Fence and drag him back to the academy myself."

"I have one," admitted M. "And it's a good one, but there's one catch . . . and there's one thing we have to promise each other."

"I'll promise anything to stay out of that hole-in-the-ground academy," said Merlyn.

"We have to promise to come clean with each other about everything," said M. "Spill the secrets. It's going to be hard, but if we do that, we may have a chance of solving the mystery of the *Mutus Liber* and the traitorous Cal."

One by one, the group all agreed to an honesty pact. Even Keyshawn looked up from scouring the closed-circuit public spaces of London and nodded his head.

"Now that you've strong-armed our integrity, Freeman, what's the catch you mentioned?" asked Ben.

"I'm pretty sure that if we follow this lead, we'll be walking straight into a Lawless trap."

Night fell while the train crossed the English countryside. The stars hummed with a cold brightness in the dark that made M feel like she was staring through the atmosphere and into the deepest point in an ever-expanding universe. She refocused on her reflection in the window, which was wet from the conflicting temperatures, inside and outside. The train ride had been quiet, but it was time to unleash their secrets, put them on the table, and reconstruct the whole truth. Luckily they were blessed with an empty car, probably because it was the last train to run from London to Leeds.

Ben looked at his phone. Seventeen messages from home base. He shook his head slowly. Keyshawn had come up with a haphazard collection of products to scramble the team's trackers. Layers of tin foil, plastic wrap, wet bandages, and small magnets chafed against their arms, but the effect drowned the signal.

"Since we're avoiding telling the truth to the base, maybe now's a good time to tell the truth to one another," said M. "Let's start with the Fulbright Academy."

"What do you need to know about?" asked Ben.

"Why were you holding Cal hostage?"

"Didn't Cal just answer that question at the library?" said Ben.

"Total honesty, Ben," said Keyshawn.

Ben relented, uncrossing his arms and leaning toward the group. "All right. He was a liability and a special case. When we pulled him from that river, Mr. Fence demanded that we get him healthy and leave him unquestioned. He was looking for a father-son reunion, until Cal came to and had a different idea. He slipped past his direct one night and contaminated the cafeteria meals. Made the entire school sick. It was awful. Never seen anything like it." Ben turned green just thinking about the whole rancid deal. "Then, while the infirmary was at capacity, Cal took advantage of our depleted man power and hacked into our system. We finally cornered him moments before he took over the entire school. After that, any other student would have been treated worse than an enemy combatant. But not Cal. No, Mr. Fence convinced everyone that detention and observation was the best response."

"Classic Cal," said Merlyn.

"You captured another Lawless student that night," said M. "What happened to him?"

"The Foley kid," said Ben, looking very uncomfortable. "Yeah, our team brought him in. Pulled him out of the fire he started, actually."

"No way, you guys started that fire!" exclaimed Merlyn.

"We did?" said Ben. "In the official report, it was started by two Lawless kids, this Foley guy and another girl."

"Yeah, and who wrote the report?" asked Jules. "And either way, it's not like the Fulbrights tried to put *out* the fire. Those irreplaceable masterpieces were torched."

"Excuse us for trying to save the world," said Ben in a low, steady tone behind his clenched teeth. "If you want to serve a greater good, then you learn to look past the little things."

"The little things are important," replied M. "You learn that at the Lawless School. Now let's talk little things. What happened to Foley?"

Ben shifted in his seat. "He . . . he was delivered to John Doe for interrogation."

"And?" cajoled M.

"And that's it," he said. "I swear. I'm a direct, not top brass. When a prisoner gets the call-up, they are out of sight, out of mind to us."

"Is that how you felt when Mr. Fence had you taken to a Glass House for the night?" asked M. "That everyone should look the other way and let whatever happened happen to you?"

Ben sat stone still, grinding his teeth at an audible volume, which made the hair on the back of M's neck stand at attention. She'd finally broken through his Fulbright shell. She saw the realization in Ben's eyes, how easily roles can be reversed, and how even those who stand against everything you believe in are still people, at the end of the day.

"It's okay, Ben," she said. "What they did to you wasn't fair. You were doing your job and hardly deserved to be punished. And I believe everything you're telling me now. But I don't believe you, Keyshawn."

"Me?" asked Keyshawn, shocked. "How did I get dragged into this?"

"We're all in this," said Jules.

"You know something about Foley, don't you?" inquired M.

"Total honesty," echoed Ben, turning in his chair to stare down Keyshawn, who kept up his charade of surprise.

"Tell them, Keyshawn," said M. "Let's start with Foley in the infirmary. Tell them about how he's in a coma. Tell them about how he's wearing more wires and tubes than a mainframe server. Tell them, even though he's unconscious and strapped to a hospital bed, that he's still being kept under surveillance by cameras."

"What!" gasped Merlyn and Jules at the same time. Their stares turned full force on Keyshawn.

"That's my guardian, man!" yelled Merlyn.

"That's our friend," said Jules.

"He's a bad guy!" Keyshawn blurted out. "Come on, Ben. Tell them. Foley is a bad apple. You're with me on this, right?"

"What do you know, Noles?" demanded Ben.

"I — I," stammered Keyshawn, now manic, with his knees bouncing up and down uncontrollably. "I know so little about . . . you see, it was direct orders." Sweat dampened the neck of his sweater. "John Doe said Foley was an imminent danger; that he would never turn to the Fulbrights; his mind was totally corrupted, so this was the best way."

"What was the best way?" said M.

"Forced deep sleep," he said. "But it was a direct order from John Doe. No one says no to Doe."

"You did," sniped M. "You said no to Doe earlier today. Tell the others why."

Keyshawn raised his head slowly before placing it in his hands and covering his face. "Yes." It was a simple, rugged word that fell from his lips. "My family, Doe said he'd take care of them."

"So you did this to make sure your family became wealthy?" demanded Merlyn.

"No," said Keyshawn. "Doe said he'd take care of them if I *didn't* follow his orders."

"And what were his orders, exactly?" said Ben.

"Keep Foley under, but stable," Keyshawn admitted. "Develop new technologies. And test the Lawless students."

"Don't you mean *train* the Lawless students?" asked Vivian.

"No, he meant *test*," said M. "The shot you gave us on our first day, it wasn't the same thing given to all the other Fulbrights. We're the trial run for the next generation of Fulbrights, aren't we?"

Keyshawn nodded. "It's true, everything she said."

"So why does John Doe need Foley?" asked Merlyn.

"He didn't tell me," said Keyshawn. "Honestly, I don't know."

"Then can you tell us why there's a stockpile of spare organs in the infirmary, enough to rebuild an army?" asked M.

"What?" asked Keyshawn. "No, I don't know anything about that. I swear."

"You told us we had two weeks to train," said Merlyn. "What was supposed to happen after two weeks?"

"The serum takes two weeks to fully fuse with the host," he confessed. "Over that period, the serum maps your instincts, your brain waves, adapting to the way you think and act, bolstering your every attribute. Once its work is done, well, in theory, you'll become the perfect you."

"We know that already," said M. "Total Persona. What really happens after two weeks?"

Keyshawn shook his head apologetically. "It's my family."

"What happens?" repeated Jules, grabbing him by the collar.

"Once the serum is fused with the body, it can also be removed, taking with it all of your special skills, like a copy of your DNA." He looked like he was going to be sick. "Then, technically, it could be used to grant someone else all your gifts. To create the perfect Fulbright."

"You're not just stealing our identities. You're stealing everything we are!" Merlyn said angrily.

"You tested this on Foley, too, didn't you?" asked M.

Keyshawn held his head in his hands and slowly nodded yes. "I gave him an early version, but something went wrong. This level of science is more of an art. He had an adverse reaction, but I learned from my mistake. I got your doses right, didn't I?"

"You're a monster," spat Jules. "A monster and a coward."

"He's not a coward," said M. "Because he took the serum,

too. Didn't you? That's why you built a Fulbright suit for yourself."

"What?!" said Ben.

"So when did you take your dose, Keyshawn?" M asked.

"Almost two weeks ago," he said.

"And that's why you were so adamant about us getting our act together," she said. "There was never a field mission to save the world. There was just an end date to the test, a deadline for proving you got the right formula for Doe's super-soldiers. And if you did, then your family would be safe and John Doe has a new weapon of mass destruction in his fight against all things evil."

The group collectively exhaled as they processed the magnitude of the revelations. Another moment of silence filled with the steady clicking of the train before M started again.

"The *Mutus Liber*. It wasn't originally in the cards for us to find one, since we were just the lab rats. So why are we out here now?"

"I can't claim to know what's going through John Doe's mind," Keyshawn said with frustration. "But I'm sure he has his reasons."

"Then what does John Doe want with those books?" asked Vivian.

"The books make something," said Keyshawn. "They work in unison, but I have no idea how. Only John Doe himself knows."

"No, someone else knows it, too," said M. "My mother, for one. And my money is on Ms. Watts, Dr. Lawless, and Zara Smith."

"What makes you think they're involved?" asked Merlyn.

"A little birdie sent me this card," said M, holding up the slim piece of sturdy paper, "inviting me to New York City. And the delivery of the message was hallmark Lawless."

"Well, I'll be," said Vivian, looking up from her tablet. "It looks like there's been a coup in the black-market book world in the past hour or so, because according to my feed, the two remaining first-edition copies of the *Mutus Liber* were just purchased by an anonymous buyer in New York City."

"So that's your lead and that's your trap," said Ben. "Are we all game for visiting the Big Apple and taking a bite?"

"We need to get those books," said M. "I don't know why, but I have a feeling that they lead to something that this world doesn't need to experience. And since we're being totally honest here, here's my crazy proposal."

"What's that?" asked Keyshawn.

"I propose that from here on out, we only trust one another. Even above your precious John Doe. He may be out for justice, but he's not a good man."

"Careful, Freeman," said Ben. "John Doe is our leader *and* he was one of your father's most trusted companions."

"Yeah, well, my dad's not here to vouch for him and I'm making my own decisions now. And I say Doe is not who you think he is."

"Ben," said Vivian, whose face had turned bleach white. "I'm prone to agree with M."

"What?" he snapped. "Breaking protocol for a greater good

is one thing, but I'm afraid you've damaged your gauge of right and wrong. When did this Lawless garbage leech into your head?"

"When I did some hacking and saw this," she said, and flipped the tablet around to show the address and name of the *Mutus Liber*'s no-longer-anonymous buyer. The address meant nothing to M. It looked like any other address in New York City: a series of numbers with a *W* and an *ST* thrown in. But the name of the buyer was loud and clear and terrifying, because the name of the buyer was none other than John Doe.

The train rattled onward as the passengers contemplated this news. Maybe it was a good thing that Cal had made off with the fourth copy of the book, thought M. Trees and valleys flew by outside the windows, flickering past her at seventy frames a minute. Agonizing over whether they'd made a bad decision striking out on their own, Ben looked like a Fulbright without a country.

"What are we supposed to do now?" Merlyn spoke up. "I mean, 'John Doe' could be anyone, right? That's the name police give to unidentified people, so it's probably not *the* John Doe, right?"

"Seriously, Merlyn," said M. "What are the chances that another John Doe is going to be attached to those two books at this very particular moment?"

"It could be someone from Lawless," said Ben.

"I don't think it is," admitted M. "The person who left me this message is from the Lawless School. And I don't think she would have waved a red flag and invited us to disrupt one of her own schemes."

"You trust her?" asked Vivian.

M thought about this question as it pertained to Zara Smith. "I trust her about this."

A hush fell back over the train car as the group realized what they were about to attempt: an off-the-books strike against the leader of the Fulbrights.

Keyshawn was the first to break the silence. "I'm in."

"Me, too," agreed Vivian.

"I never liked that creepy old guy, anyway," said Jules.

"Ditto," said Merlyn.

The group all stared at Ben, the most loyal Fulbright of the bunch. His eyes were empty and his face was flat as the train shook slightly and clicked along its path. He looked up at M. "Your father, in his video, said that there was an evil in the world that was bigger than the Fulbrights could handle. Do you think this is what he was meant?"

M thought back to the video she had been shown only a few days ago, even though it felt like years.

Do as they say, not as they do.

"I don't know," she answered. "Ben, all I have to go on are the facts that we've found. We know that John Doe had us injected with a chemical that could create a mega-army. We know that John Doe wanted us to collect that book in Prague, but he didn't want us to know what the book was or that it was a piece to a larger puzzle. And we know that someone named

John Doe bought the remaining two copies of the *Mutus Liber* off the black market. To me, that's a lot of John Doe."

Ben sighed. "I've always heard you were different, M Freeman. But I never dreamed I'd find myself agreeing with you. I'm in."

"Then it's settled," said M. "New York, here we come."

CHAPTER 20

IF THE GLOVE FITS

As the jet's engines silently lit up the meadow, M steered the ship westward and prepared for another long journey. Luckily she had a copilot, this time, in Merlyn. He couldn't help fly the jet, but she appreciated having some company.

"What did you think the first time you met me?" asked Merlyn.

"I don't know," said M. "You talked a lot; that's what I remember."

"Yeah, well, back then I felt like I had a lot to say," said Merlyn with a laugh.

"Do you think the Fulbrights have Crimers?" she asked.

"Sure, but they probably call them analysts or detectors, something that doesn't sound half as cool," he said. "Hey, M, do you ever miss it? The Lawless School, I mean."

"Yeah, I do," she said. "I actually miss it a lot." Merlyn's question took her back to her original interview with Ms. Watts. To the time when M had no idea what the Lawless School was and she thought she was interviewing for a posh boarding school, where she'd be hobnobbing with future politicians and world leaders, not lurking in society's shadowy underbelly with criminal masterminds. "You?"

"Yes and no," said Merlyn. "I mean, yes in the sense that it was challenging and exciting. Cracking practice codes, solving practice problems, I loved the theory of it all. But when it became real, when we were in Hamburg, when Cal went under the ice, that's not what I signed up for. I'm a tech geek, M. I like the problem solving and I'm good with gadgets. That's what I bring to the table."

"Hmmm, I never thought about what I bring to the table," said M. "I guess, if you're the brains, then Jules would be the acrobatic, unflinching brawn. And Cal would have been —"

"Wait," interrupted Merlyn. "Why are we even talking about Cal? He's not a member of the team."

"But he was," said M. "I think there's a reason we were all given that serum, Merlyn. I thought it was because I insisted I have you guys with me, but I think you would have been pulled into this whether I'd made that demand or not. We're all members of a team, we all bring something to the table. But I can't place Cal in all this. . . ."

M trailed off, deep in thought about Cal. From day one, he'd been a very likable idiot, yet he'd managed to outsmart a number of people: M, during Professor Bandit's mark challenge; Foley, during the deep-freeze chase; Devon, during the class clash; Ben, in the Magblast duel; Adam, in Prague; and finally M again, in the British Library. "Why didn't I see it before!" she exclaimed. "He's a Smooth Criminal, Merlyn! Cal's a Smooth Criminal. The first in and the last out of a con . . . just like Zara described on my first day at Lawless. Awkward, likable, and always three steps ahead of their mark."

"And we were the mark," said Merlyn. "He was playing us all along. Now I feel completely stupid for not seeing it."

"Don't," said M. "None of us saw it."

Light wisps of clouds hung in the sky as the jet rushed through the evening. The sun was gone but the full moon cast a murky glow on the stratospheric view, which stretched forever in all directions. M and Merlyn sat, privately recounting their past year and how it had led them to this very moment.

M had already let a black hole slip through her fingers and she wasn't going to let this new disaster, however big or small, get past her.

The jet touched down in an abandoned warehouse lot somewhere deep in Brooklyn. The area was empty and barren, surrounded by husks of buildings and hangars that probably once housed airplanes, boats, or large props and sets for movies. Either way, it was the perfect location to secretly land and stash the plane. There was even a subway close by to carry them into the city.

Dressed in their Fulbright uniforms, the crew was relieved to find the subway car empty. But that didn't last for long. Slowly the car filled up, despite the late hour. No one confronted or questioned the crew, though a couple of older kids could be heard laughing and giggling, clearly at their expense.

One boy snickered. "Oh man, I didn't know this was a ninja train."

"Is there a dork convention in town?" guffawed the other.

"Yeah, yeah, yeah," said the first, barely catching his breath. "It's like, 'take me to your dweeber.'"

Ben kept his cool and, under his breath, urged everyone else to as well. "Let them laugh. They have no idea what's really going on here."

M was thankful when their stop arrived and the crew left the train behind, pursued by the echo of croons, whistles, and tasteless jokes from complete strangers. "This is why I hate New York," said Jules. "Everyone's got an opinion and they think everyone else needs to hear it."

"I could tap into the transit system and make that train run nonstop all night," said Keyshawn with a laugh.

"You can do that?" asked Merlyn.

"Sure, it's easy," said Keyshawn. "I gave a presentation last year at the academy, all about how unprotected infrastructures are around the globe. I could reroute this whole city if I wanted to."

"Sounds cool, but it's not why we're here," said M, trying to keep everyone focused.

The streets were not completely empty at this time of night, which surprised M, but she had always heard that New York City never slept. However, once they got off the busier avenues, the side streets were quiet and still except for the thrashing gusts of wind blowing periodically in from the Hudson River. M wished she could put on her mask, if only to protect her ears from the cold, but the crew looked suspicious enough as it was, and they couldn't rely on camouflage in such a populated setting.

The street they wanted began as a residential neighborhood with picturesque brownstones walling them in, but on the next block, the surroundings turned instantly industrial. There was a commercial bus line storage and cleaning service in one warehouse, next to a row of what looked like delivery hubs, where lines of truckless flatbeds sat along the street, huge and dirty white, like dinosaur bones unearthed and left behind.

Finally they arrived at John Doe's address. Slipping on their masks, the crew spread out to get a better look at the building, which didn't look all that impressive from the outside. It was a low structure by New York standards, standing only four stories high, with a façade that was mostly made up of twelve-foot-tall, wide-panel windows that lined the upper floors. The glass was old and grimy, covered in a filth that looked like it wouldn't even be washed away by rain. It reminded M of the layers of dust that had covered the Lawless yearbooks back in Dr. Lawless's office in West building seven. It was an impenetrable dust. There was no way to see inside.

The ground floor, devoid of windows, was a mass of concrete blocks, with a metal door set back in a shadowy entryway. It was covered in tags and graffiti, swipes of color that wove over and over one another, making a twisted artistic piece that was forever unfinished.

"Not the rich digs I was imagining," said Vivian.

"Well, he did buy the books on the black market and not at a Christie's auction," M reminded her. "This is another perfect place to hide something you don't want found. The last forgotten part of Manhattan."

"But not for long," said Keyshawn, motioning across the street. There was new construction going up, scaffolding platforms built layer by layer into the sky, walling off what was probably the beginning of the block's first condo high-rise.

"That's our in," said Ben. "We can climb the scaffolding to get even with the roof and then set up a zip line across. Once on the roof, we'll either find an entrance inside — fire escape, or what have you — or we can go down the side and cut through one of those dirt-encrusted things that are attempting to be windows."

"Or we could go in the front door," said Jules. "It's already open."

Indeed the door was open, slightly ajar and cloaked in the shadows of the vagabond vestibule. As M tuned her ears to the sounds of the night, the delicate creak of the door on its hinges became obvious. Jules had probably heard it without cranking the volume levels of her mask. It was one of her great tricks: She could hear a pin drop on a pillow.

Suddenly aware that they might not be the only ones here, M perked with anticipation. "Let's see what there is to see, then."

Switching her visual sensors to pick up both full light and full heat, she slowly opened the door and snuck inside. The first room was wide and open and completely empty — there was nothing in sight other than a set of stairs in the middle of the room. Moving forward, she felt a thin breeze on the air.

"Wait, do you guys feel that?" she whispered.

"It's called a draft, M," said Ben. "Not unusual for a dump like this."

Jules took a step, but M quickly held her back. It wasn't just one simple breeze; there were several different breezes coming from every direction in the room.

"It's a trap," M said, scooping up dust from the floor and blowing it into the air. The cloud of dust scattered lightly and caught in the breezes, forming a crisscross pattern of X's throughout the room between the crew and the stairway to the next level. "They're using air instead of lasers. Impossible to see without tripping, even with aerosol sprays. Our masks won't help us."

"Looks like we go back outside, then," said Merlyn, who took one step back toward the door.

"No! Wait!" screamed M, but the door slammed shut. Merlyn had tripped a switch and there was no telling what would come next. "Everyone, down!"

The crew dropped on their stomachs and a mysterious shadow covered them. A series of air-splitting *ziss*es and *zass*es whisked wildly above them, striking the concrete walls with deadly-sounding pings. When the whizzing stopped, the shadow retreated, too. It was Keyshawn. He had expanded his suit to create a shield around the entire crew. M stood slowly, surveying the once-empty room that now looked like a pincushion. Small metal quills with razor-sharp tips were nailed into almost every inch of the walls around them.

"Okay," said Ben. "Not just a draft. I can admit when I'm wrong. But you need to make me one of those suits if we get out of this alive, Keyshawn."

Keyshawn smiled. "Yes, sir."

"The door," said Vivian, trying to open it. "It's locked."

"Looks like it's up we go," said M. "Be on your best behavior, everyone. We're guests in this madhouse."

After checking the stairwell for signs of another trap, they began their ascent. The second level was also vacant and the windows were plastered with old newspapers, which blocked out what little light might have entered the space. Jules had taken three steps in when she noticed a squishing coming from under her feet.

"Maybe there's a leak?" said Jules. "This floor is pretty wet."

"I don't like the sound of that," confessed M as Keyshawn followed up the rear and stepped into the room.

SLAM! The door to the stairwell clamped shut behind them. M turned and saw the walls begin to bleed. . . . No, it wasn't blood. They were leaking water.

"Hold your breath!" M hollered as a gush of water flushed through openings along the walls, the floor, and the ceiling, trapping the crew in an instant deluge, which pummeled them in every direction. Suspended in the water, M couldn't tell if she was facing up or down. She swam over to the windows and kicked against the glass, but it wouldn't give.

"Relax, everyone," Keyshawn's voice came through her comm link. "Fulbright masks have an air supply in them. You can breathe underwater, so please don't hold your breath like our friend M suggested."

M exhaled and took a deep breath. That alone made this experience very different from her time back in the freezing waters of Hamburg. "When were we going to get underwater training?" she snapped.

"I had it scheduled for next week," Keyshawn laughed. "No time like the present, though, huh?"

The crew swam over to the next stairwell door and shredded it open with their Magblasts. The water rushed in and leveled out halfway up the stairs. M followed its lead and climbed up to the next level.

"I think it's safe to assume that if there were another person trying to break in here, we'd at least have seen their corpse by now, right?" asked Vivian.

Through the door at the top of the stairs, the third level looked every bit as empty as the previous levels. "Maybe we're too late?" suggested Merlyn quietly. "Maybe Doe packed up everything and ditched this place because he knew we were coming?"

"Or knew someone else was coming," said Ben.

"No, whatever this place is, it's not abandoned," said M. "That's what he wants people to believe. Look at the floor. It's impeccably clean."

"Who cleans floors in a run-down place like this?" asked Keyshawn.

"Same crazy person who tries to drown or make voodoo dolls out of his visitors," said Jules.

"Someone who doesn't want you to see their footprints in the dust," added M. "There must be an entrance on this level that he could slip in and out of without having to deal with the first two levels." She walked over behind the stairs and there, just as she had expected, was an unlatched window looking out over a fire escape. "Bingo. I don't think John Doe let too many people know about this place. It's made to be secret."

"So was the academy," said Vivian.

"True, but that's tucked away in a far-off corner of the globe," reasoned M. "This is smack-dab in the middle of New York City. This isn't the same kind of hidden; this is discreet."

"Wait. First floor, metal darts, earth. Second floor, water," said Keyshawn urgently. "Third floor . . ."

But before Keyshawn could finish his thought, a hissing sound erupted in the room like millions of snakes set loose, followed by an unmistakable odor.

"Gas, FIRE!" screamed M.

Suddenly the room exploded into an inferno of rippling torrents of flames that twisted and bit in every direction. A blast of heat surged and slithered around M, and she felt her suit bend and warp against the tremendous temperature change. The stench of scorched concrete filled the room as she pulled the door open and ushered her friends through to the next level. But Ben stayed behind, walking through the fire. M adjusted her mask so that the brightness wasn't so blinding.

"What are you doing?!" she screeched.

"Trust me," said Ben. "We don't want the fire department showing up and getting in our way." Then, using his Magblast, he lifted up a giant scoop of water from the second level and cast the liquid in every direction, snuffing out the sparks in the hidden flamethrowers.

"You did it!" cheered M.

"Yeah, let's just not do it again, okay?" said Ben as his suit, singed, trailed a line of gray smoke behind him.

They crept up the final flight of stairs, entering a small corridor that ended at a closed door with light flickering underneath it.

"I'll bet anything that this level is going to be completely different from anything we've seen so far," said M from the rear.

At the front, Vivian nodded. "I hope you're right." Then she slowly closed her hand around the doorknob and twisted. The room on the other side of the door wasn't anything like the first three floors, but it was disturbingly familiar to M — it was almost exactly like the library from her old house. The furniture was arranged in the same way. The bookshelves were crammed with volumes of books, so many that the room had the same sweet odor of leather and old paper.

"What is it, M?" asked Merlyn.

"It's the smell," she said. "I know that smell."

Sensing that they had finally reached the inner lair, everyone cast over the room, looking for anyone else who may be hiding, but there was nowhere to hide. Except for two chairs and the bookshelves, the room was clear.

"Well, at least this library won't try to eat us alive," said Vivian. She walked up and down the bookshelves that lined the wall.

"Spread out and find those books," said Ben. "If they're even here."

Jules took a moment to look out of the windows. "Hmm, is it weird that these windows are so clean?"

"Everything about this place is weird," said Merlyn. "Now let's please get this over with, because I don't want to wait around for whatever is going to happen next."

The group combed over the shelves, looking for the familiar spines of the *Mutus Liber* but a quick scan proved futile. The black market books weren't mixed in with the other titles. There was something that caught M's eye, though. It was a small picture frame, stuffed deep in between two giant world atlases. *What would John Doe keep in a frame?* she wondered. She reached in, pulled out the frame, and nearly jumped out of her skin when she flipped it around. It was a picture of her with her father. He looked so happy to be holding his daughter while the younger M posed with a funny face, hamming it up for the camera like a carefree kid with her father on a sunny afternoon. She gazed at the drastically different world through the glass and couldn't believe it. Finding a fatherly memento here — it was surreal, disarming, and, worst of all, a reminder of her dad's connection to John Doe.

"M, what did you find?" hollered Keyshawn from across the room.

Dazed and confused, M turned and tucked the picture behind her. "Nothing. I mean, I grabbed what I thought was a book." But when she tried to replace the framed photograph, a giant atlas tipped off the shelf and crashed to the floor.

"Look!" said Ben, pointing behind her. Above M, a false row of books had flipped open, revealing one of the remaining *Mutus Liber* volumes.

Standing on the thick atlas, M stretched to reach the top

shelf and pull down the *Mutus Liber.* A slight cracking sound came from the atlas under her weight and she worried, irrationally, that she might have damaged its spine.

"Guys, we did it." Merlyn smiled. "Way to fumble your way to victory, M."

"No, we didn't," breathed M, gripping the tome to her chest. "There's only one book here. Where's the other?" *And what in the world is this place?* she wondered. It was so much like her home, so familiar, too familiar, and it struck a chord inside of her that had warbled softly at first and was rising into a crescendo. Clutching the book, she twisted her foot one more time and felt the atlas beneath her buckle. "I don't think this place belongs to John Doe. We were wrong. We were so wrong and we've got to get out of here before —"

But M's thought was interrupted by the sound of glass smashing behind her, followed by a swift kick to her side that sent her reeling. She landed hard on top on the *Mutus Liber,* the wind knocked out of her.

"Before what?" came a calm, slithering voice. "Before you realize what was right under your feet?" It was Zara, dressed in black, with a zip line attached to her harness. While the crew was stunned by the surprise attack, Zara swiped the atlas, flipped open the false cover that M had crushed, and pulled out a hefty-sized rock. "Poor M, don't you know it's true what they say? You can never go home again. Sayonara, suckers."

Suddenly her zip line snapped tight and launched her back out of the window, where she disappeared into the gaping night. Without thinking, M leapt to her feet and charged toward the same broken window.

"M, what are you doing?!" screamed Ben. "We've got the book!"

"But Zara's got the moon rock!" M yelled as she dove out of the window at full speed. Falling through the air, she flung out her hands and her suit produced two long ropes that latched on to the scaffolding across the street. To anyone on the street, she must have looked like a real-life Spider-Man, but M wasn't concerned about who saw her anymore. The only important thing now was getting that rock back.

She landed on the scaffolding with a thud and surprised Zara, who was placing the stone in her side pocket.

"Still don't know when you're beat, aye, M? Cool suit not-withstanding, it's best for you to run back to your friends now." Zara kicked M again, squarely in the chest, knocking her against the railing. Zara then grabbed a metal pipe and swung it, but M dodged the blow, shaking out her wrist to form a dark sword from her suit's programmable matter. On Zara's next attack, M sliced the pipe in half and used the other girl's momentum to shove her over the railing. But Zara caught herself on another rung and swung back in one floor below. M heard Zara running below her and let loose a Magblast in the direction of the sound. With one shot the wooden beams burst open, and M leapt down to Zara's level.

"You don't know what you're doing, Zara," cried M. "Ms. Watts could destroy the Earth with a rock that size."

"And what, I should give it to you and the Fulbrights?" snapped Zara. "Yeah, that's a good idea, because no black holes have ever come from that."

Zara kicked a paint can at M and a wave of white splashed over her, coating her hand and the lower half of her suit. M didn't even flinch, just aimed her Magblast at Zara, who had turned to run away, but the Magblast failed. "Paint beats the Magblast?" she complained frantically.

"M!" Jules's voice came over her comm link. "Where are you? Can we help?"

"I've got this," yelled M, and her voice echoed down the city block. She retracted the sword and wiped the paint off her other glove before screaming, "If you're not going to stop running, I'm going to do something really stupid!"

But Zara wasn't going to stop running. She had almost slipped to the bottom level when M reached out and waved for her friends, who watched from the broken window, to stay put. "Here goes nothing." She aimed her Magblast at the scaffolding anchor and fired. The anchor knocked loose and the levels of scaffolding buckled violently, unlatching from the new high-rise's skeleton, which crumbled into the street. M held on to a pole and braced for the impact as it all came crashing down, but when she hit the cold ground, she was flung aside so hard that she bounced twice.

Staggering to her feet, M refocused her visuals to light the street and see past the clouds of dust that blanketed the area. Then she saw Zara running away again.

"She's like a cat," said Merlyn in M's earpiece. "She's got nine lives and always lands on her feet."

M climbed out of the wreckage and ran after her. "I'm right behind her. We've got one of the books, correct?"

"Yes," said Vivian. "But where's the other?"

"Don't know. You guys keep looking and I'll stop Zara," huffed M as she picked up speed. She turned the corner just in time to see her old roommate racing down a subway entrance.

"She's gone into the subway," M reported while she pulled her sleeve up, tearing away the tin foil and bandages. "Use my tracker to follow me."

Skidding down the stairs, she startled some late-night passengers, who yelled as she rushed by, but the next sound she heard was the train in the station. Jumping over the turnstile, she ran to the door, but it closed just before she got there. She looked quickly up and down the train until she spotted Zara inside, one car up from her. The train began to roll and M raced alongside it until she reached Zara's car. Blasting the door open, she careened inside.

"Don't stop the train," Zara said to the shocked passengers as she turned and flew to the back of the car. And indeed the train didn't stop. It kept on its path at full speed. Zara banged through the exit door and into the next car like a waiter gliding between the kitchen and the dining area. M tried to keep up, but the doors were trickier than she thought.

"Keyshawn, I need for you to stop the train when I say so," said M.

"I'll try, but we've already wired into the network," said Keyshawn. "It looks like someone else is controlling this thing and they've put up firewalls galore."

"It's Code," said Merlyn. "Give me the computer, Keyshawn. I can undo this."

M raced past openmouthed strangers and people in head-phones listening to the disturbingly loud clack and crash of snare drums and cymbals. But she focused only on Zara, who was getting ever closer to the last car of the train.

"Soon, guys, or she's going to escape out the back," said M.

"Okay, got it," Merlyn's voice crackled. M was getting too far away from the transmitters. "Hold *shhhhh* tight."

But M didn't hold on to anything. Instead, as the brakes seized and the train abruptly stopped, she jumped forward into the air as Zara, caught off balance, was thrown back-ward into M's ready tackle. Pinning Zara to the ground, M leaned up and pointed her Magblast directly into the other girl's face. "Maybe you know what this is and maybe you know what it can do, but you have no idea what I'm capable of if you don't give me that rock right now."

Zara smiled a bruised smile. "Wow, did Eaves just crack Code's code? I'm proud of you guys. We taught you well. But there's one lesson you never learned."

"Give me the rock," demanded M.

"Never take on the Fulbrights by yourself — *I* sure don't," said Zara. A bag swept over M's head, her arms were pulled behind her back, and a vicious shock of electricity jolted through her body. "Gotcha."

CHAPTER 21
DISAVOWED

The comm link was totally silent under M's hood. That blast on the train must have short-circuited her supersuit. This was exactly why Professor Bandit warned her about relying too heavily on weapons. Well, lesson learned the hard way. Hopefully the tracker in her arm still worked.

Having exited the train's rear door, Zara and at least two other people were marching her through the muddy tracks of the New York subway system. When a clicking sound started, they guided her carefully from one track to another, followed by a rush of air and the cacophonous rattle of a train speeding by. Her captors didn't say anything to one another the entire time, leaving M alone with the sound of her own shallow breathing.

Underfoot, M felt nasty, indescribable things, and based on the awful smell, she was probably better off not knowing what kind of refuse she was walking through. Sewage and dead rats were only part of it. Then the sound of live rats assailed her senses. Tiny nails clicked and slid over metal and plastic, a whole nest scared and rampant due to the unannounced visitors in their home. M shivered thinking about the thronging mass of rodents that surrounded her. It crossed her mind that she should be more concerned about where she was being taken, that the rats were at least more predictable than Zara and her cronies.

"M," said Zara, and her voice tumbled in the wide darkness. "What did you want to be when you grew up?"

"You mean, did I see myself underground in a sewer, handcuffed with a hood on my head?"

"No, I mean, really, what did you want to do with your life? Before getting caught up in all this."

M knew exactly what she'd wanted to be. "An artist. Like my mother and father."

"But your father wasn't an artist . . . and really neither was your mother," said Zara.

"They were to me," said M.

"Some people see the glass half-full and some people see it half-empty, but you, M Freeman, you see a cold, refreshing drink, don't you?"

"Where are you taking me?" M asked with the most relaxed tone she could muster.

"Right here," Zara answered as the march ended. She pushed M against a wall and latched her bound hands to a hook. Then Zara removed M's hood, snatching her mask off at the same time. M couldn't see anything in the pitch darkness. "Listen up, because we only have a few minutes before they come for you."

"Who?" M asked.

"Did I say, 'Hey, M, start asking questions'?" Zara cracked coldly. "No! I said, *listen.* Same old M. So maybe this will make you feel more comfortable."

"M." The voice that came from the darkness was familiar. It was her mother's voice, and it reached into M's chest and tore out her heart.

"Mom? What are you doing here? What are you doing *with* Zara? She's got the rock, Mom, the moon rock. And it's, like, ten times bigger than mine was!"

"I know, darling." Her mother was closer now, but M still couldn't see her face, just shadow. "I asked her to help me."

M listened hard to hear if there was any stress in her voice, some telltale sign that her mother was also being held captive and not really working with Zara. Then a hand reached out and lovingly cupped M's face in the darkness. M felt the warm palm, the long fingers, and the gentle touch that definitely belonged to her mother.

"I don't know you anymore, Mom!" M screamed. "What are you doing, working with *her* instead of *me*! And you kicked me off the helicopter, you left me there to die, when all I was trying to do was save you!"

"M," continued her mother. "This will all make sense soon."

M burned inside worse than when the Fulbright serum had rewired her guts. Her last remaining family member had double-crossed her, used her, and now could only talk to her when she was tied up. M had always known they didn't have the most healthy mother-daughter relationship, but she'd had no idea it was this broken.

"What was that loft?" asked M, so angry, she could have spit venom. "Why was there a picture there of me and Dad?"

"You already know the answer to that, don't you, M?" her

mother said calmly. "The apartment belonged to your father. But that's not what's important right now. When the Fulbrights come, they will take you back to our old house. Your father prepared for this day. That is to say, he prepared *you* for this day."

"What do you mean?" asked M, still straining to see her mother's face.

"There's a message he passed down to you and only you, M," her mother said cryptically. "Somehow, when the time is right, you'll see it, you'll decipher it, and you'll know exactly what to do to save us."

"Save us?" asked M. "Us who, Mom? Like you and me? 'Cause I don't know if I'd ever help you again."

"The world, you doofus," Zara chimed in. "One minute left. Last chance for good-byes."

"One minute until what?" demanded M.

"This is going to be the hard part," her mother said. "Soon this place will be flooded with Fulbrights coming to retrieve you and you will have to go with them."

"No!" said M defiantly. "No. You've never given me a choice in my own life. If you leave me now, I'm going to hunt you down. You won't be able to hide and I'll make you pay for what you've done. Do you hear me?!"

"I love you, M."

The sentence hung in the darkness as Zara slipped M's mask back over her head and took off. M quickly tuned her visuals to the brightest setting and could see four figures running toward a service exit: her mother, Zara, and the Flynn twins. As they fled, M could hear footsteps, hundreds of footsteps. She turned to look down the tunnel and could see the Fulbright horde, with green eyes aglow, heading toward her from the distance, slowly and carefully, as if they were going to get the drop on somebody.

"They're gone," she yelled. "You can stop creeping around and come save me already."

Her mother was right. As soon as M was pulled from the depths of the subway system, she was escorted to a helicopter and airlifted to her family home. During the flight, she struggled to find any possible answers her father could have hidden for her to find. Staring out the window, lost in thought, she suddenly realized that she wasn't panicking from the height. Either she had finally conquered her fear or . . . she flexed her fists and felt the suit react, bristling to attention. The power was back on.

As they landed, M sat back and braced for whatever was going to come next, whether it was her father's big plan or John Doe's fury. She suddenly realized how much she truly despised waiting. Earlier in her life, waiting had seemed like a happy option. It gave her time to prepare, perfect, and plan. But after the Lawless School, after the Fulbright Academy, waiting had become torturous.

Finally the Fulbrights led her out of the helicopter and in through the door that led to her family's library. The rest of her crew was already there, sitting in chairs well-known to M from her years of reading in those very spots. Looking more closely, she realized that they weren't moving. She'd seen this state before. She'd even felt it. Jules, Merlyn, Ben, Vivian, and Keyshawn were all in a deep freeze.

At the head of this particular nightmare, John Doe was seated in her father's favorite chair, with two large Fulbrights at his side.

"Please, make yourself at home," said M ironically. "Can I get anyone anything? Water, tea, crumpets?"

"Sit down, Freeman," wheezed Doe. "You were contacted by a rogue operation. Tell us what happened, what they asked you."

"I was caught by surprise," said M, her voice level. "They disarmed me, tied my hands behind my back, and put a hood over my head. Then they told me that the Fulbrights would come and take me to my house. How did they know your next move, sir?"

"That's for me to worry about," said Doe.

"So's this!" said M as she jumped up to Magblast him, but her weapon puttered out.

"Tsk, tsk. Did you think I wouldn't disarm you?" asked Doe, holding up a remote control. "Not as smart as I thought."

M seethed with anger and lunged at him, but one of the Fulbrights grabbed and held her tightly.

"Oh, I knew you'd be trouble from the very start, M Freeman. That's why I wanted you taken off the board. Back on your very first plane ride to Lawless. My spy rigged it to crash, but we underestimated you, didn't we?"

"You expect me to believe Devon did that?" asked M. "No way. She may have been your eyes and ears at Lawless, but there's no chance she had that kind of access."

"Well, you're right on that count. Maybe you are a little smart, after all?" Doe smiled. "Still, not smart enough to see the whole picture."

The Fulbright next to Doe pulled off his mask and revealed the hard, multicolored eyes that had haunted M in her dreams. Professor Bandit stood in front of her, studying her coldly. "She has a talent for finding bad situations, Doe. I told you that from day one."

"Professor! It was you? You tried to crash my plane?" asked M, astounded and confused. "But you, you failed Devon. And saved us from Watts. How could you be working for them?"

"Ms. Freeman," replied Bandit in his righteous voice. "I failed Devon Zoso because she deserved to fail my class. She earned it. And I saved you from the Box because it wasn't Ms. Watts's place to finish the job."

"How could you?!" yelled M. "You were friends with my father! If he knew what you were . . . he'd —"

"He'd what?" asked Bandit. "Roll over in his grave? Rise from the dead to avenge you? Grow up, little girl."

As M pushed forward, the Fulbright behind her tightened his grasp, pinching her muscles into her bones. But her arms merely tickled as her suit dispersed the pressure from the Fulbright's grip. The programmable matter was still working? Would Keyshawn have kept that detail secret from John Doe?

"Well, now that we are all on the same page," said Doe,

addressing his captive audience, "I have a gripe with a few of you. Ben, you broke protocol. I'm sorry to see such a good recruit dragged into this mess. We'll deal with you when we return to base. Vivian, I can understand your role in this. Your knee wasn't the only thing broken by Freeman that night. I'm afraid we will have to let you go. We can't have a Fulbright who doesn't follow orders. But, Keyshawn, you've hurt me the most. And not only me, but your entire family. I can assure you they will be quite disappointed to learn that you failed to get the moon rock and the remaining *Mutus Liber* books."

M froze. Doe knew about the moon rock. Not only that, but he had been using her to find the moon rock all along.

Keyshawn's eyes shined as he struggled against the deep freeze. M almost thought she could see his hands move, but that was impossible. "I . . . got . . . them . . . here," he said through clenched teeth.

"Yes," Doe admitted. "Yes, you did bring my experiments back home, but in a roundabout way that has necessitated a great deal of effort on my part. And you know how it pains me to travel in this condition. Now, as for you, Miss Byrd and Mr. Eaves, Professor Bandit will escort you to the other room while Freeman and I have a private discussion."

Bandit walked over and lifted Merlyn up onto his shoulder. M glared, but Bandit wouldn't meet her eyes.

"And I think, Professor Bandit," said Doe as if it were an afterthought, "we should add Mr. Noles to the menu, too. Oh and, of course, we can't forget Mr. Foley."

"Yes, sir," said Bandit, and he directed another agent to grab Jules while he gripped the fabric of Keyshawn's suit and, still carrying Merlyn, dragged him out the door and down the hall.

"Ah, Freeman, at last," said Doe. "So where do I begin? For a long time, I've watched you grow up from afar. I have all of your old teacher reports and doctors' files, which made for fascinating reading. It may also surprise you to know that I was very close to your father, until his *accident*."

The word sounded violent when he said it.

"You were on a wonderful path until that little roadblock. Then your mother took over and the reports stopped being sent. And I was content to let her have that small privacy, until she sent you to the Lawless School. That wasn't part of the plan, you see. But in the end, plans can be revised."

"What are you doing with my friends?" asked M defiantly.

"The same thing I'm going to do with you, my dear. I'm going to drain you. Because, you see, we put something precious inside you. It's what some people used to call the philosopher's stone, though that term is so misused and misunderstood nowadays."

"Wait, you already have the philosopher's stone?" she said. "So that's not why you want the *Mutus Liber* or the moon rock."

"Oh good, then you have been paying attention," said Doe. "No, my dear, we cracked *that* code last year. Keyshawn did, as a matter of fact. And then he made it so much better than it was before. Who wants to turn lead to gold? Gold is easy to come by. Why make gold when you could make more life instead?"

M shouted as loud as she could, "Total truth, Keyshawn! You promised to give us the total truth!"

"Don't blame poor Keyshawn," said Doe. "He was only protecting his family. Though it was foolish to use the concoction on himself. He's a smart one, but too in love with his own science. Hmmm, I hope I don't inherit *that* trait."

"You're crazy!" said M. "You think you can eat us like food?"

"Freeman, I know I can," said Doe. "The serum has been inside you, cataloging your best attributes. Soaking up your intellect, your drive, your ceaseless ability to get under people's skin, and I plan to take that from you and put it into me. Along with your vitality, of course."

She had a realization then. The body parts from the infirmary — the countless eyes, hearts, lungs, spleens — they were all plastic, all labeled, and all meant to replace the broken pieces of John Doe. To keep him alive while his ultimate plan came together. She looked at him, at his gray skin, false teeth, and sunken eyes. How had she not seen it before? The man was basically a zombie.

"How old are you, anyway?" asked M.

"Almost old enough to finish what I've started," Doe said, "once I've caught Fence's boy and uncovered the final missing book that your no-good mother has hidden along with the moon rock, of course. Ah, but I must be boring you with such a deluge of information. You've been through enough floods for one day, I hear."

"What's in those books, Doe?" demanded M.

"Dear Freeman, those books hide a map that will make sweet Devon's sinkhole pale in comparison. Ah, your father would have loved to have seen it. But now I must ask you to do your part and give up your ghost for the greater good. What a pity. If you had chosen the Fulbright Academy to begin with, we would be in a very different position right now. Perhaps you would have been in Devon's place? Or in Bandit's place, carrying bodies to the chambers."

Hearing Doe say *chambers*, M suddenly thought back to the oversized, coffinlike machinery at the academy, which she had climbed over to find her mother, in the room with the canisters of gas. They were meant for her all along.

"The moon rock's no good, you know?" she yelled. "You don't have the meteorite anymore."

"Oh, Freeman, have you ever been so wrong?" said Doe as he held up the amber stone, the same stone Dr. Lawless had given her, the same stone Devon had supposedly used up completely. "It's a tricky science, alchemy. To create the *umbra mortis*, one must use equal parts lunar rock to a particular comet debris. And the results are quite fetching, wouldn't you say?"

M had heard enough. Full of rage, she morphed her suit into dozens of spikes, which cut into the hands of the unsuspecting Fulbright who held her. The move shocked John Doe, too, and she took advantage of his surprise, lunging forward and grabbing the meteorite. Doe struggled to hold on, but M raked her fingers across his face and kicked him ferociously back into his chair.

M pulled back her hand and saw it was covered in gray and black soot. What *was* this guy?

Tucking the stone into her suit, she turned to Ben, whose wide eyes screamed for her to run. She knew what he was thinking: More Fulbrights would arrive any minute. She mouthed an apology to Ben and Vivian and bolted from the library.

M dashed into the art gallery she had always called the once-living room. There she found Jules, Merlyn, Foley, and Keyshawn locked in the chambers, which were all wired together like futuristic sarcophagi. Another two chambers stood open and empty: one for her and one for Doe. M tugged at Jules's chamber, but it wouldn't budge. Then she heard Doe's stern voice down the hall, calling out.

"The meteorite!" screamed Doe. "Get the meteorite!"

M hoped that maybe she was an important part of Doe's life-stealing equation. If she could stay out of his grip, there was a chance that the others would be safe.

She heard something in the front yard. Looking out the window, she came upon a horrible sight. Professor Bandit was standing next to five holes in the ground. He was digging graves, just like in her nightmare.

In a panic, M's instincts took over and before she knew it, she was heading down into the basement. She ducked under the low beam, like in the Maze, then closed her eyes and fol- lowed the same path. She swept past stacked boxes and came to the end of the room, where she felt the cracked foundation with her feet and faced her father's rusty tools, hung on the wall. But now what was she supposed to do? In the Maze she had simply been corralled into a trapdoor. *Could it be?* thought M. She pounded her foot against the floor, but it didn't give. Maybe there was a hidden switch? She reached out and started pulling tools off the wall. A hammer, a wrench, a hacksaw, until finally a paintbrush would not come free of its hook. M tried twisting the paintbrush, kicking at the crack in the foundation . . . and then the earth dropped out from underneath her.

She fell hard, fast, and head over heels down a sloping tube slide until she landed in a bizarre room that she had never seen before. M pulled on her mask to survey the space. It was wooden, like a log cabin, but it had to be buried deep in the ground, given the distance she'd tumbled. She flipped a switch on the wall, and a buzzing erupted overhead as a long halogen bulb slowly came to life. The light was eerie and unsettling, but it allowed M to see without wearing the mask, and that made her feel more like herself and less like one of John Doe's henchmen.

The room was empty except for a chair and a desk. What was down here that her father wanted her to find? M raced over and tried to move the desk to block the slide that she had come down, but the furniture wouldn't give an inch. She sighed and sat down to regroup her thoughts. Why in the world would her family have built an underground shelter? Then she paused and felt the air. The room was cool and reminded her of the British Library's lower levels. M opened up the desk's top drawer, and sure enough, there was a single book inside. She pulled it out and stared at the cover.

Lawless School, Year One.

The book had the school's insignia stamped into the cover, a skull with keys for its mouth and the motto, *Chaos infinitum enim*, Chaos forever. M opened the book carefully and looked through the faded pictures of the students, all kids just like her. Why would her family have this in their house? Were they preserving it for some reason? It seemed like a perfectly innocent collection of photographs from a very, very, very long time ago — even if the subjects of the photographs were not innocent themselves. M kept flipping through the pages of criminal headshots, searching for a connection, and when she found it, her blood stopped cold.

M stared at the photograph and couldn't believe her eyes. It was John Doe. But it wasn't a younger version of the madman. No, it was John Doe looking just the same as he looked today, just as ancient as he'd appeared fifteen minutes ago, when she'd swiped at his face.

But the timeless photograph wasn't the reason M felt like darkness had crept inside her and stolen all the warm thoughts she'd ever had. It was the heading over the portrait:

FOUNDER, PRINCIPAL, AND FIRST DEAN OF THE LAWLESS SCHOOL: JONATHAN WILD.

M closed her eyes and opened them again to make sure that she was actually seeing what was in front of her, but each time she did it, John Doe's picture and Jonathan Wild's moniker were still there.

The sound of the trapdoor above her made her cringe and slam the book shut, tossing it onto the desk. This was it, her last stand. M braced herself to fight, turned out the light, and pulled her mask back down, wishing more than anything that Doe hadn't disconnected her Magblast.

Someone tumbled down the slide, a familiar figure who landed on his feet.

"Well, this is fine mess you've got us in, M."

It was Jones!

"Jones! You've got to stop doing that!"

He smiled and threw his arms around her, squeezing hard. "I apologize for the surprise, but this place is swarming with Fulbrights. Lucky you found your father's panic room."

"It wasn't luck," said M. She took a deep breath. "Are my friends . . . are they going to be all right?"

"What's most important is that you escape," he said. He pressed down upon a beam of wood and the rear wall slid open. "There's an escape pod back there. It will take you to safety."

"Wait," argued M. "I'm not going to escape! I can't leave my friends up there. I can't let Doe steal their lives."

"Right now, you don't have a choice," said Jones. "M, I'm sorry to do this, but I'm pulling rank. There's far too much at stake. We need to get you out of here."

"But what about me, don't I have a say in this?" asked M. But looking into Jones's eyes, she knew the answer already. She didn't.

"I love you like a daughter," he said and hugged her tightly. She was so confused that she didn't know whether to hug him back or shove him away.

"I love you, too, Jones," said M. "Mom has the moon rock."

"That's good," he said flatly.

"And Cal Fence stole a copy of the *Mutus Liber*," she said.

"That's better," he said.

"And I have the . . ." But before she could finish, a Fulbright agent came crashing down the slide. Judging by his shredded gloves, he was the same Fulbright who had held M in the library. Jones lunged forward, but the Fulbright Magblasted him up and against the ceiling — hard. Jones went limp and crashed back down to the floor. A pool of blood formed around his head.

"No!" cried M. The intruder stepped over Jones's lifeless body and walked toward her. He held a finger to his wire-laced lips. Then he charged his Magblast and aimed it squarely at M.

M shook her head and flicked out her sword from her programmable matter again. The blast was furious and just missed her. Swiftly and instinctively she slashed downward, lopping off the Fulbright's weapon. Blood spattered as his four fingers fell to the floor, writhing like worms in the sun. Still, he didn't miss a beat. He brought a heavy punch down on M's right shoulder. Using the strength and momentum of his attack, she spun around on her heel and let her sword follow its natural path. The Fulbright couldn't block in time, and she felt the sickening resistance as the sword struck true. By the time she'd completed her spin and faced him again, he was already lying on the ground, his breathing labored.

"Who are you?! Who are you?!" was all M could scream, but the Fulbright didn't move. With her sword aloft, she knelt down to pull off his mask.

But with a cackle, the Fulbright plunged a syringe into her neck. M stumbled backward, kicking him in the face, and pulled the needle out. "What was that? What did you . . ."

The room shifted like a carnival ride. Quickly she grabbed the yearbook from the desk and turned back to see the carnage in the room. Jones wasn't moving and neither was the Fulbright. M stumbled backward and fell, barely making it into the escape pod, which looked like something out of a sci-fi movie. It sat at the mouth of a dark tunnel, which shushed with a continuous blast of cold air.

"You can't stop me, Wild!" she screamed. "I'm going to find you and put an end to this once and for all!"

Then her head went woozy with a headache that made it feel like her very brain were being rewired. She couldn't remember what she was shouting about or why. Memories that were solid and true one moment faded away the next. Her father, her mother, the Lawless School, the Fulbright Academy, they all started to disappear. And as the pod closed, M felt her body drift away, too, light as air and flying soundlessly away toward a brave, new nowhere.

ACKNOWLEDGMENTS

It takes one person to dream a story. It takes many more people to build that story into a book. Then even more to make a trilogy. We are not alone.

First, I want to thank you for reading this book. Then I have to thank the people on every floor of Scholastic HQ for believing in this story, especially David and Nick, the increditors. Thanks to Phil for the new cover digs. And thanks so much to Scholastic Book Fairs and the Scholastic Reading Club for supporting M.

Josh and Tracey Adams also deserve a standing ovation for being terrific innovagents.

Thanks to my friends, Geoffrey Todd, Ganesh, and Timmy G, who are always up for adventure and really bad movies. Christopher Michlig, Sam Shaw, Ben Barnett, Pete Swanson, Paul, and Kirsten, who helped me through my own fish-out-of-water story way back when.

Mom and Dad will always have my love for their never-ending support for my creativity and because they are two of the most amazing people I know.

Thanks and congrats to my brother, Matt, and his wife, Ashley, for being in love.

To my daughter, Wren, thanks for listening to so many of my stories. Even the bad ones. There were a lot of bad ones.

To my son, Dez, thanks for laughing. Keep laughing. It makes the world go round.

And to Adrienne, thanks for laughing at all my bad stories. And making me better.

ABOUT THE AUTHOR

Jeffrey Salane is the author of *Lawless*. He grew up in Columbia, South Carolina, but moved north to study in Massachusetts and New York City. After spending many years playing in several bands, he now works as an editor and author. He lives in Brooklyn with his wife and kids.

You can learn more about this law-abiding citizen at www.jeffreysalane.com.